THE SAGEBRUSH HOTEL TONTINE

Luminare Books by L. Wade Powers

NOVELS

The Home

The Party House

New Albion Sunset

SHORT STORY COLLECTIONS

Falling In Love and Other Misadventures

Confronting the Boundaries

The Sagebrush Hotel Tontine

A Tale of Treasure and Treachery

L. Wade Powers

LUMINARE PRESS

WWW.LUMINAREPRESS.COM

The Sagebrush Hotel Tontine
Copyright © 2021 by L. Wade Powers

This is a work of fiction, and the characters are derived from the imagination of the author. With the exception of recognized historical figures and events, any resemblance to actual persons, living or dead, is purely coincidental.

Printed in the United States of America

Cover design by Roslyn McFarland, Farlands Publishing

Luminare Press
442 Charnelton St.
Eugene, OR 97401
www.luminarepress.com

LCCN: 2021919832
ISBN: 978-1-64388-773-9

For those in out of the way places

and open spaces,

in rural communities that live

in peaceful obscurity but give

their strength to friends and neighbors

whose trust and honor is the ultimate security.

To the people of Sagebrush, California,

the Paiute bands of Modoc County,

and the gamblers and ramblers

who live by the creed,

"Anything Is Possible."

Table of Contents

Preface ix

Prologue: Gold Rush Days (1864) 1

1. Arrival (1977) 10

2. Not the Only Game in Town (1957) 14

3. The Trove Group 36

4. The Tontine 58

5. Together Again (1967) 80

6. The Trophy 101

7. Unsettling News 119

8. Surprises (1977) 138

9. Confrontations and Decisions 161

10. Family Affairs 183

11. Disposing of the Trove 207

12. Accusations and Consequences 227

Epilogue 254

Author's Notes 258

Acknowledgments 261

About the Author 262

Preface

Tontine. A financial agreement between two or more people to share an amount of money or other asset over an interval of time, with a survivor or survivors to receive the proceeds. Terms of longevity and distribution vary with purpose.

Dead pool. A list of individuals, events, or other topics for which people wager money on which person or item will expire, terminate, or fail first or last. The individuals in a pool may be members of a tontine, where the survivor is the winner. All others, by definition, are losers.

There is no clear distinction between a tontine and a dead pool if the participants have bad intentions.

Poker. Any of several card games in which players attempt to win more money than they risk. The winners (survivors) end the game with more than they started and the losers with less than they started. A key element of the game is to learn the tactics and strategies of the other players to one's advantage. Deceit is part of the strategy, just like in real life.

Prologue

Gold Rush Days (1864)

THE THREE BROTHERS RECEIVED THEIR GOOD FORTUNE WITH humility and appreciation. They were righteous men, moderate in their habits, kindly disposed to their acquaintances, and prudent in their relationships toward the miners working adjacent claims. The rich veins of gold they worked cut across the Scott River on the eastern edge of the gold fields of northern California, but they never announced their discoveries or revealed the amount of gold they had been able to extract from the creek beds. To others engaged in the backbreaking and often unrewarding labor, they were like everyone else, barely able to eke out a living to pay for food and supplies and infrequently joining the others in rare moments of celebration or recreation.

Working farther up the river than most of the other prospectors, their efforts of more than three years were slowly but generously rewarded. Unlike so many of the other pan miners, Daniel, Andrew, and Abraham Hatcher quietly stashed their nuggets and flakes around their staked property until they could melt and consolidate them into ten-pound doré bars, each resembling a large potato or crude loaf of bread. They hid the gold-speckled bars in grain sacks covered with oats or barley, and buried the sacks in a vertical shaft behind the lean-to shanty that passed as their living quarters. The brothers had few visitors, and they were careful to avoid handling or melting the gold if anyone was nearby.

By 1864, they had accumulated enough gold to exceed their most optimistic expectations. By that time, most of the gold rush fever had passed on the Klamath River tributaries, including the Scott, Salmon and Trinity Rivers. It was time to say farewell to their few friends and discreetly withdraw. By working carefully to remove impurities, they estimated the doré bars contained about 80 percent gold and silver, most of it gold. They had more than a hundred of the bars, more than a half ton of concentrated precious ore.

The brothers purchased a heavy wagon, constructed from sturdy lumber and reinforced with iron, to haul their treasure and supplies back to Utah and home. With two horses and half a dozen oxen they left their claim on a fine day in May and made their way east and north through the rugged mountains to reach the Klamath River. They traveled east along the river and then turned south to the bustling mining town of Yreka. After several days rest and purchasing final provisions, they continued the trek east and north on the Yreka Trail, passing a steady stream of Argonauts, late-ar-riving gold seekers, and other settlers and farmers in wagon trains accompanied by livestock. The brothers made steady progress at two to three miles per hour. With good weather and abundant daylight, they covered about thirty miles a day on even ground. They had several miles of heavily forested mountains to climb, but passes were well maintained for the immigrants.

Abraham preferred to hike, so he often drove the four hitched oxen as he walked on their left with a short whip to start, stop and turn them. Daniel or Andrew rode one of the horses, scouting ahead for water and to survey road conditions. The two extra oxen and the other horse were tied to the rear of the wagon and rotated so that the team animals were fresh. Fortunately, traffic from the east had slowed from the peak years of the rush during the 1850s and grazing areas had mostly recovered along the trail.

The brothers had two rifles, a double-barreled shotgun, and gear to fish. They were mindful that encounters with roving bands of Paiutes, some of them hostile to the immigrating whites, were a possibility as they crossed the desert stretches to the east. Their main fear was having their horses stolen, but the frequent presence of settlers on the trail helped decrease the danger and provide some assurance. By mid-June they reached the juncture of the Applegate Trail, leading westward into the Willamette Valley of Oregon and eastward into northeastern California and northern Nevada.

They camped that night on the southeastern shore of a large shallow lake, accompanied by several other wagons headed in the opposite direction. They shared some of their dinner with four horsemen who said they were returning to western Oregon to work on a cattle ranch. Asked where they had been and where they were bound, Daniel said they were coming from the Marble Mountains and were headed home to Utah.

"Been prospecting for gold?" asked one of the horsemen.

Abraham looked at his brothers, letting them know he would do the talking. "We tried it for about a year but didn't find enough to meet expenses. Looks like most of the area has played out, and we just lost the heart for going anywhere else. Guess we'll head back to the family farm outside Provo."

"Going through Lassen's Pass then?"

"Yep, we came that way headin' west," said Andrew, not wanting to be left out of the conversation.

"Then you know it's steep on both sides, especially the east slope. Be prepared to slow your wagon headed down."

"Thanks for that. We usually drag a log on the steep ones," said Abraham.

One of the horsemen took special notice of their wagon wheel ruts and how deep the rims sank into the soft lakeshore soil. He casually glanced into the wagon and saw the large number of grain sacks visible under the cooking and camping supplies. The horsemen offered some whiskey, but the Hatcher brothers refused it, citing their Mormon teachings.

After dinner and coffee, the riders bid them a good night and settled down a ways from the camp. They quietly discussed the possibility that the brothers had fared better than they indicated and might be returning east with more than just food for the animals.

"Quite a wagon load for three men just trying to get home," said Bill, the one who had observed the grain sacks.

Bob, their leader, said "There's nothing behind us on the trail for several days. I reckon if we leave early tomorrow morning and cut back a ways, we can have a closer look see at that wagon. We can wait for them where the road starts up into the mountains." The four agreed and went to sleep, anticipating some excitement after several boring weeks in the desert with the large immigrant wagon train.

* * *

After breakfast, the Hatcher brothers hitched their oxen and bid farewell to a few of the settlers. The late spring day was clear and it promised to be a hot one. The large alkaline lake they left behind was only a preview of the hundred miles of desert they would need to traverse on the other side of the mountains. The pass was more than six thousand feet above sea level and it would offer some respite from the heat. There was no oncoming traffic as the road narrowed and they approached the mountain rise. Just before noon they stopped at a creek and waterhole on the right of the trail, giving their oxen and horses a drink and allowing the men to stretch their legs. With each mile on the trail, their anticipation increased for a joyous homecoming and being with their families and close friends after a nearly four-year absence.

Daniel saw them first—the four men from the night before, riding from behind a grove of nearby trees. One of them had a rifle across his saddle and two had drawn pistols. They were on the brothers before they could make a move for the weapons in their wagon. Andrew had a pistol, but he dared not draw it. They raised their hands as two of the men remained mounted, one holding the rifle at Abraham's head. The other two walked quickly over to the wagon. One climbed up and started opening the bags.

"Nothing here but grain and a bunch of old rocks," he said. He looked closer. "Hey, these rocks have gold in them." He heaved one of them to the man standing at the back of the wagon, who examined it, shifting it from one hand to the other, rotating the crudely shaped stone in the sun. It sparkled like it was on fire.

The man looked up at his mounted comrades. "Hey Bob, looks like these here boys were plannin' on stealing some of California's precious gold." He grinned and handed the oval bar to the smallest and thinnest of the four.

Bob passed it to Denver. "Well, guess we can't permit that, can we? We'll just have to return it to where it came from. Good thing we were headin' that way."

Red, so-named because of his straggly flaming hair, climbed from the wagon. "There must be dozens of sacks in there. Probably gold bars in every one of them. Quite a load." He looked at the silent brothers, still standing like pines with hands high. "What should we do with these three?"

Andrew spoke up. "This ain't stolen. We worked for it hard and honest. It's ours."

"Honest, huh? You weren't too honest with us last night, pretendin' you were worn out and goin' back to a life of sod bustin'. Shame on you. I thought you were upright Mormon fellers."

This brought laughs from the others except for Bob. He was in deep thought or what passed for it among the four. He and his boys had experienced a few minor run-ins with the law, mostly for drinking too much and creating public disturbances. They had stolen a few things here and there, but never did anything that would merit serious jail time. What to do?

"I'll tell you what, fellers. This is probably a hell of a lot of money and you won't really need it back on your farm. Suppose we relieve you of most of this weight, makin' your trip across the pass a lot easier, and we'll let you keep your pious lives, even your horses. We'll head west with the wagon and agree never to see you or bother you again. What say?"

Denver frowned. "Now Bob, I'm not so sure that's a great idea. What's to stop them from following us or going to Camp Bidwell and siccing the troopers on us? We ain't gonna be able to make fast tracks with that wagonload."

"Well, we'll have to relieve them of their guns. If they show up at our backs we'll have to treat them like varmints and dispose of them as such. Seems like a fair deal to me. They live, we leave." Bob turned to the brothers as Red reached behind Andrew and drew the man's pistol from his holster.

"Bill, get any guns in the wagon and on the horses." Bob turned once more to Abraham. "You look like the oldest. You willing to skedaddle on your horses and not look back? You can make it to the camp in a few hours and maybe buy another horse and saddle from the soldiers. I'll give you one of your bars. You can lower your hands. How's that?"

Abraham looked at Daniel and Andrew. They gave brief nods. He glanced up at Bob. "Can we take our canteens and a bit of food?"

"Sure, that'd be Christian of us. Least we can do, right, men?" He gave a short laugh and dismounted, leaving Denver to cover the Mormons in case they attempted something desperate.

Daniel and Andrew gathered up canteens, a sack of grub, and a small tent. They used the horses as pack animals and walked them up the climbing trail to the pass, about three hours away. As instructed, the brothers left the wagon and the four thieves without looking back. It was another five or six hours to Camp Bidwell, a small open garrison located in hostile Paiute territory. They wanted to be within its protection by dark.

As they disappeared around a curve, Bob instructed Denver to follow them but to stay back and be discreet. If they continued on for a mile or two, he was to return and help them unload the wagon.

"Unload it? Here? I thought we were going to take it somewhere else," said Red.

"Where would that be?" said Bob. "We'll each take a bar. That should hold us until we can recover the rest. There's more here than we can deal with at this time. Let's move the wagon back toward the lake but well off the trail. We'll bury the sacks and join the wagon train later tonight or tomorrow. I doubt if anyone else knows the brothers had gold so we should be in the clear if we show up with their wagon and oxen. We can say we bought them to help the poor busted prospectors."

After taking the wagon west a few miles but staying outside of the lake's highwater marks on the shore, they traveled a quarter mile north to a small creek lined with willows. The ground was soft and easy to dig and the three men were able to excavate a six-foot pit in less than an hour. The sacks were lifted two at a time from the wagons and tossed in the pit. Four sacks, minus the bars, were retained and filled with some of the grain to provide evidence of cargo in the wagon along with the supplies and equipment the Hatcher brothers left.

As they unloaded the last of the sacks, Denver rode up and dismounted.

"Just in time," said Bob. "Any trouble with our Mormon friends?"

"Nope. They had their heads down and I'm sure there were plenty of grumbles, but they were probably thanking God for their lives. Which, by the way, I'm still not so sure was a good idea."

"Hey, let it go. We might be caught and held for robbery but not for murder. If we get away with this haul, we'll be set for life, here or anywhere."

Red called out, "That's one hundred and twelve bars, and that doesn't count the four we're taking with us." Red and Bill laughed and whistled as they shoveled dirt over the pit, scattering the extra soil and tamping it down.

"I drew us a map marking the spot on the creek, the big tree over there, and the boulder next to it. It appears to be due north of the trail where we left it at the wide curve." Bob handed the map to Denver.

Red climbed into the wagon and guided it back to the Lassen Trail as the other three rode alongside. Each horse's saddlebag held one of the doré bars. Bob was whistling and Denver was spouting a continuing series of fantasies about what he would do with his share. After several months of hard labor and little to show for it, the hijacking had been miraculously easy, and their boastful chatter was anything but subdued.

Their joy was short lived. Before they could rejoin the road, a marauding band of mounted Indians overtook them. The silent approach of nine warriors from the foothills on the east went undetected until the braves broke cover. It wasn't a battle. Bob and Denver were cut down by bullets. Bill was able to get off a shot, wounding one of the braves, but he was knocked off his horse and knifed through the gut. Red scampered back into the wagon to grab the shotgun, but it wasn't loaded. He was looking at it when one of the Paiutes climbed into the wagon and slit his throat. Red was thrown to the ground to lie with the others. Bill wasn't dead yet—that would take a few more hours. He would have time to think about what might have been if they had made it back to the wagon train.

The Indians ignored him and the other whites—they were after the horses and guns. Discarding the saddles, they threw them into the wagon. They looked at the four dirty loaves and noticed the sparkle but dropped them. They removed the shirts Red and Bill wore and claimed them as trophies, and the map in Denver's pocket was also discovered but thrown away. After releasing the oxen, they used Bob's matches to set the wagon on fire.

The burnt-out remains of the wagon wouldn't be discovered until many years later. Vultures, coyotes, and time removed most traces of the men except for boots, belts, a few scraps of cloth, and four stones that eventually disappeared, merging with the surrounding ground cover.

———◆———

THE HATCHER BROTHERS DIDN'T FARE ANY BETTER. DESCENDing the pass and moving north along a trail between the eastern slopes of the mountains to their west and a large alkaline lake to the east, they were met by another small band of Paiutes. Camp

Bidwell had been established for less than a year, but its presence infuriated the native inhabitants. Any whites they encountered would pay the price for the restrictions on freedom and hunting the pony soldiers imposed. Without weapons, the brothers succumbed on their knees in prayer. The Indians bashed their heads with stout clubs and rode away with two additional horses and a black broad-billed hat.

The remains of the three Mormon men were found two days later by a patrol from the camp.

CHAPTER ONE

Arrival (1977)

The weathered clapboard hotel stands just off the dusty road. Two stories in height, it dominates the nearby cabins and shacks lining the main street of a high desert town that refuses to die despite several opportunities to do so. A few blocks farther down the street lies the central district, boasting a few more-modern buildings to conduct business for the surrounding agricultural countryside. The sun's almost down and it's been hotter than hell. Robert John Templeton is back, ready or not.

He is sweating through everything, clothes clinging with Great Basin stubbornness. The flop-eared dog along the wooden rail follows his progress and gives half a tail wag—too much effort for the full greeting. The man can sympathize. He's out of breath and hindered by a painful right knee, and the two short steps onto the landing are more work than he wants at the moment. It's been a half-day's hike from the state highway. Some traffic, but not enough to hitch a ride into town.

Across the porch and through the double doors, the dark, cool lobby brings welcome relief from the stifling heat. A small faded sign near the front desk reads Welcome to the Sagebrush Hotel, Established 1894. The all-too-familiar musty odors of ancient carpets and overstuffed furniture, dust-laden drapes, the dim light over the front desk, towering ceilings, the perpetual ticking of the grandfather clock in the corner. The memories return like a flood, clear and concise, as if he hasn't been away for ten years. It's all here, waiting like some Western gothic snare from the past. A glass chandelier hangs over the lobby and, at the other end, facing him as it did then, the mirror. It's as tall as the man, a bit wider, framed in ornate oak. The glass is weathered and permanently spotted with age, yet it remains, as it has for more than eighty years, guarding the long carpeted hall, returning the images of countless visitors. He sees himself passing the few closed doors to each side. He is also weathered and spotted, if not with age then with living out of pocket.

Pausing in front of the mirror, he sets a black leather bag on the carpet. Hitching his pants and tilting his hat forward, he quietly studies the reflection. Middle aged, rough-hewn, more than a bit on the scraggily side. *Could use a haircut, definitely a shave, need to clean up. I must smell like the underside of a semi. No, probably not that good.*

The reverie is broken by the hesitant inquiry behind him. "Can I…can I help you mister?"

Turning, Johnny faces a young man, probably in his late teens, neatly dressed, wearing glasses. *Looks like the studious type. Probably goes to college somewhere.*

He stands with his hands clasped in front, trying not to stare at the road tramp in front of him. Johnny gives him what he considers a friendly smile, but he realizes his less-than-civilized appearance doesn't help.

The boy clears his throat and tries once more. "If you're lookin' for a room, we got one for sixteen dollars a night, payable in advance," he states with growing confidence. "And that includes breakfast."

Johnny picks up the bag and walks slowly toward the lobby. The boy steps back while facing him, maintaining a cautious distance. "I'll take it." His voice sounds gruffer and louder than intended.

The clerk continues to back into the lobby, reaching the counter and slipping behind the dark wooden barrier. He stands erect and alert, eyes pivoting to the man between glances around the room, at the doors, and the guest register in front of him. This he shoves forward, together with an old-fashioned fountain pen.

Johnny counts out two twenties, a five and three crumpled one dollar bills, smoothing each on the counter. Ignoring the pen, he looks again into the clerk's eyes. "Relax, I just need a room and a bath. This should cover three nights. I'm almost human and I've been here before. You might say this is a homecomin' of sorts."

The boy doesn't fully relax, but his eyes focus on the man's face for the first time. "Do I know you, mister?"

"Doubt it unless you're a lot older than you look. How old would that be, anyways?"

"I turned nineteen three days ago. Why are ya asking?"

"No reason. Got a room key?"

"Aren'cha gonna sign in?" the clerk asks, pushing the pen toward the man.

"I'd prefer not to." Johnny stares at the register while pushing the bills toward the boy. He doesn't recognize any of the scrawls on the lined sheet.

"No one wants to sign the register anymore. Must be an invasion of outlaws." The clerk hesitates and smiles briefly but takes the bills, placing them in a drawer under the counter. He turns to the wall and reaches for a key.

"Can I have room 23?"

The boy looks at Johnny, pauses, turns back, and takes the familiar key from its hook. There are few keys missing from the board. Checking the number, he passes it across the counter. Johnny picks it up slowly, reaches for the bag, and turns toward the hallway. The clerk starts around the counter, obviously intending to show the man to his room.

"I know where it is," Johnny tells him softly, almost reverently.

Pausing in mid step, the clerk lets the man pass and walk out of the lobby. Several steps down the hall, no stairs to climb, one turn to the left, and the door to room 23 is in front of Johnny. The large metal numerals on the door haven't changed. Neither have the brass doorknob, the primitive keyhole, or the half-opened transom. He could have left here yesterday. Maybe he did.

He starts to slip the key in and turn the lock, but instead he twists the knob and the door opens. Thinking about the number of years that are about to unwind, he enters a room that overwhelms him with smells and sights from the past. The single-width brass bed is in the same position, but the color of the covers are different. Pull-down shades and blue curtains. A beat-up dresser that could have been delivered by wagon train. It is all as he remembers from ten and twenty years ago. Dropping the bag on the bed he walks to the closet. Opening the door, he searches for the initials he had carved on the inner side of the doorframe. *For what? Posterity? My anticipated return?* A few more have been added over the years, but his are there, "R.J.T. 1957." A distinct relic of an earlier presence, a lifetime ago. He turns back to the room as a momentary dizziness sweeps over him. It passes while he sits on the bed, expecting the familiar sponginess of the overstuffed mattress he had slept on so many times in the past, but the mattress has changed. It's thinner and firmer, reminding him of where he is and how long it has been.

This is not that time and I am painfully aware I'm not that person. Nor is anything else, despite casual impressions to the contrary. She might not be here this time. Only the stage remains the same, that and the unquenchable memories of those times. The kid in the lobby…is he connected to any of this or just a walk-on player in this edition of the performance? I shouldn't know him, just another hire for the hotel, but there was a strange look about him. I must be more tired than I thought.

A twinge of leg pain reminds him of the recent trek from El Paso and it's physical cost. Slipping off the boots and unbuttoning his shirt, he lies back on the pillow and looks up at the ceiling. He can still see the old cracks, not completely disguised by recent coats of plaster and paint. *This is going to be one helluva tomorrow. Best to rest tonight. Even the road grit can wait.* His eyes close and *helluva tomorrow* repeats over and over in dimmer and dimmer echoes as he walks down an endless road filled with twenty years of wind-blown dust. Even that fades as the relief of nothingness replaces a dingy room in a forlorn inn.

CHAPTER TWO

Not the Only Game in Town (1957)

The Friday night poker game at the Sagebrush Hotel was three hours old. Ray Gordon, the town's hardware store owner, was experiencing a disastrous run of bad luck. In poker, that meant second best, good enough to bet, bad enough to lose. He was getting hands but raking few pots. Although he had relatively deep pockets, he was increasingly anxious and that was transforming into desperation. The others at the table knew it and they had no intentions of providing him peace of mind. Ray was a decent player and usually held his own, winning his fair share of the modest stakes, so no one was going to shed tears. Ray had also been drinking a bit more than usual and he was one of those souls whose happiness decreased as his blood alcohol increased.

Johnny was on a heater. He had won three of the last four pots and was feeling the sweet zone. His biggest competition at the table, as it was often, was Brandy Charlebois, a striking eighteen-year old brunette who knew her way around a deck of cards. She had been in town for about a year, waiting tables, helping out at a clothing store, and hustling drinks and favors when the opportunity rose. Not legally old enough to drink, it mattered little in a high desert town in the middle of nowhere.

Modoc County in northeastern California had a larger community north of Sagebrush—Alturas, the county seat, but there was no nearby metropolis. The few hundred people of Sagebrush didn't care. They were rugged individuals, proud of their independence, hardy in their ability to survive on what appeared to be minimal resources, and always, as they were quick to remind you, self-reliant. If a good-looking gal who played poker wanted to drink and be an adult, they weren't about to stand in her way. Most of those who played against Brandy or had any dealings with her knew that standing in her way wasn't a profitable option.

Johnny grew up in Sagebrush on a small farm outside town. He was twenty-two, had served two years in the army, and returned primarily because he had nowhere else to go. His parents had died in a car accident while he was in the military. He had the skills to be a mechanic, a plumber, or any number of other worthy trades, but a stint overseas and endless payday nights of poker and craps had soured his taste for hard labor. When he had to, he worked as a carpenter and general laborer, earning enough for his modest needs. He was slim of build, ruggedly handsome, and more than a bit arrogant, or so his friends indicated. He was generally well liked, could handle his liquor better than most, and had enough smarts to avoid most of what passed for trouble. Accumulating sufficient money to leave town and venture to farther horizons was his announced objective.

Johnny shared a trailer on the edge of town with a woman named Sonya Markova. Her Russian parents had been farmers near Lakeview in Oregon, but Sonya had followed a cowboy to northern California. She never married and was able to avoid getting pregnant. The cowboy rode into the sunset and Sonya remained in Sagebrush to work as a seamstress and occasional waitress. Although she was two years older than Johnny, they were a comfortable couple—not overly romantic but filling each other's needs in a town where loneliness, especially for younger adults, was not unknown. It was Sonya's trailer and Johnny spent many comfortable nights there, but he also had an informal open reservation for room 23 at the Sagebrush Hotel, one that was usually available when he wanted to walk from the poker room to a nearby bed after a night of convivial drinking. He built and repaired things at the hotel in exchange for the occasional lodging.

Johnny and his live-in mate had been together for over a year. Despite the comfortable relationship he had with Sonya, she talked about saving enough money to leave Sagebrush in the rearview mirror.

Oddly enough, there was enough loose cash in town to make such a goal feasible. There weren't a lot of distractions to spend money on, so weekend poker games, sports betting, and a few other suspect enterprises were well-frequented attractions for some of the locals. The modest hotel was their resort, casino, and party house.

Rodney Haas had been a friend of Johnny's parents. Five years older than Johnny, he also served in the army for two years but at an earlier time and in a different outfit. Physically, he was the opposite of Johnny. Somewhat overweight, of medium height, Rod had a large jowly face, often unshaven, and dark unruly hair. At twenty-seven, there were already signs that his hair was thinning, which was not helping his overall looks. He drove trucks on contract for local farmers during their asynchronous and diverse harvests and also worked with Ray on occasion at the hardware store. Frequent trips to Reno helped indulge his primary passion for cards and craps and it was rumored he occasionally acted as a courier for shadowy clientele. Although he sometimes acted the ladies' man, especially after several drinks, he professed to be a confirmed bachelor and his manner indicated that he didn't care much for the female persuasion other than for an occasional romp in the proverbial hay. He enjoyed the long-term, low-cost rental of room 21, paid by running errands for the hotel.

Ray, Rod, Brandy, and Johnny were the core of the frequent players club, always up for a game. The stakes were usually moderate—most pots averaging ten to fifteen dollars, some much less—but several hours of playing could result in losses or winnings of a hundred dollars or more. Other regulars joined in the contests: Justin, manager of the hotel and the nominal host when the games were played in one of the larger second-floor rooms; Ken Williamson, the town barber; Pete Roberts, the manager of the local bank; Steve Woodward, a field biologist for the Bureau of Land Management, and his wife, Donna Woodward, an elementary school librarian. A few others from the farms or friends passing through occasionally joined the games. With a rare exception, Brandy and Donna were the only women at the table.

Sonya never played, preferring to stay at home with the television but always wishing Johnny luck for both of them. She displayed no jealousy or sense of possession when Johnny decided to stay the night at the hotel. She and Johnny were free to come and go as they wished and with whom they wished. Despite occasional opportunities to indulge in other sexual ventures, Johnny rarely responded, preferring to sleep off a night in the hotel by himself.

Brandy had a small place of her own: a studio apartment above the mercantile store in the business district. Her comings and goings were discreet and no one among the poker group had ever been invited to her place for the evening. It was a point of considerable curiosity for those inclined to speculate about the mystery and growing legend surrounding the winsome brunette. On occasion, when the game ended later than usual, she occupied the room next door to Rod's, two doors down from the room Johnny sometimes used. Although their proximity started the rumor mill going—it didn't take much—Johnny was regarded by most as usually faithful and not the type inclined toward lechery.

At the table, Donna played conservatively and held her own, but Brandy did a lot better. No one was sure why the young woman seemed to excel, but Ray and Rod were especially anxious to take Brandy down, both at the table and in more intimate surroundings elsewhere. Although Ray was married, his eyes and comments spoke of his unrequited desire to taste the young black-haired one. He wasn't the only one.

Rod openly challenged Brandy to try him on the wild side. "My daddy told me years ago to take a rowdy woman to bed," he announced to the group after several drinks. Not for the first time he displayed a self-satisfied smirk and indulged in prolonged eye contact with Brandy.

She glanced at Donna and innocently asked, "Is he talking about you or me?"

Steve casually said, "Yep, she's rowdy all right." He also didn't make it clear which woman he was referring to.

It was a typical slow weekend night in Sagebrush. The usual game, the usual players, and as likely as not, the usual winners, but tonight would be different in one respect. It would be later remembered as the last night for most of the members of the group to regard poker as the only game in town.

EMMA DODSON WAS A TEACHER AT SAGEBRUSH ELEMENTARY. She was in her mid-fifties and had been teaching for more than thirty years—first in Alturas, the last twenty in Sagebrush. Fifty-seven kids were enrolled, spread over eight grades. She taught a variety of subjects for the sixth, seventh, and eighth graders. Science was her favorite and she delighted in leading her pupils on frequent field trips around the valleys, desert plains, marshes, and nearby foothills.

On occasion, Steve Woodward accompanied her group and lent his wildlife expertise to their education. Steve was in his late twenties and knew the backroads and wild places of Modoc and Lassen Counties from several years of fieldwork and surveys.

Emma and Steve were in the field on a bright and hot Saturday on April 27, 1957, to scout out a student trip for the following weekend. They wanted to take the combined seventh and eighth grade class of sixteen to the eastern shore of Goose Lake, a high desert alkaline body of water that straddled the Oregon-California border. The lake edge was marshy and home to a variety of shore birds. A small stream, Willow Creek, flowed from the eastern foothills of the Warner Mountains into the lake. Emma and Steve spent the morning at the lakeshore before driving past the small Willow Ranch community along a rural road.

They turned onto County Road 4, the approach to Fandango Pass Road, once part of the Applegate-Lassen Trail. Steve parked his car to picnic near the creek edge under a majestic willow tree. A large boulder some twenty yards from the tree was a perfect place to relax and take some photos.

They finished their lunch and were about to depart for home. Steve was packing the blanket and picnic basket in the car while finishing a beer as Emma strolled along the creek, watching a white egret moving stealthily along the opposite bank. With her eyes fixed on the magnificent bird, she stumbled and almost fell into a shallow depression set back several feet from the water's edge. The ground was soft due to heavy rains and high water a few weeks earlier. Except for mule deer tracks, it didn't appear that the area had been host to visitors in recent times.

"Steve, come here. I think there is something buried here."

Steve put down his beer and hurried to her side. Peering down at the sunken ground, he could make out the surface of rough cloth, resembling gunnysack. "Let me get a shovel," he said and returned to his car. A few minutes later, he was clearing the edges of the pit and exposing the ragged remnants of several sacks lying a few feet below the surface.

"Something's buried here, that's for sure," he said as he continued digging. "I'll get one of these and we'll see." He handed one of the deteriorating sacks to Emma, who took it and set it on the grass next to the hole. The sackcloth fell apart to expose two large stones. There was also some residue that appeared to be badly spoiled grain in the cloth remnant.

Steve lifted a roughly oval stone, about three times longer than high or wide. "I estimate about ten pounds, but what is it?"

Emma was the first to notice the sparkle—specs of golden light flashing in the sun and embedded throughout the stone that looked like a giant spud. "Steve, what is this? Iron pyrite, maybe?"

He looked closer, tilting it this way and that. "I don't think so. It's too flaky. Doesn't look like pyrite crystals, and if they were, who would bury several sacks of them in the ground?" It was obvious to them that the sacks with the sparkly spuds had been deliberately hidden. "Let me fetch my magnifier."

Steve went to the car and returned with a watchmaker's headpiece: two magnifying lenses set in a headband that he often used to examine larval insects in streams. He gave a low whistle, hefted the stone again, and handed it to the schoolteacher. "I think this might be gold. Possibly gold and silver." He examined the second stone.

"Really, Steve? What would these be doing out here and why do they look like a loaves of bread or a baked potatoes?"

Instead of laughing, Steve returned to the hole and retrieved an additional sack. Opening it, he uncovered two stones, about the same size and shape as the first ones. Each sparkled in the sun as they examined them in amazement.

"How many of these are there do you think?" asked Emma.

"Don't know, but if this is gold, it wouldn't take many of these bars to add up to a fair amount of money."

"But who does it belong to? This isn't private property." She frowned. "You called them bars. Like gold bars? Aren't they square or rectangular and smooth?"

Steve retrieved and opened another sack, which displayed the same contents. "There are apparently a *lot more* sacks here. You're right, this is federal property, and, I believe, these are called doré bars. They were usually produced at the mining site from nuggets and flakes. They would be from sixty to eighty percent pure, usually mixed gold and silver, possibly some mercury minerals, but cleaned of dirt and other materials.

"Why would they look like this?" Emma asked, as she rotated one of the oval stones in her hands.

"Bars are made from melts in a mold. In the case of these crude ones, they were probably poured into a trough in the ground. This made transport to a refinery or official smelter a lot safer and convenient. It is difficult to account for individual flakes and nuggets but these could be weighed and counted, helping to prevent theft or loss."

"Hoarding gold is illegal, I thought."

"Yep, since the early 1930s. FDR signed an executive order to help banks recover during the Great Depression, because our financial system was based on the gold standard. It's still illegal to retain gold except for jewelry and antiques."

"Who do you think these belong to?"

"Ownership might be a legal or even a historical issue. These may have been here quite some time and wouldn't have been exposed if not for the spring flooding."

"Should we report this to the BLM or to the Treasury? Suppose this is a stash from a robbery?"

Steve shook his head. "If so, it had to be a long time ago, nothing recent. Although there are some high-grade mines in the county, they're all commercial ventures. No one would be producing crude doré bars at this time. I bet these date back to the 1800s, possibly to the California gold rush days. The Applegate-Lassen Trail was a major roadway for immigrants coming west but also for prospectors returning east."

"That sounds about right. I've mentioned Peter Lassen and the Applegates during some of my classes. What now?"

"Let's rebury these, fix the surface so it doesn't look disturbed, and carefully seek some help in town. I'll keep one so we can verify it, but we need to be cautious. I'll also take a few photos to be sure we can relocate this site. I suggest we don't delay—tomorrow would be better than the day after. And Emma, don't say anything about this to anyone until we know what we're doing."

She nodded. They replaced the sacks, covered them with dirt, and smoothed the surface. On the way back to Sagebrush, Emma was lost in thought, marveling at how quickly an unexpected discovery had inserted itself into her quiet routine and sometimes lonely life.

Steve was quiet and decided to forego the Saturday night poker game. It wasn't going to compare in excitement with the serious talk he and Donna would share that night or the sparkly stone he would show her.

On Sunday morning, Emma and Steve began their mission to find the help they needed in order to recover the buried horde. Steve had informed Donna the evening before, and she couldn't wait to see the rest of the suspected treasure. Emma suggested Justin Gonzales, her friend and manager of the Sagebrush Hotel, as a reliable source for assistance. Steve had played poker with him for a couple of years and agreed.

Justin often ate Sunday breakfast in the hotel dining room before attending early Mass at the small Catholic church. They found him, as expected, reading a newspaper and having his second cup of coffee after the breakfast dishes had been cleared. He looked up and smiled as they approached.

"Good morning, Miss Dodson. And Steve! What brings you two into the hotel at this time?" Justin folded the paper, laid it to the side and motioned to two empty chairs. "Care to join me for coffee or something to eat?"

"A cup of Earl Grey would be nice," replied Emma as she took the chair opposite.

Steve pulled out a chair and sat. "I'll take you up on the coffee but I've already eaten. Sorry to bother you before you run off to Mass, but we have something important to share with you and we don't believe this can wait. It needs to be kept confidential, in every sense of the word." He looked at Emma and she bowed her head in agreement.

Justin motioned toward the waitress and told her what they needed. She returned with a tea bag and hot water and poured coffee for Steve as the three exchanged pleasantries. When the waitress had withdrawn, Justin leaned forward, like a conspirator planning a revolution. "Now what is this all about?" He said it in a mischievous manner, relishing the mystery and the deviation from his usual weekend routine.

Justin was in a good mood, having stayed ahead of the money in last night's game, not a trivial feat against the better players. He was twenty-six, slim, and ambitious. Born of a mixed Hispanic family of modest means, he had graduated high school, taken two years of business at a community college, and been hired to manage the hotel. The elderly Bay Area owner had long ago lost interest in the town of Sagebrush and several times indicated he would sell the building at a fair market price. Fair market price was subject to different interpretations in Oakland and in Sagebrush. Justin was interested in purchasing the hotel but lacked the financial means to do so.

Emma shrugged and turned to Steve. "Why don't you tell him? You know more about this and the complications than I do."

Steve took another sip, set the cup down and leaned forward so that his face and Justin's were about a foot apart. "Justin, you have always been a clear thinker and we, that is Emma and I, trust your judgment and…your discretion. What we have to tell you is nothing short of astounding. In fact, we don't yet know *how* astounding, but we'll let you judge for yourself."

As Justin sat back and sipped coffee, he listened carefully to Steve's account of their discovery by the creek. Emma occasionally interjected a comment, but Steve provided most of the details. He indicated he had one of the bars concealed at his house. Justin asked only a few questions before Steve finished. The clock showed it was time for Justin to leave for church, but he dismissed it, saying he would make the late morning service instead.

"I think we need to make some initial decisions right away," Justin said in a low voice. A few hotel guests and townies had entered the dining room and were being seated. "Let's retire to my office. I have a map of the county. Are you willing to show me where this stuff is buried?"

"Yes we are and I have a crude map showing some landmarks at the creek." Steve patted his pocket as they left the dining room, walked behind the front desk in the lobby, and entered the manager's office.

Justin sat behind his desk while Emma and Steve pulled two chairs to the front of the desk. They spoke in subdued voices. "It's just the four of us who know about this?" Justin asked.

"So far. I figure we will need the help of a few others, as few as possible, to transport the materials to some place for safe keeping. Then there is the problem of disposing of the…ahem, property. We will need someone with appropriate contacts and know how to market it." By common agreement, they decided to forego any mention of gold or treasure. It was a small town and like most small towns, there were big ears and big mouths in abundance.

Emma said, "We exposed only a few bags, but we don't know how many are there. Might be a dozen or more. We need to return in a car, make sure no one is around, and get them back here or someplace else."

Justin smiled. "Well, Emma, another side to you is revealed. I do believe you are enjoying the intrigue for its own sake in addition to the potential for profit."

"I have been a schoolteacher all my life. As you are well aware, I never married, although in my younger days, a few of the gentlemen caught my fancy. Never worked out though and I wasn't desperate enough to settle for just any hayseed farmer. I was going to marry someone whose intelligence I could respect or fly out to some other nest, but neither occurred. A bit of mystery, even a hint of danger, might be a fit payback for years of monotonous waiting. I'm not complaining, mind you. I enjoy my job and I feel fortunate to have good health and good friends," she looked at Steve, "that I've had, but what we saw yesterday, I confess, has put a new bounce in my step."

"You should have seen her at the creek, Justin. When she realized what she had found, she was like a young girl. Neither of us could believe it. However, I have to caution you. I believe these are miner's bars. They were placed in sacks, but those have mostly fallen apart. We don't know how many or anything about their origin. It might not be gold at all." He hesitated, having used the forbidden word. "We won't know until we can get a piece of one assayed."

Justin rubbed his chin as he sat back in his reclining chair. "Then there is the legal issue, right? We will need to find out how and when to exchange the material for real coin of the realm. Who do we know who has the possible means?"

Steve thought a minute. "Rod Haas makes frequent trips to Reno. He knows a number of pawn shop operators and has mentioned a few others, some shady types of his acquaintance. Probably not mafia or anything heavy duty, but he might be the one member of our poker group who has connections or knows of someone who does."

Emma sighed. "I don't know how trustworthy Rodney might be. He brags a lot, especially when he's drinking, which is much of the time. Do you think he can maintain a secret?"

"If it's worth some real money, I'm willing to bet he will." Justin said it with conviction but then softened. "However, I have been known to lose a number of bets on occasion."

"That would make five of us," Steve said. "Anyone else?"

"Not until we see what we are dealing with. If we are talking about a few bars like the one you described, weighing about ten pounds, let's see…" Justin pulled a manual calculator out of his desk and his fingers flew over the keys. "Ten bars at ten pounds is sixteen hundred ounces, times roughly thirty-five dollars per ounce, is…wow, about fifty-six thousand dollars. Even divided five ways, that's more than ten thousand for each of us." Justin frowned. "Steve, Emma, are you sure you want to divide this equally? It's your discovery. Rod and I might be satisfied with a nominal assistance fee. In fact, I'm not sure what my role in this would be. Why do you need my help?"

Emma didn't hesitate. "For the very reason that you are asking that question, Justin. I have known you all the time you were growing up, before you went away to college. You have never shown a trace of greed or selfishness. Second, you have a head for business, which I certainly do not. I don't believe that is Steve's forte either." Steve smiled but didn't contradict her. "I think you will more than deserve a share in helping us. I agreed that Steve and Donna would get a larger share, since I have only myself to look after. I don't need that much to have a good time and I will retire in a few more years and have that as well."

"Tell you what," Justin said, folding his hands like a steeple. "Let me attend Mass today, and then let's drive out to the creek tomorrow. It will be Monday afternoon and from what you tell me, the site is well off the road and isolated from likely visitors. I'll get an extra shovel, and we can load the stuff in the trunk of my old Merc. We can be back here by evening, and I can put it in the cellar where we used to keep the prohibition booze."

The Sagebrush Hotel had been an oasis during Prohibition, providing beer, wine, and homemade alcoholic drinks to selected customers, most of them local. The enterprise was so successful that it allowed the original builder and owner of the hotel to retire to the Bay Area after Prohibition was revoked. He never set eyes on his moneymaker again.

There were two cellars: an outer one and a well-concealed inner one. The outer one had contained a few kegs of beer, a wine vat, and several cases of bottles, mostly cheap whiskey and vodka. The inner chamber stored additional quantities of liquor including some of the high-priced brands. If the hotel was raided, the federal agents would find and confiscate the cheap stuff, leaving the hotel to continue operations. A raid was occasionally rumored but never happened. The desolate desert town didn't seem to be of intense interest to the booze-busting feds.

"Monday at one, then, right after lunch," said Steve. "I'll tell my office that I'll be following up on a survey on the western Warner Mountains."

"Monday is a school day, so I won't be able to help. Can you boys do it without me?"

It was a rhetorical question, and they knew it, but they gave her reassuring smiles and told her they would get together with her Monday evening at the hotel.

Emma returned to her bungalow on the edge of town, singing quietly to herself. Steve was right—she felt like a schoolgirl and couldn't wait to discover what the near future would bring.

When Monday afternoon arrived, three people rode in Justin's 1950 Mercury Monterey sedan. Justin drove and Steve sat alongside of him. Donna, nourishing dreams of adventure, was in the back seat. After Steve's description of the hidden cache, she wouldn't consider passing on the Willow Creek trip. Like Emma, she worked for the local school and needed some spice in her life. The recovery of a possible small fortune in gold was too exciting to leave solely to the men's pleasure. Fortunately, she could take that particular Monday off.

About an hour later, the dark-green Mercury pulled off Highway 4 and crossed a short field behind a low rise. The ground near the creek was soft, and the car was parked about twenty feet from the water's edge.

While Donna laid a tarp in the spacious trunk, the men wielded shovels at the burial site. It took only a few minutes to expose the sacks, most of them in shreds, few of them intact. They began lifting the sacks out of the hole and Donna ferried them to the car.

"Nothing like a pretty woman with a strong back," said Justin as they dug deeper, recovering more sacks.

"Yeah, and she sure can cook," said Steve as Donna approached for two more bars.

Sometimes there was no sack to lift and they simply removed the bars from the ground. The stones were much alike, looking like bread rolls in the shade but revealing their characteristic sparkle in the sun. A few minutes later, they had removed thirty bars from the hole, and there was no end in sight. They paused to confer.

"If there are many more of these, we might need to make a second trip, possibly with a truck," said Steve.

Justin grinned. "Remember I calculated that ten bars might be worth as much as fifty-six thousand dollars? It seems we have at least three times that and, who knows, maybe a lot more."

Donna wiped the sweat from her brow. "What do you want to do? The trunk will hold a few more in terms of space, but if you are right about the weight, we have about three hundred pounds in the rear. We probably should put some of them in the back seat. How much weight will your car carry?"

Justin could see the car from where he knelt. The rear bumper was noticeably lower and he was concerned that the car might get stuck in the soft soil. "Tell you what. Donna, transfer some of the bars to the rear seat to even the load and we'll stop for the day. It's good news that there are more bars, but we need to come back for the rest."

"We have another problem." Steve nodded toward the gaping hole in the ground. "We'll have to do some ground replacement to disguise the site. I suggest we do that while Donna rearranges the load in the car." He smiled at her and she shrugged in agreement. "We can return tomorrow with a pickup truck. Ray has one I can borrow. I'll tell him I'm hauling a couple of dead deer from a ranch."

Instead of immediately covering the remaining bars, they brought them all up, determined how many they had, filled the cavity, and put the bars back on top so they wouldn't have to excavate the entire hole again. It required another hour to remove the remaining bars and sacks, gather dirt from a wide area to minimize signs of disturbance, place the bars back and cover everything with a foot of soil. They were all sweating when they got in the Merc and drove back to Sagebrush.

It was late evening, not quite dark, when they parked at a small loading dock at the rear of the hotel. Justin opened a delivery door and walked down a flight of stairs to the storage cellar. He unlocked the exterior and interior storage room doors and brought several gunny sacks back to the car. "Anyone poking around?" he asked.

"All quiet on the Western front," answered Steve.

They began unloading the rear seat first because the bars were only partly covered by a blanket. They worked quickly and efficiently—Steve removing two bars at a time, putting them in a sack and carrying it to Donna, waiting inside the door. She carried the sack to the flight of stairs to hand to Justin who placed them in the interior storage room and returned the sack to Donna. Fifteen minutes later, the car was empty.

"Now I'm more than ready for a beer," said Donna. Her blouse was wet, matching the men's shirts.

"My treat at your choice of tavern," said Justin. He locked the cellar doors and the delivery door, drove the Merc around to the front of the hotel and parked it. Satisfied that they had earned some cold suds and that no one had observed the transfer, they walked down the street toward the Sagebrush Watering Hole.

"I'll borrow Ray's truck tomorrow," said Steve. "Looks like we have about a hundred or more bars—I lost count—so somewhere over four hundred thousand dollars."

"If it's really gold and the purity is good," added Justin in a hushed voice. "We'll be trying to move this outside of the usual banking and metals market, so we'll probably have to settle for a percent of its real market value."

"True enough, but it will still be a tidy sum," answered Steve as they reached the front door of the tavern. "Time for worry about that later. Let's enjoy a few cool ones."

"What about Emma? We told her we would meet her tonight." Donna hadn't forgotten the original claimant to the discovery.

Steve stopped inside the door. "Oops, you're right. I'll call her and see if she wants to join us here or would like us to come to her house."

"If we're going anywhere else, I'll need to take a shower and change." Donna looked at Justin and Steve. "I suggest you two might want to do the same."

Emma saved them the additional hassle by joining them at the tavern. She didn't often patronize the local bars, but it was one of the more acceptable night spots in town in her opinion. She pointed out after joining them, this night was a special occasion. When they told her how much of "the stuff" they had uncovered, she was delighted.

"Do you think there might be even more buried nearby?" Emma asked, nursing a gin and tonic.

Steve shrugged, his hands wrapped around an amber bottle. "Hard to say, but this is quite a haul. I saved a couple of the intact sacks to see if we can determine an approximate date and place. One of them had a feed store label from Yreka, so my guess about the California gold fields could be right. If that's the case, this might be a miner's stash that was abandoned or lost for some reason."

"Would the feds have a claim on this?" asked Justin.

"Could be the State of California or the feds or both, if they knew about it." They all lifted their bottles or glasses and there seemed little doubt among them that government authorities would not be apprised of the find.

As they walked back toward the hotel, Justin told them quietly that he would take a small chunk of one of the bars to an assayer in Alturas for a preliminary identification and value estimate of the material.

"Take the one we have," Steve said, "it's better to keep everything in one place."

* * *

Tuesday morning, Steve paid a call at Ray and Jay's hardware store. Ray's brother, Jay, was working in the back, unloading lumber from the truck that Steve needed. After a quick approval from Ray, Steve helped Jay finish the task and told Ray he would return the truck that evening with a full tank of gas.

"And clean up any deer guts or blood, okay?" Ray wasn't unhappy about lending his truck—he owed Steve for helping him locate deer and elk during hunting seasons—but he wanted to have the vehicle tidy if he needed it the next day.

"I'll use a cover and there won't be a mess. Thanks, Ray."

Steve drove away to pick up Justin, who was waiting at the hotel. They had a large tarp to put in the truck and were on the road to Willow Creek by noon. Donna wanted to join them again, but they gently advised her to keep her day job for the time being.

They were relieved to see that no other tire tracks had been laid since the day before, and a glance at the burial site confirmed that it was undisturbed. A few minutes later, they uncovered the bars and began transferring them to the truck, laying them on the tarp in even rows. Justin had brought along a few small sacks in which to place the bars on top and the men kept count as the truck filled. They made a cursory attempt to fill the hole but it would take a few more rains and additional high water to completely ablate their excavation.

When they finished covering the horde, Steve announced the inventory. "Eighty-two bars in this load. With the thirty from yesterday, that's one hundred and twelve bars. Justin?"

Justin pulled a pencil and a small tablet from his pocket. A few seconds later, he whistled. "That's about four hundred and seventy thousand dollars, depending on the actual weight and purity." He paused and looked at Steve. "That is, if they are. If this is gold, then someone lost track of one hell of a fortune. Hard to believe that you and Emma lucked into this the way you did. I'll get the sample to Alturas tomorrow and then we'll know for sure."

Steve was no longer paying attention, focused on thoughts of a future he could not have imagined a few days earlier. Justin smiled and climbed into the passenger seat, numb from the magnitude of what they had undertaken. Legalities aside, it was a game changer for everyone. A few minutes later, Steve climbed behind the wheel.

The transfer inside the hotel took longer, but when they finished, one hundred and twelve brown bars, minus a small piece of one, were stacked neatly under gunny sacks in the inner cellar.

The transfer did not go unwitnessed. A man strolling by the hotel noticed the truck parked in the alley and two people unloading bags of something from the back. It was dark and he couldn't make out what they were doing, but he stepped around the corner and decided he would inquire later.

⁂

Thursday evening, Emma, Justin, and the Woodwards had a quiet dinner at the hotel, served late in the empty dining room. Justin's trip to Alturas had been mostly successful. The assayer, an experienced prospector and rockhound, gave Justin a positive identification on the gold with intermixed silver. Justin showed him only a small, rough chunk, nothing to associate it with a molded bar, but the assayer was curious about the character of the minerals. He could tell this wasn't a direct removal from a stream or a cliffside. Justin averted further questions by telling him the rock was borrowed from a friend and he was only attempting to verify whether it might contain precious minerals.

"That it does, Mr. Gonzales, but it looks like material that may have been melted and concentrated from jewelry or something like that."

"Could be. Can you tell me anything about what the purity might be?"

"Hard to tell unless I melt it down, separate the metals from the rest, and weigh it. Do you have more of this?"

"I don't and I'm not sure about my friend. Can you make a rough estimate based on what you see, without melting it?

"Don't hold me to this, but it looks like more than half, possibly as high as sixty to eighty percent. What part gold and what part silver, I can't say."

Justin gave him twenty dollars for his time and trouble and left with the sample. He didn't provide an address or any other contact information.

The encounter left the group satisfied that they had a cellar full of precious metal, the total value to be determined. Justin laid the nondescript fragment on the dinner table as the group talked and ate. No one else was in the dining room except for an occasional visit by their waitress. "When we know what we are going to do, how and when, we'll get a formal analysis from a professional assayer, probably in Reno or Sacramento," he said.

"I think our ballpark estimate will suffice for now," said Emma. "Almost a half a million dollars. I never imagined." She looked around the table. "Can we do this? I mean, do we have the knowhow to do this without going to jail?"

Steve sat forward, put his fork down and swallowed a bite of meat loaf. "Emma raises an important consideration. We will need to be cautious about what we do during the next few weeks or longer. No one should change their living habits drastically. No new cars or houses purchased, no trips to Europe planned. Agreed?" The others nodded, as each realized that the difference between good fortune in the present and a bad ending in the future could depend on the words chosen and actions taken.

Donna had the next question. "Will our gold be safe where it is and, if so, for how long? The secret cellar is probably known to others in Sagebrush, especially old timers. Does anyone ever venture into that room?"

Justin answered. "We use the outer cellar for additional long-term storage. It is supplemental to the usual kitchen stores. No one has used the inner cellar since Prohibition days. I have a secure lock on both doors and there are only two keys to the inner door." He reached into his pocket, retrieved two large keys, and placed them next to the gold fragment.

Steve picked up one of the keys. "Looks ordinary enough. I suppose the local locksmith knows the pattern?"

"Long gone. These are the keys that unlocked those doors during the 1920s. They can be duplicated, of course, but I don't believe that anyone else has a copy, not even the owner in the Bay Area."

Steve's brow furrowed and he placed the key on the table. "Owner? That's right, I forgot. You manage for an older guy who no longer wants the hotel. If I remember correctly, he was trying to sell it. What happens if this place suddenly changes hands?"

"We lose our poker palace," said Donna.

"We lose our safety cellar filled with a half a ton of gold," replied Justin.

"If we sell a few bars now, we could buy the hotel and guarantee that nothing will be disturbed." Everyone looked at Emma. She had been quietly following the conversation and the others knew she was fully engaged in the operation.

Justin sat back in his chair, his left hand holding a glass of red wine. "I would like that. I started thinking about what I wanted to do with my share. I'd like to put it toward projects about town to help us improve our local economy—fix up the streets, get equipment for the volunteer fire department, things that would make life better for the community. I don't need much for my personal use, but the chance to buy the hotel, to own it and manage it as I see fit, yeah, that would be something to dream about."

Donna said, "Steve and I have talked about putting some of our share to good use as well. Yes, we'd like to take a nice vacation somewhere and get a newer car, but if your estimate of the gold's value is anywhere close, we'd have enough money to support a number of projects."

Emma smiled at Donna and announced that she would like to provide support for the school, perhaps even remodel the building that had been built as a Civilian Conservation Corps project during the Great Depression. "We could also provide a decent athletic field and an indoor basketball court. That would help alleviate some of the guilt over the legal issues, I'm sure."

"Emma, I think you should have one of the keys. Keep it in a safe place. I'll retain the other." Justin handed her a key and put the other in his pocket.

"I guess that brings us back to Rodney, doesn't it?" asked Steve. "If we are going to part with a few bars to buy the hotel, we'll need his help, or someone's, to sell it without risking a lot of questions. He would be another partner, but with all of the material we have, each share will still be generous. Should we cut him in or pay him a fixed fee?"

Justin responded. "If we pay him a fee, he may have a lot of questions about where we got the bars and if we have more. If we make him a full partner, the risk to his stake is the same as ours, and he won't be inclined to ask questions or snoop around for answers." Justin sat back and looked at the others for confirmation or rejection of his proposal.

Emma was the first to answer. "I'm not enthusiastic about Mr. Haas. I've known him for a good number of years. I don't think he is a bad man, as far as that goes, but he does drink and at times he can be loud and boastful. All of you play poker with him, so you know him better in the social sense than I do. If it is necessary that we have him act as our gold trader, then so be it. I do hope, however, that we can trust his discretion."

"All the more reason for him to be a partner. He shares the reward but also the guilt and the loss if we make any grievous errors." Justin looked at each person for agreement to proceed.

Steve sighed. "Emma is right, but I support Justin's proposal." He turned to his wife. She nodded and looked at Emma. Emma smiled and gave a brief nod of her head.

"Okay. I'll approach him tomorrow night, privately, before our game. If he agrees to do it, we'll have him take six bars to Reno and see what we can get. He can say they came from Nevada, keeping any inquiries off our doorstep. At the same time, we'll get a proper assay and learn the value of our treasure."

"That first," said Steve. "Otherwise, he won't know what he is bargaining with. If he can get between twenty and twenty-five thousand dollars, that should be enough to put a substantial down payment on the hotel and get your deed."

Justin laughed. "My first thought was that Old Man Godfrey, the owner, would wonder where I came up with that kind of cash, but I suspect he'll be so happy to unload this property that he won't ask."

"If he does, tell him you are working with a group of real estate investors in Sagebrush, which is true." Donna smiled at her companions in crime.

Justin called for a toast and the meeting was adjourned. All were pleased with the progress they had made. Emma and Justin were especially happy about their plans for community improvement. Donna was consulting her husband on her idea for a train trip across Canada.

CHAPTER THREE

The Trove Group

The group of four began referring to themselves as the Trove Group but not within earshot of others. They refrained from using the words *gold*, *treasure*, *hoard*, or other revealing references to their secret cache. After removing six bars for immediate cash purposes, Justin moved an old refrigerator and several crates against the door to the inner cellar. As agreed, he and Emma retained a key, but decided against having copies made.

Justin met with Rod for dinner before their Friday night poker game. Rod was affable and a regular participant in the weekend get-togethers. As Emma had indicated, he was not a stranger to a bottle and not particular about what form the alcohol took: beer, wine, whiskey—it was all the same to him. Most of the time he held it well, a result of more than a decade of dedicated practice starting at the age of fourteen. By the time he graduated from high school he had obtained sufficient resistance to the numbing effects, a trait that served him well in the military. He could booze with the best and still retain composure and a measure of control.

His other passion was gambling and he wasn't restricted to a specific game or format. His favorite was cards, but craps, horses, sports betting, other casino games—they were all good in his book. Like many gamblers, Rod could be flush with recent winnings or dead broke after a bust, but he never mooched from his fellow table-mates and he paid the occasional debt on time. His best friend at the table was Johnny, a restless risk-taker possessing a spirit somewhat like his own. Johnny was partly settled into semi-domesticity with Sonya, whereas Rod had never found a woman to his liking other than a wild night in the sheets now and then. Then was more frequent than now as the years passed and he began putting on weight. That didn't stop him from looking and scheming, despite the paucity of available females in Sagebrush. Available was a relative term and Rod wasn't picky about looks or personality. Besides, any intended relationship with the opposite sex would be short lived and well defined.

Rod was mystified by his two formidable tablemates. Johnny didn't seem to be in play with Brandy during the games or, as far as Rod could tell, afterward. Rod's room was next door to the room Johnny used in his occasional stayovers and the walls of the old hotel weren't particularly thick. Either Johnny was remarkably discreet—hard to believe after a night of boisterous drinking—or the prospective liaisons never took place. The other possibility was that his friend occasionally made his way to Brandy's flat, but that had never been apparent. Johnny smiled and usually flirted when Brandy did, but his loyalty to Sonya didn't appear to be in doubt. Ray Gordon and Rod didn't keep their unfulfilled aspirations hidden, but they were also on the outside looking in.

Justin bought dinner, although Rod had ample money for the meal and the game that would start around eight that evening. The young hotel manager hadn't revealed the reason for the unusual treat, but Rod figured it had to be something important. Justin made sure that no one was seated near them and he cautioned Rod about the private nature of their meeting and discussion.

After a predinner drink and the first course, a hearty beef and barley soup, Justin broached the subject with a few questions. He had spent a good part of the day rehearsing what he would and would not say to solicit Rod's assistance without revealing critical details until he was sure Rod would be cooperative and could be trusted.

Rod finished the last of his soup and sat back in the chair with a relaxed grin. He pulled out a small package of cigars, better ones than he usually carried, and offered one to Justin. The manager declined and Rod lit up as they waited for the salad to arrive.

"Guess you must have something big in the wind, huh? Never thought you'd be wanting to cut me in on anything. What have we got?"

Right to the chase. That's good. We won't have to dance around. "Well, Rod, your perception is on the money. We have something that I think you might be interested in, but first, I need to remind you again that what we talk about is not to be shared with anyone outside our group. You'll understand why after I give you the particulars."

Rod sat forward, cigar in his right hand. "Group? There's a group? Who?"

"A few of us in Sagebrush, people you know well. We share information on a certain discovery made not far from here. I can fill you in on details later, but the important thing I need to ask you is whether you are willing to do something that might not be completely legal."

"What the hell does that mean?" Rod flicked ashes into the tray at his side. His voice, gruff as usual, was offset by a face-wide grin, as if Justin had suggested an evening of entertainment to supplement the forthcoming card game.

"I mean to propose that we engage in an activity, a sale of some items that might not be prescribed by the law of the land." Justin looked in Rod's face, noting the amusement and anticipation.

"Shit, Justin, I love all your big words. What? Drugs, guns, what?" Rod held his cigar out to the side, the grin still evident, an indication he was not shocked or intimidated by dancing at the edge of legal boundaries. "I hope that doesn't refer to assassinating or kidnapping someone, Justin. I'm no angel, I assure you, but I have never dropped to that. At least not yet."

"You won't have to. Our group is in possession of some material that is against the law to retain in large quantities. The materials aren't illegal, just possession of large amounts."

"Ah, it must be gold. Somewhere, somehow, your little group has gotten their hands on some gold. What is it? Jewelry, coins?

How much?" Rod leaned forward, keeping his voice low. "A certain amount of that is legal, especially family jewelry and collectable coins. I know, because I have some friends who are pawnbrokers and they hold a fair amount of that for their customers." He sat back and took another slow drag on his cigar.

"Exactly the reason why I am…why we are consulting you. You know something about these types of commodities and have some connections with, let's say, professionals who can negotiate a sale of the same. Interested?"

"I hate to be offish or come across as selfish, but I have to ask. What's in it for me?"

"A share of the proceedings. We would ask you to take some of this material to your contacts, arrange the sale of it, and bring the proceeds back to us. We would divide the remaining assets equally among the group members, including you."

Rod thought and shifted in his chair. "If we are talking about some jewelry or coins, why wouldn't you do this yourself? Pawnshops are perfectly legal and selling gold items is not a problem, unless it's stolen property. Are you asking me to fence things that aren't yours?"

"No, no, not at all. Well, maybe, but it's not something we stole, and it's more than a few coins or pieces of jewelry." Justin hesitated as the moment of truth arrived. It was now or never to inform Rod of what they were up to and if he didn't, Rod's curiosity had already been aroused. There didn't seem to be any way to erase what he had revealed. "Rod, we have in our possession a considerable amount of raw gold. It is in the form of old miner's bars, not refined, but in quantities that appear to be worth upward of several hundreds of thousands of dollars."

Rod sat back, sporting a different type of smile—not conspiratorial but relaxed, as if he had been let in on a hilarious joke. "You're putting me on, right? You're telling me you and your group, whoever that is, have a treasure chest or something like that full of gold?"

"That's what I'm telling you, Rod. That's why the need for discretion and why I have been dancing around about the details. We need your help, and we're willing to share our find, but the amount and type of material we have is well beyond the federal limits established for possession. Are you willing to help us?"

"Who is *us*? Who are the other partners in crime, so to speak?"

"Steve and Donna Woodward, Emma Dodson, and myself. It was Emma and Steve's discovery and Donna and I have been helping with the interim tasks. I took a small fragment to Alturas to confirm what it was."

Noticing that Justin was hesitant to name it aloud, Rod followed suit. "And this material is in what form?"

"Do you know what a doré bar is?" Rod shook his head. Justin glanced around the room, but only two couples were seated some distance away and engaged in conversation. "Well, neither did I, but Steve identified them as the physical form miners melted their flakes and nuggets into for easier transport and accountability. They are usually sixty to eighty percent pure gold and silver. The man in Alturas estimated, without a proper assay, that our fragment could be that pure."

"So you have a few bars and want me to sell them somewhere for you? Doesn't seem like a big problem. Just need to ask, though. What's to stop me from making the sale and disappearing with all the proceeds? Could be several thousand dollars and that would keep me content somewhere besides Sagebrush."

"We'll trust you with six of the bars. They weigh about ten pounds each, and they might bring twenty thousand dollars or more, depending on purity. They represent a small fraction of what we recovered. You would be a partner in the full amount, which I can assure you is worth many times more than what you could run away with."

"Trust is relative, heh?" Rod grinned and put out his cigar as the salads arrived at the table. The dining room clock indicated that the card game would start in an hour. "Let's eat up, and maybe we'll have time to discuss this a bit more before we play. Yeah, Justin, I'm definitely interested, and thanks for bringing me in." He picked up his fork and started to eat but paused. "Emma Dodson. Really? I would never guess that she would be in on something like this."

Justin ate the greens in a slow, deliberate fashion and watched Rod as he attacked his salad with eager enthusiasm. *I hope I haven't made a mistake. We need someone like him and he appears to be candid about the temptation to run off with the money. Will the promise of a bigger payoff be enough to guarantee his cooperation and discretion? In this and any other aspect of life, what is a guarantee?*

Rod and Justin finished the dinner with a cocktail. Justin provided additional information about the find but not specifically where it had been found or relocated. He remembered Emma's question about whether there might be additional caches of bars. Although it seemed doubtful, the last thing Justin wanted to instigate was an out-of-control treasure hunt that brought the feds and others into Sagebrush. He told Rod that the hoard was stored in a safe place and that he would reveal the details after consulting with the group and after the bars had been evaluated. Rod said he was prepared to leave for Reno on the following Monday and would have an answer by Wednesday or Thursday of that week. Justin said he would deliver the bars to Rod Sunday evening at the hotel.

THE FRIDAY-NIGHT GAME INCLUDED JOHNNY, ROD, JUSTIN, Steve, Ken the barber, and Brandy. Donna opted out. Earlier, Justin had informed the biologist of Rod's cooperation in the venture. Rod occasionally glanced at Steve, but neither of them indicated anything about events beyond the game.

Ken was doing well, taking some pots on last cards and an aggressive lucky streak. The drinks were flowing freely and no one seemed overly concerned about where the chips were piled. Brandy, usually among those ahead at the table, was down several dollars, as was Johnny. For Rod, the game seemed more of a distraction than the featured attraction of Sagebrush weekend nightlife.

Johnny noticed the subtle difference in the table atmosphere. Rod was usually boisterous, especially as the night wore on and the alcohol accumulated. Justin, usually soft spoken and mild in his approach to betting, seemed loud and reckless. Not a lot, but enough to alter the dynamics of play. Looking at his diminishing stack, Johnny remarked that it didn't seem to be his night.

Rod put his hand on Johnny's shoulder. "Might be the case, Johnny-O. Maybe it's time to get back to the trailer and take some comfort in your Russian woman."

"Not yet, you slimy bastard. I still have a few hands left in me and if it gets late, I know where my room is."

"So does everyone else," replied Rod, giving Brandy a leering stare as she replenished her drink from the bar set up on a rolling cart against the wall.

Brandy glanced back at him and flashed one of her enigmatic smiles. "Knowledge isn't the same as access, is it Rodney?" She sat down, prepared for her turn dealing the cards. It continued the commentary between Rod, Johnny, and Brandy, much to the amusement of the others at the table. Even when she was the only woman at the table, the brunette could hold her own and provide a suitable retort. Ken, in particular, was alert to any indication of change in the status of the three. Despite Johnny's woman friend, these three were the only unmarried regular players. When Pete, Ken, Ray, or Justin played, their wives waited faithfully at home. They rarely went out with the guys to barhop or participate in any of the other male activities. Donna and Brandy were the exceptions.

<hr>

Rod sat in the hotel manager's office on Sunday afternoon. To Justin's surprise, Rod had shaved and donned fresh, pressed clothes and polished shoes. He had his hair cut the day before, which had brought favorable comments at the Saturday night game.

"Looking slick, like a high roller." Justin leaned back in his chair, displaying a sincere smile to a man unlikely to earn a best dressed award.

"Never hurts to present an image of casual affluence when you're playing in the business world. So where are the bars?"

"I have them out back, hidden on the loading dock. Sixty pounds worth, so I thought we would load them direct from there."

Justin still hadn't revealed the location of the trove. That would come after Rod returned with the funds. In the meantime, he had inquired about purchasing the Sagebrush Hotel. The owner was interested and a purchase price and conditions were floating between his agent in Oakland and Justin's real estate friend in Alturas.

The men walked to the back of the hotel and emerged from a door looking over the alley. Justin instructed Rod to bring his car around and pull up to the dock. While he was doing so, Justin uncovered a wheeled cart that contained two boxes. Each box held three bars, covered in paper scraps. They carefully transferred the boxes to the trunk of Rod's '53 Chevy. No one appeared in the alley, but if they had, they would have seen nothing to get excited about, just some boxes. They shook hands, Justin wished him good luck, and Rod drove off to earn his admission to the group.

Justin returned to his office to draft a few notes for the transaction and reflect on how the pending purchase of the hotel would change his life in a substantial way.

THE SAME SUNDAY AFTERNOON ANOTHER MEETING OCCURRED. Steve and Donna were relaxing in the small town park, sitting on a blanket. The grass was fresh and green from the recent rains, preceding the expected summer drought when greenness was a rare commodity anywhere in the high desert valley.

Ray parked his pickup truck along the park side curb. When Steve looked up, Ray motioned for him to approach. Steve winked at his wife and got to his feet, walking toward the truck with a smile.

"How ya doing, Ray? Nice day, huh?" Steve leaned against the open passenger side window, noticing that Ray didn't seem to be having a nice day.

"Get in the car, Steve. We need to talk." He was all business, particularly odd on a Sunday afternoon. Ray often spent the day off at home with his wife and brother, occasionally eating out or picnicking out of town.

Steve opened the door and sat. "Thanks again for loaning me the truck last week. Preciate it."

"That's what I wanted to talk to you about." Ray fixed him with a hard stare. "You told me you needed to haul some dead deer. If you remember, I'd asked you to make sure the bed was clean when you brought it back. It was dark when you returned it, so I didn't pay much attention."

"Damn, Ray, it was clean. I told you we would use a tarp and…"

"Yeah, it was clean. No problem, because you didn't haul deer with it. I don't care why you borrowed it, but no need to lie to me about it, and what's this?" Ray held up a small, rough brown pebble that glittered in the sunshine from the windshield.

Steve recognized the fragment. A piece of one of the bars must have broken loose while loading and probably rolled under the tarp. In the dark alley, they hadn't noticed it. "Looks like a rock, Ray. What's it look like to you?" He smiled, as if Ray was pulling a trick on him. "I mean, I don't want it, so you can keep it if you like."

"I didn't say anything to you until now because I didn't know what it was, but a rockhound friend of mine thinks it might be gold. Where did you get it?" He held the rock up, halfway between his face and Steve's.

"What makes you think I got it anywhere? It might have been in your truck before I borrowed it."

"There's more to it," Ray stated firmly, putting the rock on the dashboard. "I happened to be walking by the hotel alley on Monday night. Although it was hard to see, I could make out you and Donna transferring something between my truck and the hotel loading dock. A whole lot of something. It took several minutes, but I know they weren't deer. What the hell's going on, Steve? What did you find and what does the hotel have to do with it?"

Steve thought a minute. *What to do and say? Got to stall him.* "I can't answer that right now, Ray. There are others involved and

I will need to consult with them. I'll try and get you an answer if you will promise to do one thing."

"Promise? I don't promise nothing. If you're up to something illegal and my truck is involved, I promise nothing. However, I'll give you a break. Meet with your partners, whoever they are, and tell them I want to meet with them myself. I can be persuaded to go along if the rewards are worthwhile."

Steve lowered his head, realizing he was caught between a gold rock and a hard place. Anything said further would only make it worse. As useful as Ray and his truck could be, he was one of the last people in Sagebrush that the group would want to share the secret with. He looked up. "Okay, Ray, you've got a deal. It may take a few days, but I'll try to arrange a meeting before the next week is done. Give me that much time and we'll talk."

"Yeah, but don't pull any fast ones. I'll be keeping an eye on the hotel and when I can't, I'll have Jay checking on it." He motioned to the door.

Steve climbed out and walked to Donna without looking back. He heard the truck drive away as she looked up at him. "Anything wrong, dear? You don't look like you've had a neighborly conversation."

"You're right, it wasn't friendly. Ray found a piece of one of the bars in the truck bed. He believes it contains gold and he saw us unloading the truck at the hotel. He wants in on whatever."

"Does he know?"

He sat on the blanket, hugging his knees. "Not much, but enough to be a dangerous source of rumors. I told him we'd get back to him after I talked to other people. He probably suspects Justin is in on it, but there would be no reason for him to include Emma or Rod. Which reminds me, Rod won't be back for a couple of days and we'll need to include him in any decisions. Shit! Bad timing and even worse interference. We'll need to make some hard decisions."

⸻ ◆ ⸻

Steve informed Justin about Ray and the possible threat to their group early Monday morning in the hotel dining room before he drove to work. The conversation was brief and Justin cautioned him about doing anything further until Rod returned with information about the bars and, hopefully, the money they needed to back their offer for the hotel. Justin didn't see any need to bring Emma in on it until the group met following Rod's return.

Rod returned to Sagebrush Wednesday, flashing a triumphant grin and smoking a five-dollar cigar. Wearing slacks and a new tweed sport jacket, he portrayed the picture of success, a man who knew his way about town, not difficult in Sagebrush, and one who had the means. He and Justin met in the manager's office at seven-thirty in the evening.

"We're good to go," Rod said without preamble, leaning back in the chair, legs splayed in front of him. He pulled a large manila envelope from his coat pocket and tossed it on Justin's desk.

The manager resisted the temptation to grab the envelope and open it. He sat back in his chair, regarding his courier-seller quietly as if trying to decide whether he should continue to use his services. *Too late, now*, he thought and opened the envelope. It contained 215 one-hundred dollar bills, three tens, and two ones, a total of $21,532. Justin laid the money on the desk, the hundreds wrapped in paper bands of fifty bills each and five loose bills.

"The bars averaged 78.5 percent gold, plus a small amount of silver. The assayist, a friend of a friend, was amazed not only at the purity, but also the form it came in. He wanted to know where I got them, but of course, I played dumb." Rod laughed. "Actually, I can do that pretty well. The market value came to 26,564. Their fee to assay and handle the transaction was 18 percent, leaving a net proceeds of $21,782. I deducted my expenses for the trip—gas, food, and a place to stay—holding out $250. Is that agreeable?" Rod rolled it off his tongue as if he had rehearsed it a number of times.

"Sure, sure, that's fine. Apart from curiosity about the bars, were there any other problems? Do we need to be watching our backsides?"

"Don't think so. Some of the people who handle this make six- and seven-number deals, so this isn't a major effort for them. My contact said they would melt the bars and purify it and that was part of their fee. If we brought additional gold to them in real bars or ingots, they could reduce the fees to, say, 16 percent. I didn't confirm that we had additional bars."

Justin rubbed his chin, his eyes on the money spread across the desk. "Something to consider as we decide what to do with the rest of the haul. In the meantime, I better get this into the hotel safe." He placed the bills back in the envelope and wrote a note to himself to record the amount. "I'll continue with the offer for the property, but let's plan on meeting with our group tomorrow evening. At that time, we'll decide what to do about Mr. Gordon."

"Ray? What's with him?" Rod, like some of the others in the poker group, was not particularly fond of the hardware store owner, but he tolerated him for the sake of the games.

"Seems our friend is suspicious about our secret. He found a pebble in the bed of his truck, the one Steve and I used to recover the material. He doesn't know anything for sure at this point, but we need to come up with a plan to quell his curiosity."

"Quell his curiosity, huh?" Rod imitated a gun with his hand, pulling back the trigger with his thumb.

"Nothing that drastic, although it is a thought." Justin gave him a grim smile. "But we'll decide that as a group."

"Sounds good. Now, can you tell me more about this find? Where was it, who found it, and how much more there is?"

They were both standing. Justin moved to the wall safe, spun the combination while blocking Rod's view, and tucked the envelope inside. He closed the safe and turned back to Rod. In his hand, he had thirty-two dollars. "Enough to have a couple of drinks, and continue our discussion, heh?" He grinned. They shook hands and left the hotel to wander over to the nearest tavern.

Not close enough to hear their random chatter, the men were observed from a block away by Ray Gordon, sitting inconspicuously in the dark shadow cast by a cabin on the main street. He watched them enter the Pioneer Barroom. *Need to have a talk with*

Mr. Gonzales. He walked into a nearby alley, climbed into his truck and drove slowly home, trying to grasp the relationship between Steve Woodward, Justin, and Rod Haas. He knew them all and had played poker with them often enough to know they were different from each other and that none of them should be connected to the gold fragment he found in his truck. *What the hell is going on?*

———◆———

Justin wasted no time in having his real estate agent contact Godfrey's agent in the Bay Area. He made the offer on the hotel, proposing a $20,000 down payment and terms to pay off the note within ten years. He had thought about offering a larger payment, but didn't want to attract attention or questions about where the money originated. The smaller amount seemed safe enough and this would permit the group to discuss the logistics of selling additional bars, dividing the proceeds, and, not to be forgotten, what to do about Ray Gordon. What did he suspect and what would he believe? The manager passed the word to Rod, Emma, and the Woodwards to meet Thursday evening. Emma agreed to host the group at her home. They would gather at eight o'clock, after dinner, arriving over a fifteen-minute interval to avoid notice by Ray.

Their hope was doomed to fail. Ray had his own contacts with Alturas realtors and had learned about Justin's offer to buy the hotel. He kept an eye on the building, suspecting that a meeting or a decision was imminent. However, he was surprised when he cautiously followed Justin and Rod to Emma's bungalow. The Woodwards had already arrived and he surveyed the scene from a nearby high spot with binoculars.

Emma served iced tea and oatmeal cookies as the group settled in her living room. Rod was wearing his new slacks and sport jacket and Emma gave him a reassuring look of approval. Justin and Rod discussed the initial gold sale in Reno and the offer to purchase the Sagebrush Hotel. Steve reported on the Sunday meeting with Ray at the park and the inherent threat to their project. It was a sobering moment. Until then, everything had proceeded smoothly, under control. Following the initial discovery by Emma and Steve, each member had been brought in with the group's approval as it grew. The five now faced the prospect of admitting someone who none of them trusted or wanted.

"There will be quite a payoff at some time." said Donna. "Maybe we shouldn't be too greedy."

"It's not about greed. It's about a man who threatens us if we don't include him. No one else here joined under those conditions." Justin looked at Rod and smiled. "We had some hesitation with regard to you, if the truth be known, but you didn't pressure us and you have earned your fair share of the proceeds. Ray is a whole different kettle of corn."

Rod picked up a glass of tea and shook his head. "Probably need something stronger than this." He looked up at Emma and grinned. "Later, of course." He took a large sip. "I've known Ray for a good number of years. Most of the time, there has been nothing to complain about. He plays a fair hand of poker and has always been a help with hardware and repair issues. I work for him on and off and he always pays me when the work is done. He can be demanding at times, occasionally nasty, but this, this is not a good sign."

Donna sat forward on the couch and looked at Rod, Steve, and Justin. "Do we have a choice, really? If we don't make him some kind of offer, what could he do?"

"You mean, besides blab his fool head off?" This was from Emma, usually gentle and soft spoken. Ever since the discovery, she had assumed a different persona, one that displayed considerable determination with a toughness that had not been considered one of her major attributes. Donna smiled and shook her head.

Justin looked up at the ceiling, searching for an appropriate response. "I think we need to press on quickly for the purchase of the hotel." He paused. "News about the recovery of a large amount of a forbidden mineral will not help us in negotiating an affordable price for the property, nor will it play well with the federal govern-ment. Remember how much of this stuff we have."

Steve spoke. "That may actually play into our hands. If Ray becomes a shareholder in the enterprise, he will face the same potential penalties as the rest of us. I suspect he'll enjoy a walk on the dark side, but that imposes some restraints as well."

"He is also a talented locksmith. He might be able to help secure our assets until they are sold," said Justin.

"That might be tricky," said Rod, finishing his glass of tea. He shook his head when Emma offered a refill. "If Ray provides the locks, we may find it hard to control the number of keys and who has them."

They sat silent for a moment, trying to think of another approach, an answer to the dilemma the hardware dealer posed. No one offered an alternative solution.

"So it seems we are going to let the weasel into our hen house." Emma sat back in her easy chair, hands wrapped around her chest and looked at Justin. "Will you be the one to inform him?"

"I think Steve and I should do it together." Justin looked at the biologist. "You are the one he confronted and I am the current guardian of our little trove, but we will need to set some conditions to keep things under control. That is, better control than we have at the moment."

The others indicated their agreement and the meeting drifted into a general discussion of what might change in their individual lives as a result of the windfall. "If we can cash it in safely," said Donna.

After an hours observation, Ray drove home to await further developments and reflect on the group he would be dealing with. Were there others? How deep did this go and how much money was involved? *It must be enough to warrant a fair amount of secrecy, but this is not more than I can handle. A matronly school teacher, a biologist and his wife, and a nowhere hotel manager. Rod might be more of an obstacle. He might be an even match if it gets physical, but he walks in an alcoholic mist half of the time. Nothing that Jay and I can't handle.* Thinking of his brother and wife, Ray thought it best not to reveal current events to them. Barbara knew too many women in town and there was no telling what his twin brother might say or who he might say it to.

AT TEN O'CLOCK ON FRIDAY MORNING, JUSTIN CALLED RAY TO meet him and Steve at the hotel. "How about a late lunch, one-thirty or thereabouts? We'll have it in my office. Just let me know what you would like."

"How about a steak with the trimmings? Can you afford that now Mr. Gonzales?" The mockery in his voice could have been written in neon lights. Ray felt full of an almighty and self-justified dose of confidence. He could demand what he wanted and he had them in the grip of his powerful fists. Time to squeeze.

"No problem, Ray. See you in a few hours." Justin called Steve, confirmed the time and indicated that Ray was hunting for big game.

"Do you think we need Rod there?" Steve asked.

"Not this time. Let's give Ray a chance to play his hand without revealing our down cards. We'll hear him out and see what we can come up with. If necessary, we can defer any final decision until we pass it by the group." As usual, Justin's voice was calm and level, reassuring Steve that the meeting was unlikely to descend into a storm of threats. Poker analogies had their place.

Justin and Steve opted for less opulent meals, but Ray was served a New York steak, medium done, with a baked potato and fixings, a tossed salad, and a large draft. The men sat around a table set up in the manager's office. They ate mostly in silence without mention of the group or the suspected treasure. Steve and Justin exchanged an occasional glance as Ray consumed his steak, inhaling it as if there would be no food in the foreseeable future.

Ray wiped his mouth on an oversized napkin and sat back with a grin, satisfied with the moment, the concerned look on Steve's face, and the silent contemplation of Justin. *Don't know what to do with me, do you, you pompous bastards? I'll let you know before we're through here, bet your ass on that!*

Justin leaned forward, put his folded hands on the table, and looked directly at Ray. "As you are probably aware, a small group of us are in possession of some material that is illegal to possess but has a modest potential value to our community. Since we are alone, I can confirm your suspicions about the material being gold, a partly refined ore that was probably mined during the last century."

Ray sat up straight, putting his hands on the table, consciously mimicking the hotel manager. "How modest, Justin? What are we talking about? A few thousand dollars? How many people in this group of yours?" *I know who some of them are, but who else?*

Justin looked at Steve, who said, "Ray, you found a fragment of some bars that Emma and I discovered while doing an informal reconnaissance near the Warner Mountains. We were looking for field sites for her school kids and the find was an accident. We didn't have any prior knowledge of its presence."

"On public or on private land?" Ray was looking for any angles that might give him an upper hand and the other men knew it.

"Public land," answered Steve.

When he didn't say anything more, Ray became more aggressive. "Where is this? Somewhere near here? Can't be more than a few hours because you didn't have my truck that long."

"You're right," answered Justin. "Not far from here, but you can understand why we aren't in a terrible hurry to provide further details. We need to reach some agreements about this before we answer your questions."

"Agreements, huh? Like I keep my mouth shut about your discovery in turn for a share of whatever it is. Does that sound like what you mean by an agreement?"

"Crudely put but basically in line with what we have in mind. Listen, Ray, you know it is gold and that possession of large amounts is against the law. We don't have any evidence related to prior ownership, but revelation about the site or the amount could result in confiscation of everything. No one in Sagebrush will benefit from that. Agree with that so far?"

"Sure, sure. I'm not a dunderhead. Listen boys, we've played poker for a number of years. I'm a businessman here, work hard, have a family, and I'm not wanting to spoil this big find for anyone. I just want a small part of it for myself. I want to be a part of the group, so who all is involved in this?"

Steve and Justin exchanged glances. Steve answered. "Emma and I discovered the bars and Justin obtained the first identification and estimates of value. Rod Haas got us a better estimate and exchanged a few for some working capital. My wife, Donna is the other member of the group."

"There are only five of you, that's it?"

"That's it," said Justin. "You would make six, each having an equal share of the pot."

"How about Barbara and Jay? What about their shares?" Ray looked from one to the other, searching for a sign of weakness, but only stony faces stared back.

"Not going to do that, Ray. A sixth share is more than adequate for the loan of your truck and your silence. We'll take the risks of negotiating and handling the transactions. We might need your truck for transportation later, but you'll be well compensated for your minimal efforts."

"Good, I was coming to that next. What is a share of this? How big is the pot?"

"Several hundred thousand dollars, by our best estimate, Ray. We have more than one hundred bars of gold."

Ray sat back and whistled. "Jeez-us Christ almighty! No wonder all the secrecy." He narrowed his eyes and grinned as if he had hit the hidden full house. "You must have this stuff here at the hotel, because that's where you unloaded my truck. Right? Must be in your cellar, behind the kitchen."

Justin nodded. There was no need to say anything further about the location. "Ray, is it worth your confidence and cooperation, I mean full cooperation, to have a one-sixth share? It should be a substantial amount once we figure how to dispose of it without official intervention by the State of California or the feds. What say?"

Ray leaned forward and extended his hand. "You gotta deal. Can I share this with my wife and brother? I won't tell them the details, just that I have something working to ensure a brighter future."

Steve shook his hand. "Your call, Ray, but tell no one outside of your family, and you need to reinforce their confidentiality. Rumors spread fast in a small town like this, and the less anyone suspects the better. That includes the others at our game tonight. No hints, no references."

Ray agreed to the conditions. After he left, Justin consulted briefly with Steve. "Do you think he'll play by the rules?"

"I think so. Just as we proposed with Rod, the amount is sufficiently large enough to exercise caution. Ray isn't real bright but he isn't stupid, just ornery at times. I don't completely trust him, but as long as he has that much to lose, I don't think he'll betray us. He needs us more than we need him."

That afternoon Steve informed the other group members of their arrangement with Ray. Despite some concerns, they were relieved to learn that the meeting had been cordial. No mention of the hotel purchase had been made, but Justin decided to expedite the transaction.

THE FRIDAY NIGHT POKER GAME STARTED TENTATIVELY. UNTIL a few drinks had lubricated the players and eased the tension, the conversation seemed artificial, almost as if the table consisted of strangers. Much of the usual banter and insults were muted except for Brandy and Johnny, who along with Ken and Pete, were blissfully ignorant of the real game in town.

By ten-thirty, the table talk had descended to its usual low level of integrity. Rod had been drinking steadily, producing a familiar baritone slur. His eyes kept returning to Brandy, whether she was in the pot or not.

Johnny sat next to her, across the table from Rod, and noticed the hard stares and undisguised leer. "See something you want, Rod?" he said, folding his cards. He had also consumed a fair share of whiskey and felt agitated enough to challenge his older friend.

"What's it to you kid? I'm looking at the only thing seated here worth lookin' at. If she don't mind, no reason you should. You got an old lady to go home to."

Johnny leaned forward to offer a rebut, but Brandy intervened. "Let it go, Johnny, I can take care of myself and I can handle Mr. Haas. For all you know, I've handled him before."

That brought a laugh from the other men at the table, who were always amused by the rowdy exchanges. Donna was absent, so Brandy was indeed the only person at the table worth looking at.

Rod smiled, pleased with her response. *Couldn't have done better myself.* "Maybe later, then," he said, hopeful for a late night rendezvous.

"There is always maybe, baby, but don't bet your entire stake on it." She gave him an eyelash flutter, laid down her winning straight, and scooped the pot.

Ray made a mental note of the repartee and wondered if Rod was capable of maintaining the confidence that the group was supposedly committed to. He kept his cool and played with a minimum of emotion, smug in the knowledge that a bigger stake awaited if everyone did what they said they would do. He counted every drink Rod consumed and watched him slip into a sedentary state, all too familiar to the weekend card group.

The game broke around one o'clock, and most of the poker gang stumbled out of the hotel. Brandy decided to stay at the hotel that night, something she occasionally did when the game ran late. She had already dropped off some sleeping clothes in number 19, next door to Rod's room. Johnny left the hotel to join his live-in lady, clearing the way for Rod to make his move.

Brandy had consumed a fair share of drink, and though she held it well for an eighteen-year-old, she was in a strange mood. She wasn't sure why she had responded negatively to Johnny's attempt to defend her and she was even less sure whether she wanted him to or not. He flirted and teased her, like many of the others, but had never come on to her with any serious intent. She barely knew Sonya and had no reason to make a move of her own, but it left her wanting something.

Rod stood in the hallway before her, a hand on the knob to his room. He had mellowed as the night wore on and he looked at her now, displaying more desire and less raw lust. His voice was softer, almost gentle despite the vocal gravel. "Would you have an interest, lass? Perhaps for a nightcap or to snuggle for a while?" He was lonely, didn't entertain the ladies often, and was more interested in company than sex at the moment.

Brandy seemed to sense this and took his hand. "Do what you need to do and then come to my room. I have better booze there than you do." Indeed she did, having grabbed a bottle of Glenlivet from the bar as she left the poker room. She smiled and walked to her room and entered.

Rod stumbled inside his room, used the bathroom, removed his pants and shirt but retained his underwear. He nonchalantly walked the few steps to her room, knocked on the door, and entered when she answered. She was wearing conservative flannel pajamas, not the seductive negligee he had hoped for, but she had two glasses of scotch poured. She invited him to sit next to her on the bed. They talked and drank and he attempted to put his arms around her a couple of times, which she permitted but didn't aid his clumsy attempts to go further. She smiled and cooed and figured if she talked long enough he would fall asleep.

However, it didn't work that way. Instead, his mumbled sweet nothings turned to something far more seductive. He told her that he was a partner in a local enterprise that would make him wealthy enough to never have to work again. At first she chalked his prattle up to the deliriums of alcohol, but then he told her about Steve and Emma and the gold bars, his trip to Reno, and the secrecy needed because the gold was stored in the very building they were in. As he confessed, Brandy realized that this was not mindless muttering but a revelation to which, for whatever reason or result, she was now a privileged recipient.

About three o'clock, he fell asleep and soon after she did the same, sharing her bed with the man who had promised to give her half of his share in the cached fortune. When the morning came, Rod barely remembered what he had told her, but she gave him a kiss and promised to keep the secret. He was not happy about his lapse of trust and could only hope it had been worth it. He wasn't sure if they had made love or not, but she seemed friendly enough. His real fear was what the other group members would say if or when they found out.

CHAPTER FOUR

The Tontine

The Saturday night game progressed without any referral to the trove group and Rod remained silent about his dalliance with Brandy. She apparently did the same, and her table behavior toward him was no different than on any other night. She occasionally flirted and often insulted him, along with the others. Her eyes, however, drifted toward Johnny. This time she sat across from him, studying his moves, his expressions, as if auditioning him for a film or stage performance in which he was expected to play a major role.

It was almost midnight when Rod began to hint at a possible replay of the night before. He had purposely limited his intake of the good stuff, trying to maintain a sense of purpose. He was wearing his better clothes, the ones he brought back from Reno. Ray noted the change in behavior and appearance and observed the three-way drama with some interest. It was no surprise to him or anyone else when Johnny announced that he would crash at the hotel after the game. Brandy said nothing and Rod made his way to the liquor table to pour a stiff one.

After the game folded, Rod walked quickly down the hall and entered his room without looking back at Johnny and Brandy, who were several steps behind. Johnny had his head down and paused at his door, looking into Brandy's face.

Without a smile or eye bat, she said, "You know where I live." She walked past Rod's room, gave a brief look back at Johnny, still standing by his partly opened door, and entered her room. It was unusual for her to stay at the hotel two nights in a row, but this was an unusual weekend.

Johnny wasn't clear what it meant. He was used to the young woman's flirtations and general craziness, but other than the prevailing lust most men felt for the delights of the fairer sex, he had never entertained a serious move to consecrate anything intimate with her. She was witty, fun, a hell of a poker player, and always a challenge, but he already had a woman with a warm bed. He rarely strayed. In many ways, it was ideal having the freedom to wander but electing not to. The invitation was clear but what should he do about it? Like Brandy, he was curious about a fellow tablemate. He suspected that she had already slept with Rod at some time, although his older friend had never indicated such, a rare example of discretion from an otherwise unreserved blabbermouth and braggart.

Johnny left the door ajar, walked into the bathroom, peed, washed his hands and face, and stared into the mirror. He needed a shave and a clearer head, but the idea of the young, attractive brunette waiting for him two doors away was having its effect. *What do I have to lose? Sonya won't know and even if she did, would it make a difference? Would it change things at the poker table? What about Rod? Although we are sometimes competitive and give each other a hard time, we have been friends for several years and he might have an interest in the girl, woman, or whatever Brandy is or isn't, but she is an adult and so is Rod. I don't need to be overly sensitive about their reasons or actions.* He looked at his bed and at the open door to the hall. There was no sound from Rod's room. The hotel was quiet, not even a scurrying mouse to disturb the peace. *If I do go to Brandy, how quiet would that be? The walls are anything but soundproof. Is Rod still awake, wondering if he should be the one to knock on her door? The hell with it!*

He took off his boots, walked into the hallway in his socks, carefully closed his door, and stepped softly past Rod's room to stand before the door of the femme fatale of the evening. He started to knock, thought better of it, and twisted the knob. The door opened and he stepped inside. A night-light beside the table revealed her sitting on the left side of the bed, her hands around her knees, wearing nothing, staring at him. She remained silent as he closed the door and made his way to the bed.

"The socks are a nice touch, but you might want to lose the shirt and pants, cowboy." It was almost a whisper, but one exuding warmth and humor. She gave him an encouraging smile and rolled back the covers from the right side of the bed.

He sat beside her and starting pulling down his jeans. "Can I ask you why you are being so kind this evening? I beat you the last hand when we were head to head. This hardly seems in character with our usual farewells."

"I didn't plan to spend the night here. Sorry, no bedclothes." She smiled and sat back, exposing her upper body in the dim light. "Some things have changed, Johnny. I need to talk to you and I thought this wasn't the worst thing that could happen to us. I spent last night with Rod, but he slept on the bed with his clothes on. He was pretty wasted before he fell asleep. His only reward for keeping me company was a morning kiss and smile, but it's what he told me before he zonked out that might be important."

By then, Johnny had thrown his jeans into the corner and was removing his flannel shirt. That left him in briefs and a T-shirt that had seen better times. He sat on his side of the bed and leaned against the pillow propped on the headboard. "Sounds serious, Brandy. Is this something you should be telling me? Despite all of the things we say to each other at the table, Rod is a friend."

"Yeah, I know that, and I have been mulling this over all day, not sure when or if to tell you. He did ask me to keep it a secret, so I'm assuming you don't know about the scheme he is in, the one that's guarding something here at the hotel." She had turned to face him, her profile in the shadow of the night-light, but he could make out the concern on her features and the lack of tease in her voice. "Should I continue?"

She had moved mostly under the covers, but one breast was exposed. It was his first intimate glimpse of her, but as enticing and promising as the view might be, the revelation about Rod interested him most. *Should she continue? Hell yes.* He put a hand on one of hers and nodded, not sure what this was all about but knowing they had already gone too far down this road to turn back.

"Rod said that he was part of what he called the treasure trove group and that it was in possession of a large amount of gold bars, ones that may date from the gold rush days. He said Emma and Steve found them a couple of weeks ago, and they are stashed here in the hotel. Donna, Justin and Ray are also part of the group."

"Ray Gordon?"

"Yes. Rod said that Ray forced his way in after discovering remnants of a bar in his truck. Steve and Justin had used Ray's truck to bring the gold to town."

Johnny said nothing for several seconds as he processed the unexpected news. "That helps explain Rod's new clothes and more positive outlook after he came back from Reno, but why did he decide to tell you this and why are you telling me?"

"I'm not sure, Johnny. I think Rod had some fantasy about sharing it with me. He offered me half but was snoring before he could specify the conditions or what I was supposed to do to earn it."

"Do you think he wants to marry you?"

"I doubt it. He isn't the marrying kind. Maybe he was thinking of a long-term consort, to use a polite phrase. We didn't talk about it in the morning and I got the impression he was sorry he told me. Alcohol can make for bitter regrets, as we all know." She settled down closer to and facing him.

"Yeah, we do, but why me? I'm sure that none of the other members are going to be delighted that you and I are aware of their plans. I mean, hoarding gold is against the law. How much do they have?"

"A lot. Rod didn't give me an exact amount but apparently enough to make him and the others independent for some time to come. Enough for Justin to make an offer on the Sagebrush Hotel."

"Umm, and me, where do I figure in?"

"First of all, I didn't ask for Rod to consult with me and I don't want to be in debt to him, even if he doesn't mean for it to be that way. Understand?"

"Yep, I can see that."

"I also don't know how much of it is true. I didn't want to ask any of the others, and it might only be the wishful ramblings of a drunk, horny poker player."

"Yeah, both of those words can describe Rod—the first one often and the second less frequently, but I suspect true. As you said, he is not the image of the courtin' frog, but he must have felt the need to impress you. Not an abnormal desire for any normal man." Johnny smiled. "You want me to find out if there is anything to this story? Then what?"

"I'm not sure. Maybe you can talk to Rod first, let him know that I told you. We can do it together if you want. I don't want to hide anything from him or split our shared friendship. If we reassure him that we are not after his gold, maybe he won't be worried that he told me."

"He didn't seem too worried tonight, as far as I could tell."

"You probably didn't notice. He wasn't drinking as much during the game, not until you announced you were staying here tonight. He was wearing his new duds, had his hair combed, looked almost presentable. I don't know if Ray knows what Rod did, but he was busy observing every movement, every word between Rod, you and me. Rod indicated that Ray was angry when he confronted Steve and Justin, and he agreed to calm down only after he was given a share of what they call the trove."

"Yeah, I can see where this could get out of hand in a heartbeat. I like your idea of talking to Rod together. I'll set up a meeting first thing next week." He looked down at his bare legs. "I think I should get under the covers or get back to my room."

She put her arms around him and moved closer, pressing against him. "I know I'm not dressed all that seductive, but, since you're here…" She turned off the lamp.

"Seductive enough," he murmured as he crawled under the covers and they wrapped their arms and legs around each other.

BRANDY AND JOHNNY MET ROD AT THE PIONEER BARROOM ON Tuesday. It was five-thirty, and the place was mostly deserted. They grabbed a back table and Johnny ordered a pitcher of draft.

"What's the occasion, folks?" said Rod. He was in work clothes, coming off a trucking run for Ray and Jay's Hardware. It wasn't unusual for two or more of the poker group to share liquid refreshment at any time of day, but Rod's aborted soirée with Brandy followed by a probable tryst with Johnny on Saturday, had him feeling on the ropes. He accepted the glass Brandy poured and sat back to await their answer.

"I'm sure it's not a big surprise that we need to talk to you, Rod." Johnny held his mug in front of him as if clinging to a defensive weapon. "Brandy let me in on your secret, and I want to start by saying it will remain that and go no further."

Brandy looked properly contrite, her eyes lowered, but Rod stared at her as he took another gulp. "How can I believe that? She was asked to keep it a secret. That lasted one day, didn't it?"

She looked up. "Yes, Rod, it did. No excuses, I told him and I know you didn't want it to go any further, but you also told me how Ray found out and what he did and said to the others to weasel into a share. We're not asking for anything. We'll do whatever you want, but I don't trust Ray, and neither should you. Emma and Donna are sweet people, but they can't stand up against him."

"You forgot Justin and Steve. And me. We can handle hardware man just fine. I worked for him today, and there were no harsh words or threats. In fact, Ray is friendlier than ever."

Johnny sat back. "I don't have anything against the man. He has never done me a wrong turn. He can get a bit exercised at the table when he's on a losing streak, but that has happened to many of us." He gave Rod a hard glance to emphasize the point. "Normally I would have kept what Brandy told me to just us, but she didn't want this to come between us three, and she wanted to know if it was true."

"Oh, it's true all right. The stuff is lying in the basement of the hotel. I haven't seen the stash itself, but I took some of the bars to Reno, had them assayed, and brought the cash back to Justin. Did she tell you he is trying to buy the hotel?"

Brandy said, "I told him everything you told me, but I am trying to make up for the betrayal of my promise to you." She put her hand on his arm. He started to shrug it off, but he couldn't doubt her sincerity. If they had wanted to keep their alliance from him, they could have.

"Okay, I am confused, totally at sea with what is going on. You two know about the," He looked around at the bar and a couple of townspeople who had walked in. "the stuff, where it's at, and who has a claim on it. When I was brought in, it was to assure that I would share the risk if anyone found out and to give me a generous share for helping them with disposal. Ray came in because he discovered our secret. He may be helpful if we need to transport the material for sale. What would be a good reason to include you two?"

Brandy poured everyone another glass of beer. Johnny decided this was a good excuse for him to leave the table and buy another round, so he carried the empty pitcher to the bar while Brandy considered what appeared to be an offer of reconciliation from Rod.

"I did you wrong, I know, and I can't ask you to trust me. Don't blame Johnny. He never asked for this and he was willing to let it go after I told him. He is still your friend."

"Did you and he spend Saturday night together?" Rod asked without the animosity he might have had. It seemed more a point of curiosity than the critical inquiry of a would-be jealous suitor.

"We did, but it went pretty much the same as when you and I spent Friday night." She gave him a reassuring smile as Johnny paid the bartender and started back to the table.

"Pretty much? What does that mean?" Rod asked, sounding lackadaisical about the affair and still unsure about what had transpired between Brandy and himself.

"Pretty much."

Johnny sat down, pushed the pitcher to the center of the table and said, "Did I miss anything?"

"Pretty much," answered Brandy. Rod finally laughed as he reached for the pitcher.

THE THREE DECIDED TO APPROACH THE GROUP FOR THEIR DECISION about Brandy and Johnny. Rod indicated he would speak on their behalf and this would keep everything in the open during the meeting. Brandy and Johnny were well liked and they didn't expect any real problems, unless Ray raised a fuss. "I can handle him any day," said Rod.

Late Thursday afternoon at Emma's had the eight of them drinking tea. "I'm going to need a lot more tea" was Emma's response. They had waited until after five so Steve could get off work and join them. Justin was the last to arrive. Brandy and Johnny sat next to each other with Steve on one side and Ray on the other.

They knew why they were meeting. As Rod had promised, he preempted their reactions by talking to each of the trove members on Wednesday and earlier on Thursday. Ray was more than a bit indignant and Emma told Steve that she was afraid Rod's discretion was not likely to be as dependable as they had hoped. The group greeted Brandy and Johnny in a friendly manner, and Justin summarized what had happened to date. The big news he shared for the first time was that his offer for the hotel had been accepted and the sale would close within thirty days.

After a few congratulations, the focus turned to the newcomers. Ray proposed that the two should be paid from Rod's share since he was irresponsible for revealing the plan. Brandy and Johnny didn't respond, letting Rod negotiate the financial details.

Emma raised her hand, as she taught her schoolkids to do, a move that always brought a few smiles to the others. "Do any of you know what a tontine, t-o-n-t-i-n-e, is?"

Justin nodded. "I've heard about something like that. It's a financial arrangement between members of a group, an investment that is cashed in at a later date."

"Yes, Mr. Gonzales, that is correct. An A for you. They started several centuries ago in Europe and some modern insurance groups have similar plans. It commits the members to maintain a monetary interest or instrument, as they call it, for a specified time. The investment is closed, shared only by the group that formed it. The rules vary from tontine to tontine, but some have a survivorship clause."

Ray's interest picked up. "What does that mean?"

"It means that the closed group, over a period of several years, may decrease by natural attrition. The proceeds of the investment are divided between the survivors. There might be hundreds of people in the group or only a few."

"Natural attrition, huh? I don't suppose unnatural attrition was a part of any of those deals." Ray looked around at the group with an amused expression for reactions, but they ignored him.

"What are you proposing, Emma?" Donna was anxious to get the meeting over and to avoid any lingering hostilities or hidden unpleasantry that might develop.

"I suggest we consider forming a tontine, a written agreement among the eight of us. We know that it will be difficult to cash in our assets in the near future. We will need to investigate a safe mechanism for its sale and delivery. This may take several years and we should consider it in the same way as any other long-term investment, like bonds or life insurance. We can also include a survivorship clause that permits redistribution of the shares if required. Furthermore, while signing such a paper, we would include a pledge that no additional members will be invited without prior approval of the group. I suggest that six out of eight votes would be required to make a change in the agreement once we activate it."

"How many shares will that be?" asked Ray.

"Since we are just now forming this agreement, this tontine, I suggest we divide the asset into eight portions. Brandy and Johnny will each receive a portion but we will ask them to contribute to future tasks to earn their participation."

Ray started to object but a hard stare from most of the group forced him to reconsider. Rod indicated he would be willing to divide his share with Johnny and Brandy, bringing a smile to Ray's face.

Justin spoke next. "We decided early on that the participants should enjoy a significant benefit from this windfall. Make no mistake about it. None of us are more deserving than others in receiving the proceeds from the gold. If anything, it belongs to Steve and Emma. They found it and they are sharing it with us. All of us have a stake and a reason to defend the secrecy and integrity of our cache. With the sale of the hotel pending, I will have some specified tasks for our newest shareholders, duties that will help us secure and retain the material until we dispose of it. Ray, you have some locksmith skills that we might require. Everyone will have a role, but our first act must be to guard against further disclosure. That means everyone. Agreed?"

Justin's proposal was met by a round of seconds, somewhat reluctantly from Ray. Justin said he would draft a set of papers for everyone to sign. At that time, access to the gold would be determined and the rules for additional expenditures formalized. Ray indicated that Barbara and Jay would not sign the tontine, since they weren't being dealt directly into the agreement and were ignorant of the details. Johnny indicated that Sonya was also not a formal part of the agreement.

Brandy, Rod, and Johnny left Emma's house for a round at the bar. It had gone better than they expected and a celebration of the adventure was the order for the evening.

⁕

ROD WAS AMAZED AT HOW EASY IT WAS TO INCLUDE BRANDY and Johnny into the group, especially after the cautions and reluctance about including himself and Ray. Despite misgivings by himself and the others about his breach of secrecy, the new members seemed to add some stability, blunting Ray's hostile incursion.

Rod was still not sure about how he stood with Brandy or what he wanted or expected from her in the future, but he was pleased that Johnny was in, someone he knew and trusted. It was clear to Rod that there were three cliques in the group they now referred to as the Treasure Trove Tontine or Triple-T. The four original members, Emma, Steve, Donna, and Justin, composed the more conservative faction: quiet and reasonable with long-term objectives for the cash to come. Ray was a clique unto himself, and the extent his wife and brother represented any direct interests in the prize was not clear.

Now Rod had allies. He, Brandy and Johnny—RBJ—were a subgroup without long-term goals. As individuals, they were independent, but as a trio, they could be a decisive influence on how negotiations for the sale and disposal proceeded. Emma's proposal that six of the eight members were needed to approve a change in the guiding principles guaranteed that the RBJ faction would be consulted. Ray would remain an outsider, dependent on the good will of others to be influential.

In early August, the eight TTT members met in Justin's office to sign the formal agreement. There were no lawyers or external consultants. Each person signed nine copies of the tontine. One was placed in the hotel safe in Justin's office and each member received a personal copy. Justin employed a notary and made the group official via an unspecified investment agreement. There would be no other changes in plans without approval from the group.

The following week brought additional stability and a designation for the partnership. Godfrey, the previous owner, sold the hotel to the new real estate holding group, Rattlesnake Basin Enterprises (RBE). Justin and Emma were listed as the officers and the other six tontine individuals as members of the Board. Although RBE legally owned the hotel, an internal agreement designated Justin Gonzales as the future owner when funds to complete the purchase became available.

It didn't take long for Justin to make changes such as redecorating, upgrading dining room furniture, and modernizing kitchen fixtures. In compliance with the terms of his membership, Johnny provided help with some of the general labor, and Brandy offered her time serving drinks and overseeing some of the hotel room changes. She left three rooms untouched: Rod's, Johnny's night-use room, and one for herself in exchange for being a part-time assistant manager. She moved from her apartment to the hotel in mid-September. To help pay for the renovations and legal fees involved in the hotel purchase, Rod cashed four gold bars in Reno, leaving 102 bars in the cellar cache.

Ray devised a three-lock system for the inner door of the cellar. The locks were custom-designed and set into the door. Each lock had a unique separate key with two copies. The six keys were distributed so that no two close allies had the same key. Key A was given to Johnny and Ray, key B to Brandy and Steve, and key C to Emma and Rod. Justin and Donna received no keys. Ray swore that these were the only keys and because a standard pattern had not been used, it would be difficult for anyone to duplicate them.

The system required all three keys to open the inner door, now referred to as the "vault." One master key that opened all three locks was created for emergency use and that key was placed in a special safe deposit box at the Sagebrush Bank. Three of the TTT members had a key to the master deposit box, but a written agreement with the bank required three of the eight to access the box together, even if only one of them had a key.

SUMMER WAS OVER. THERE WERE FEW TREES TO SHED LEAVES, but the winds increased and the nights grew colder, often dropping below freezing on the high desert.

Johnny was feeling the itch, an increasing need to move on, to be somewhere else for the coming winter, a warmer place. Maybe Texas or Mexico, somewhere along the Gulf Coast. Perhaps some time in Florida or the Keys. It wouldn't be forever, but with the tontine in place, the waiting had begun.

Rod carefully inquired about potential venues for gold disposal, Justin assumed his new role as hotel owner, and the weekend poker games continued.

So far, the secret had held and there were no unpleasant surprises. Ray was on good behavior and the group occasionally met to share news, but there were no decisions to make and nothing to keep Johnny in town. His relationship with Sonya was steady, in the sense that there were no dramatic developments and they remained domestically comfortable.

That was the problem. Johnny was no longer satisfied with comfort. Despite the advantages of home-cooked meals, a warm bed and body, and a partner who was not possessive or demanding, Johnny needed fresh air, a long and winding road. The tension that surrounded the formation of the tontine, followed by an indeterminate wait for the payoff, left him frustrated and edgy. He had been to Arizona and New Mexico, but other southern places called and he knew he had to answer. As if anticipating the move he knew he would make, he decided to leave something for posterity. It wasn't much, but opening the closet door in room 23, he knelt, opened his pocket knife, and neatly carved his initials and the year into the door frame. As he stood and closed his knife, he thought about Brandy.

They had never consummated an intimate relationship. Despite the flirting and shared hotel bed on a couple of occasions, their relationship was strangely platonic. She had never openly resisted and he was not immune to her considerable charms, but the fires behind a smoking affair had never materialized. It might have been the long nights of gaming combined with a steady influx of alcohol. That didn't set the stage for ambitious physical romping under the covers, but they never proposed another time or place. It was enough to whisper some sweet words, snuggle under the blankets like exploring teenagers, and wake up in the morning as if it had been a night of wondrous desire fulfilled.

Sonya understood his need to hit the road. Although she had a scattered but steady income and owned the trailer, she also expressed yearnings for places other than dusty Sagebrush. She and Johnny occasionally talked about hitching up the mobile home and trekking off to somewhere. Johnny favored south and southeast and Sonya was drawn to north and northeast. "Something besides deserts" was her usual response. They rarely disagreed and had fought only twice. They seemed compatible by their neighbors' measure and most of the townspeople who knew them as a couple wondered why they didn't tie the knot. She had lived with a man before, so her domestic experience was stronger than his. They had been together for two years without further plans or a deeper commitment.

On the last Sunday of October, Johnny lingered over a cup of coffee while Sonya finished the breakfast dishes. "I think the time has come, Sonya." He looked up at her.

She dried her hands, poured the last of the coffee for herself, and sat down across from him at their small, pull-out table. "What time is that?" she said, but it was rhetorical. She knew what had been eating at him, isolating him, for the past three weeks. She knew before he said anything, that this was an exit song. The question was for how long. She had nurtured hopes of a permanent relationship—if not marriage, at least a long-term cohabitation. She didn't need the rings and bells, but she was comfortable having a man, a decent one, who worked and treated her well.

"Need to leave this town for a while. Need to see some different people, different buildings." He smiled. "Maybe find a different poker game." He caught himself. "It's not you, Sonny, you're not what I mean by seeing different people. It's the others here, the tired same-day, everyday people. Nothing new on the scene." He examined her expression, hoping she would understand. He sometimes called her Sonny, the closest he came to an actual endearment, but she didn't mind.

She had agreed some time ago to accept him for what he was and what he was not. "How long do you think that will be?" she asked gently, keeping any hard edges out of her voice.

"Don't know. Might be a few weeks, months, possibly a year. Depends on what I run across. Kind of like roadkill. Some might be worth putting in the pot but most are best left alone."

"Think you'll be back?" *The critical question. Not sure I want the answer, but best get it out if he has one. One thing I do trust—he will be honest with me.*

He looked down at his hands wrapped around the coffee cup, like a security blanket. "I can't tell, not at this time. You're a good woman, better than I deserve for sure, but I won't make false promises or try and keep you tied down while I screw around in the big, bad world. I would expect the same if you needed to roam. I might find that the scenery isn't what I thought it would be and the people not as exciting. I might miss you and this stupid town so much that I'm back in days rather than weeks or longer, but I have to find out. If I am going to stay around, I need to know that it was a choice I made, not one made for me."

She took a sip and put her cup down, making no sound other than her last question. "When do you plan to leave, Johnny?"

"In a couple of weeks. I have jobs to finish around town, including some work for Justin." He thought about what to tell her. Sonya knew nothing about the tontine or the trove group, but he decided to provide her with a small measure of reassurance. "Sonny, I have some longer term business here in town, an investment that I haven't mentioned because I didn't know when or even if I would be able get anything from it, but I'll be back at some time to check in on it. I just don't know when." He reached across the table and put his hand on her arm.

She smiled and said, "It'll be all right. Let's make these next few weeks count."

They did make the following weeks count, refreshing their intimacy and spending most of their free time together. On a cold rainy day, they ate a picnic outside, enduring the blustery wind and faces full of water, laughing like young kids who didn't know when to come in from the weather. Johnny showed up for only two of the remaining six poker games and spent none of those nights at the hotel. He owed Sonya that much and more.

He met with the TTT on November 10 and announced he was leaving town for some indeterminate period.

"Off to see the world, huh Johnny?" said Rod.

Donna had to ask. "Will Sonya be leaving with you?" Johnny shook his head.

Justin spoke. "With Johnny leaving, we will need to have a means of staying in touch. We will eventually find a way to dispose of the gold. Rod has some promising leads and it is just a matter of time and being cautious. I propose we establish a procedure to check in periodically here at the hotel. If you are on the road for an extended time, it would be nice to drop us a card and let us know you are alive. Provide a post office box or reliable telephone contact so we can get back to you. I assume most of us are staying here in town?"

Several heads nodded. Rod took a puff on his ever-present cigar. "I might head out for some meandering, too, just to shake some dust off my boots."

Brandy seconded the notion. "I have a few friends to visit here and there, so I'll be…here and there."

"Let's plan on a formal meeting here at the hotel no later than August 1967. We'll confirm the date and provide the rooms and a reunion dinner. I know that seems like a long time away and we may be able to get together sooner if we identify a buyer. If we do, I want to be able to gather or consult with everyone to make the necessary decisions and arrangements. Those of you leaving, stay in touch so that we can act quickly on a potential settlement. Otherwise, good luck to all."

Justin stood, and the meeting ended. Rod, Brandy, and Johnny had a few farewell sips at the nearby tavern.

Johnny was not at all sure how he felt. As much as he wanted—needed—to leave, he would miss Rod, his poker friends, the group, and, yes, Brandy. His friends expressed a few regrets about their parting, hoping that it wouldn't be ten years before they exchanged insults over a deck of cards. Johnny indicated he would probably be back before then, date to be determined.

Sonya and Johnny spent Wednesday night making love as passionately as their first time. She cried a bit, despite her best attempts not to, but this was accompanied by his own tears. They fell asleep with wet faces. She was gone the next morning, not wanting to see him drive away. It was just as well. They had said and done everything they could. Additional goodbyes would not help the cause.

He packed his bags and drove away from Sonya's trailer on Thursday morning, November 14. It was a dark, cold, overcast day. His 1952 Ford had a bad heater, but he didn't want to delay the exit any longer. Thanksgiving was approaching and after that the yearend holidays, a poor time to say goodbye. But then, when was a good time?

Rod left town two weeks later and spent most of the time in Reno, gambling and casually asking about gold buyers. He returned in mid-January, reclaimed his room, and rejoined the weekend poker table.

Brandy came and went, usually away for less than three weeks at a time. She kept her room and helped Justin manage the hotel.

◆

Sonya discovered she was pregnant in February 1958. She had been using a cervical cap as a preventative measure and Johnny sometimes used a condom. She could only guess that their physical passion during the last few weeks of his stay had resulted in dislocation of the cap. What to do? Abortion was not an easy option, even if she went to Alturas or to some other community that provided the illegal services. She still hoped that Johnny would return, but even if he did, would he accept the child as his? Having children had never been a topic of discussion during their time together. It was a moot point. No one had heard from Johnny since he left and no one, including Rod, knew how to reach him. "He is somewhere out there, and might even be alive," he said, unaware of the real reason why Sonya asked.

As the months passed, Sonya made arrangements to become an unwed mother. It was easier in Sagebrush because the small town lacked much of the so-called sophistication and self-imposed morality that was common then in many urban places. Neighbors were willing to help one of their own. A local physician arranged for her to deliver the baby in Alturas. On July 17, 1958, she gave birth to a healthy six-pound, seven-ounce baby boy.

Sonya was not so healthy. Three days after the birth, she was discharged and driven back to Sagebrush by a neighbor. She had acquired a respiratory infection a few days before entering the hospital, and the birth had been long, robbing her of what energy she had. The next few days were miserable and she was unable to breastfeed, so she depended on neighbors to warm bottled milk and change the baby's diapers. Despite antibiotics and daily visits by her physician, Sonya Markova succumbed to pneumonia on the twenty-sixth. Because there were no known relatives, she was cremated three days later and her neighbors scattered her ashes across the desert.

What to do with the unnamed boy? The same neighbors who supervised her funeral, George and Anna Charles, were childless and had been taking care of the infant. They kept him at their nearby farm and unofficially adopted him. No one questioned this, including Sonya's doctor. Johnny's friends were not aware of Sonya's death and the fate of the child now named Dean Charles. The few who asked were told she had probably left town, giving up on any return by Johnny.

Brandy tried to reach Johnny via Rod, but it was another year before he contacted the Sagebrush Hotel. Johnny phoned the hotel from "somewhere on the Atlantic Coast." When he asked Justin who was left, Justin said that they were all there, playing poker and as crazy as ever. They were still waiting to dispose of their assets and the reunion remained pending for 1967.

"How is Sonya?" Johnny asked.

Justin had known her but not well. "I heard she left town over a year ago and no one has heard from her since. Sorry, Johnny."

"Not unexpected. My wanderlust has taken me farther and longer than I thought it would. I'll check in from time to time. Say hello to the gang and especially to Rod and Brandy. Take care of yourself."

That was it. No further word for the next three years except annual postcards to let everyone know he was still alive. He provided a general post office box but no phone.

Dean grew up with the Charles family and adopted the nickname Charlie. Brandy increased her poker skills at the expense of others and Rod put on a few more pounds. Justin's hotel did moderately well under his ownership and Brandy's management. Emma retired from actively teaching school but still consulted in education and community affairs. Ray's hardware business flourished, and Steve and Donna produced two children. The Treasure Trove Tontine was still intact and the members continued to wait for a means of cashing the bars.

❖

IN 1962, THE MEMBERS OF TTT PARTICIPATED IN A LONG-DIStance reunion. It marked five years since the agreement was signed, and to everyone's knowledge, word of the secret trove had not been leaked to anyone outside of the group. Johnny was in South Carolina, and Rod had moved south of his usual haunts in Reno to try his luck in Las Vegas. It didn't go well and he returned to Sagebrush just before the five year check-in. Gold bullion was still illegal and Rod had not found a better financial deal for transfer. The other members were still in Sagebrush, biding time and carrying on as if no fortune awaited their pleasure.

Steve and Donna Woodward didn't get to take their Canadian railroad vacation. They had the brochures and maps, related *National Geographic* articles, and big dreams, but the arrival of a boy in 1958 and a girl in 1960 postponed their dream trip. "We'll do it as a family. What an adventure for the kids."

In February 1964, the Woodwards planned to visit Portland and spend some time among the lights and taller buildings of the big city, something their kids had never experienced. The trip through the icy Cascadian pass on Oregon Route 58 didn't worry Steve. He was an experienced winter driver and his car had new snow tires. He had the oil changed and the auto inspected and tuned before they left. They packed the car for a ten-day trip and took off on a bright clear Sunday morning.

As they drove north on Highway 97, the skies grew dark and the snow fell in increasingly heavy flurries. "Probably be rain when we get to the valley," said Steve. The kids had fallen asleep in the back seat and Donna was thinking about the stores she wanted to visit. They had saved up to shop and visit museums, eat out, and enjoy a decisive departure from the routine of their small high desert community.

Turning west onto Highway 58, they began the twenty-mile climb to Willamette Pass at the top of the Cascades. The temperature dropped steadily as they could tell from icy patches appearing along the roadside. The snowfall was moderate, and the new windshield wipers maintained visual clarity.

"Another forty minutes or so and we'll be out of this," Steve said. Donna smiled, glanced back at the kids, and sighed.

Two trucks in front of them slowed their progress at the top and they kept some distance behind the semis as they started down the steep western slope. The snowfall increased, creating near-whiteout conditions at times. The road was two-lane and twisted considerably more on the west side of the mountains, requiring frequent braking, as evident from the red rear lights in front of them. The two-lane pavement on their right bordered the mountain slopes, but across the road were numerous steep drops into the canyons below.

The truck ahead of them applied its brakes as it rounded a sharp curve to the right. Steve tapped his brakes to slow for the same spot, but no response. He stepped harder on the brake, but there was no resistance, no slowing. He tried to make the curve but the car slid across the road and over the edge. There was barely time for a curse from Steve and a short scream from Donna as the car plunged down a rocky cliff, more than a hundred feet to the stream bottom. The trucks were out of sight and there were no other vehicles following to witness the slide and disappearance.

Hotel reservations in Portland went unclaimed and no one in Sagebrush thought it unusual that they hadn't heard from the Woodwards for two weeks. Only the Bureau of Land Management was concerned when Steve didn't report for work as scheduled. They made a few calls but no one could provide information.

Two weeks later, a light plane following the highway during snow clearance operations spotted the wreckage in the canyon. It looked recent and a deputy sheriff and two volunteer hikers were sent to investigate. They confirmed that the bodies of one adult and two young children were in the demolished auto. A young woman was found several yards away. They were identified, and friends in Sagebrush were apprised of their deaths a few days later. The wreckage was hauled out of the canyon by helicopter the following week and trucked to Alturas for inspection and disposal. The accident was officially attributed to driver error on seasonally icy roads, but a mechanic noted some inconsistencies and defects in the wreckage. The results were reported to the authorities, but jurisdictional issues inhibited follow-up and the accident file was closed.

Following a closed-casket funeral and burial in the Sagebrush cemetery for the Woodward family, five of the remaining members of the tontine met at Emma's house. Johnny was still somewhere in the Southeast and they needed to wait for his next call or note to inform him of the accident. The mood, as expected, was somber. Steve and Donna had been well-liked and their sudden demise reminded everyone that life was never certain and that even treasure in the wings didn't provide guarantees of happiness or success. Justin prepared seven updated copies of the tontine agreement, dividing the shares into six portions. Ray lobbied to replace the Woodwards with Barbara and Jay, but he was the only one supporting the proposal. Approval for amendments was changed to four out of six.

Everyone signed the papers, noting that Johnny's signature was still needed.

"Maybe he won't show, and then we'll be down to five," said Ray.

"Probably suit you just fine, would it?" replied Rod. Ray's comments struck an ugly chord with the group that had gathered.

Emma was not happy. "That probably could have been left unsaid, Mr. Gordon. I'm sure we will hear from Mr. Templeton in due time." She sipped her tea slowly but her eyes remained on Ray.

Brandy was also irritated with Ray. She and Donna had become friends during the many poker games over the years, and they enjoyed the competition with their male tablemates. She had very few female friends and it was a loss she wouldn't soon forget.

Justin distributed the papers and closed the meeting with a brief prayer. They left Emma's house slowly, each lost in their thoughts, pondering a future that seemed less hopeful, with plans postponed until the ten-year meeting in 1967. They had hoped for an earlier settlement, but none anticipated the turmoil to come.

CHAPTER FIVE

Together Again (1967)

In July 1967, the tenth anniversary reunion of the Treasure Trove Tontine gathered at the Sagebrush Hotel. Rod and Brandy had their usual rooms and Johnny's room was reserved. Brandy had been a relatively stable, hard-working resident at the hotel. Rod drifted in and out, spending half of his summers but most of the winters in town.

Ray and Jay's Hardware store had fallen victim to an Ace Hardware franchise that opened in 1965 and offered lower prices. In late 1966, Ray closed his business and sold the building. Working out of his house as a locksmith, plumber and auto mechanic, he was able to stretch the funds from the property sale to cover living expenses, but he was increasingly persistent about cashing in the gold bars. He anticipated that a deal would be made during the reunion and was prepared to put up a fight if there were further delays. He needed three votes from the others to impose a plan of action. He knew that Justin and Emma were probably lost causes, so his hope for a cash out rested with Rod, Brandy, and traveling man Johnny. He had to depend on their respective financial situations and hoped that none of them were flush with funds, although no one knew what Johnny was up to. Emma wasn't getting any younger, so she might still be an ally, but he couldn't count on it.

The price of gold, under federal regulation, had remained rock steady and there seemed little hope that the economics of the yellow stuff would change anytime soon. However, the cost of living had gone up and the accumulated assets didn't have as much purchasing power as in 1957. It was another point in his favor for redeeming the precious metal for what they could as soon as they could.

Sagebrush had never been a prosperous town. The first settlers arrived in 1881: farmers who took advantage of a few wetlands along the south fork of the Pit River and part of the adjacent valley. Much of the rest of the surrounding basin was desert scrub and sagebrush. The small community slowly coalesced around a few ranchers with hardy stock that could forage on what the land provided. Dry hay farming helped supplement the diet of horse and cattle herds, that were never large but adequate to provide a minimal, stable income. The hotel was built in 1894, and a few stores and commercial businesses accumulated during the next two decades. Unfortunately, a highway, destined to become part of US 395, followed the rail line the Nevada-California-Oregon Railway laid at the end of the nineteenth century to connect Reno and Alturas via small agricultural towns in Lassen and Modoc County. Sagebrush was bypassed and relegated to be an isolated community. Prosperity briefly returned after the Great Depression and World War II when land was cheap and a few investors decided to risk effort and money in the high desert economy. It was an on-again, off-again proposition, sustainable for a population of fewer than one thousand but never realizing the dreams of its more progressive citizens such as Emma Dodson and Justin Gonzales.

Johnny called Justin from Mobile, Alabama, in June to confirm the meeting set for Friday evening, July 14. The past year had been good for him in terms of jobs, playing cards at a few pickup games, and staying out of trouble. He had saved enough for a late-model Pontiac and made a leisurely, two-week drive from the Gulf Coast to California with stopovers in Austin, Flagstaff, Vegas, and Los Angeles.

He arrived in the dusty desert town on Wednesday, July 12. This gave him time to relax, unwind, and get his bearings for what he presumed would be a decisive week ahead. Checking into the hotel late that evening, he obtained his old room, number 23. He needed sleep more than anything and skipped dinner and the next morning's breakfast.

He met Rod Thursday afternoon and they adjourned to the Pioneer Barroom for a sandwich, a steady intake of brews, and a leisurely catch-up on whats, wheres, and whos.

"Good to see you again, Johnny. It's been a long time," said Rod. He had a cold mug in one hand and his ever-present cigar in the other. "You look better than I expected. Dixieland must have been good to you."

"Can't complain. Turned some money and was happy to trade beach sand for desert sand. By the way, beach sand comes with the smell of coconut oil, the taste of piña coladas, and the sights of tiny two-piece swimsuits."

"Speaking of which, how are them Southern belles?"

"Pretty to look at but not much to recommend for anything serious, whatever that means. I haven't met too many who weren't mostly sugar but little spice. Speaking of which," he grinned, "is Brandy still around?"

"She is and she's still living next door to me. Been working as Justin's assistant all this time. She had a fling or two with a few, one a truck driver who came in and out of town from time to time. There was another guy about her age, a cowboy from Susanville, but neither stayed around and she didn't seem anxious to move on. Who would have figured?"

"Still playing poker? Her and the rest of you?"

"Yep. Same old gang, sometimes on Fridays, sometimes on Saturdays, not often both days. Justin has improved his game and holds his own, but Brandy is still the one to beat. Maybe you'll give her some competition tomorrow night."

Johnny looked around at the tavern. "Still the same. The whole town looks pretty much the same, as if the world has left it behind, around a corner, out of sight."

"Yep. Justin's made a few nice changes in the hotel, fancied it up a bit and gotten better help, including our girl." He smiled at the "our" possessive.

"Is Ray any more pleasant to deal with?"

"Don't see a lot of him since his store closed about a year ago. He shows up for most of the games and seems okay, but lately he has been dropping hints that this is the time to settle affairs. I don't think he and his family are hurtin' terribly bad, but like all of us, he could use the money." Rod held his glass up for a refill. "I guess Justin told you about the Woodwards, huh?"

"Yeah, I heard. Winter accident took out the whole family. A real shame. I liked both of them."

"Yeah, it was a shame, but I'm not so damned sure about the accident part."

Johnny looked up from his beer and into a somber face. "What does that mean, Rod? Something I haven't been told?"

Rod leaned forward and spoke slowly, in a voice low enough so that only Johnny could hear. "We need to keep this between ourselves, buddy, because it ain't official and nothing can be proved, not at this late date."

Johnny nodded. "Okay, what gives?"

"A friend of mine in Alturas, a mechanic who inspected the Woodward wreck, noted some problems with the hydraulic brake lines. They appeared worn, but not with the overall look of older ones that need to be replaced. He said it looked like there was a spot on each one, producing a localized defect as if they had been exposed to something strong and corrosive, like acid."

"Acid? You mean, he thinks the brakes were sabotaged?" Johnny sat back in his chair, not believing what he was hearing. He took a last sip from his glass as the waitress delivered a fresh pitcher to the table.

"Yeah, Johnny, that's what I'm saying. He put the observation in his report but there was no follow-up. The wreck has long since disappeared, so there can't be any confirmation."

"Damn it all to hell, Rod. Am I understanding the implications of this?"

"I think so. It certainly occurred to me, but that's not all. Steve had his car fixed up for the trip to Portland the whole family had been talking about for weeks ahead of time. Some of the work was done at Jimmy's garage, but the other mechanic who worked on it was our own Ray Gordon." Rod poured himself another glass.

"What work did Ray do on the Woodward's car?"

"Well, that's what so interesting. I had a chance to talk to Jay several months after the accident. He seemed upset and I asked him what was wrong. He mentioned how excited Steve was when he brought his car over to Ray to finish some repairs."

"And?"

"It seems that Ray worked on the brakes, replaced linings, inspected the shoes, the usual."

"Did Jay seem guilty or indicate something was wrong?"

"No, just sorry that the accident happened. He remembered working on the car with Ray, and he remembered what they did, although Ray finished the job by himself. Strange—his memory didn't seem as bad as Ray always lets on about."

"Shit, Rod. Do you think Ray might have sabotaged their car to increase his share of the agreement?"

"Couldn't say and he hasn't given any sign of it, but his reaction to their deaths almost seemed rehearsed when we heard the news. He still plays at most of our games and no one else knows what I suspect. You're the first one I've let in on what I learned. What do you think we should do?"

"Hmm. Good question." He thought. "Nothing for now, but let's keep it in mind and see what Ray proposes during our get-together. If he gets too far out of line, we can step aside with him and see what he has to say for himself."

"Be careful, Johnny. He can be a mean one if he wants to, and I know he sometimes packs. He might find a confrontation good enough reason to reduce the size of TTT further."

"We can arm ourselves as well and it might be the prudent thing to do whenever we are alone. Right now, he has no reason to suspect us, so let's keep it that way. Bears watching, for sure."

They finished the second pitcher in silence scattered with a few questions and comments about their last ten years. After ordering and finishing a pizza, they wandered back to the hotel. Johnny was tired from the cross-country drive and needed another good night's sleep.

"Stay alert," said Rod as they opened their room doors. "We should all be there for dinner tomorrow night."

Brandy and Justin were in the dining room when Johnny entered at seven-thirty the next morning. Only a few other early risers were eating. He nodded at them and was prepared to grab a table by himself when Justin flagged him to join them. He almost didn't recognize Brandy. The last time he had seen her, she wore her hair long, sometimes pinned up on top. Now it was a short pixie cut that changed the features of her face. Like him, she was ten years older, but she seemed younger.

"Morning, Johnny. Good to see you made it." Justin stood and shook his hand. "We just ordered. Get what you like. As always, breakfast is on us."

Brandy looked up at him, smiling. "You're looking pretty chipper for this time of day. Get enough sleep last night?"

Johnny sat down and a waitress arrived to pour coffee. "Eggs over easy, taters, and bacon, done hard. Oh, and a tall glass of orange juice." The waitress nodded, topped up the cups for Brandy and Justin, and walked back to the kitchen.

Johnny looked at Brandy as he took his first sip. "So, working for the man, huh. How's that going?"

She shrugged and Justin answered for her. "She's been great. Keeps me organized and takes care of much of the routine, including supervising the kitchen and cleaning staff. Don't know what I'd do without her." He leaned back, his arms over the sides of the chair like a cat stretching. "How about you? Been hard to keep track of where you were, so you must have been busy, successful, or both."

Johnny kept his eyes on the brunette. Her short hair enhanced her long neck, making her look more exotic than ever. She was dressed in a simple business-style white blouse and gray skirt, but, like the town, a few things hadn't changed. She still flashed those dark, penetrating eyes, the ones that could see inside your soul and read your thoughts, and she still sported a smile that was half amusement and half flirtatious as if daring you to make a move before she pounced. If anything, her maturity made her more physically attractive than ever. *Beware the pounce!*

"It's been better for me than for you from what I've heard." Johnny lowered his head. "Sorry about the Woodwards. I liked them. Didn't meet their kids, but they must have been a great family."

Brandy put her cup down and sat back. "Unexpected as with most tragedies. Of all of the members in our survivor's pact, the last ones I expected to go were Steve and Donna." She said it slowly, as if the pain had been yesterday instead of three-plus years earlier. "I miss Donna at the table. We haven't found another woman to give you guys a bad time."

"You are bad enough by yourself. I assume we might have a game later tonight?" The last was directed at Justin as the breakfast orders arrived.

"Yes, we'll have a game. Ken will play, and Pete will be there. So will Ray Gordon." Justin picked up and sipped a glass of juice. The simple statement and use of his full name seemed unnecessary, as if confirming some of the things Rod had shared with Johnny the day before.

Johnny looked at Brandy and back to Justin. "Is our hardware friend creating problems?"

"Nothing new. He is agitating for a sale and settlement and he'll probably try to talk to you before our dinner meeting tonight. Not much has changed since you left except for the Woodwards, but Ray wants the money as soon as possible."

Brandy was busy eating but paused long enough to say that Emma was in good health and would abide by whatever decision was made.

"Will she be here for dinner?" asked Johnny.

Justin nodded. "She'll be here. She seems to have taken a liking to you, Johnny, or at least she is concerned about your welfare. She has asked me any number of times where you were and what you were doing, but I didn't have much to share with her. I'm sure she'll have questions for you."

Brandy looked up and wiped her mouth. "She won't be the only one. I'm sure you will be more than willing to entertain us tonight with your many exploits and misadventures."

After breakfast, Johnny walked out of the hotel. He planned to take a walk about town before the heat became a deterrent, and see who was still around. He was two blocks from the hotel when Ray called to him from across the street.

"Johnny, good to see you again," shouted Ray, rushing up and offering his hand.

Johnny shook it unenthusiastically but maintained a pretense of politeness. After what Rod had told him about the accident, Johnny felt even less inclined to cozy up to the hardware guy and part-time auto mechanic.

As expected, Ray wasted no time in cutting straight to his pitch. "Glad I could catch you before our big meeting tonight. It's been ten years, hasn't it?" Without waiting for an answer, he launched on as they walked down the street as if enjoying a casual stroll like friends. "We need to put a hot probe up Justin's ass and push some of the others to go ahead with the sale of our property and get things distributed. There's only six of us now, Emma ain't gettin' any younger, and I bet you and Rod could use the money 'bout now. Am I wrong?"

While Ray ranted, Johnny was trying to decide if he should mention the accident. Ray probably wouldn't indicate any sorrow or misgivings about Steve and Donna's departure from the tontine or from the rolls of the living. *Better keep the suspicions to myself. I don't know if they're true, but best not reveal anything until I see how Ray plays this out.*

Ray stopped talking, waiting for a response. By now they were about four blocks from the hotel and Johnny wanted to be alone. "Let's see how the discussion goes tonight. I'm not against the idea of selling, but I don't know what problems we might have. We still have some legal hurdles, like last time."

"Yeah, I know, and that means we could be wringing our hands over this for the next thirty years. I'd like to use my share while I, that is, me and my family, are still young enough to enjoy it. What'd ya say?" He put his right hand on Johnny's shoulder and they stopped on the side of the street.

Johnny faced him as Ray removed his hand. "Like I told you, Ray, let's see what gives. I'm not promising anything, but I'm open to any reasonable plans." Johnny stared at him for a moment.

Ray nodded, backed up a couple of steps, and gave him a smile. "Sure, Johnny, makes sense. See you tonight." He walked away and Johnny turned, continuing his way up the street.

Gonna be an interesting meeting. Odd that Ray didn't mention Brandy. Is he depending on me to convince Rod and the brunette to come along? We have always been independent and there is no reason for him or anyone else to think we'll act in concert, but then again, who knows? I'll need to talk to the assistant manager and see where she stands in all of this. He passed Ken's barber shop, but it was still morning and appeared to be closed. Johnny noted the stores, cafes and taverns along the main street. A prominent Ace Hardware sign graced a newer building. A block farther was Ray's old store, now hosting a feed and farm supply business. *Nope, not much has changed. Still sleepy, still dusty, windswept and forlorn.*

Johnny grabbed an afternoon beer and a few pretzels at one of the taverns and returned to the hotel. It was almost two o'clock and the heat was peaking on the streets. He had three immediate objectives. The first was to see if Brandy was about and wanted to talk. After that, a relaxed shower and a nap.

A young woman stood behind the front desk as he entered the lobby. He approached her and asked if Miss Charlebois was available.

"Do you mean Brandy? Oh, I mean, yes, of course you do, I rarely hear her called by her last name." She blushed as if she had committed some deep social faux pas and put a hand across her mouth. Johnny waited, amused but patient. The woman pointed to the door behind her, which was standing open and through which Johnny could see part of the office furniture. "She stepped out to run some errands around town and should be back about three. Should I leave a note to tell her you called, mister…, mister…"

"That won't be necessary. I'll catch up to her later. Thank you." He strolled pass her to the hallway, made the turn and walked to his room. *Objectives two and three then.* He entered, undressed and started the shower.

Thirty minutes later, clean, shaven, and refreshed, he decided against the nap. He walked to the room next to his and knocked. A few seconds later, he and Rod were sharing a bottle of whiskey and discussing the day's events, including the breakfast meeting and his encounter with Ray.

"So how has Brandy been treating you?" Johnny took a small sip of the fire water, not wanting to get shit-faced before dinner. He was curious about Brandy's tenure at the hotel and whether Rod had cashed in on his near-romance.

Rod took a bigger hit, wiped his mouth on his sleeve and grunted. "Never got closer than that night ten years ago when I blabbed to her about our treasure group, but, she and I have gone out drinking a few times, played cards many, many times, and we still smile at each other. I haven't been in town all this time, but she seems happy enough to see me when I come back. Always greets me with her usual scorn and insults, so I guess she still loves me. Satisfied?"

The look on his face was hard to read, how good natured or how put off he felt, but then, Rod and Johnny had always endured an enigmatic and complex relationship with the long-necked one. For the three of them, flirtation and suggestive innuendo was the practice rather than the consumptive affairs that many of the other poker players assumed were taking place. Among the three principals, there didn't seem to be any need to enlighten anyone.

"Hell, Rod, you know I'm satisfied. Always have been." He reached for the bottle and took another sip. "I have as much fun watching the reactions of our tablemates as I do fantasizing about what might or could have been with our girl. As the wise men say, anticipation is often more delicious than fulfillment."

"Is that what they say? I'll vote for fulfillment any day. So what did Ray get on about?"

"Like you said and Justin and Brandy confirmed this morning, he wants to cash out with no more delays. Have you found out anything during the past few years that would make that more likely?"

"Yeah, I did. During my last little sojourn to Reno, I learned that my former associates have moved on, whatever that means, and a new outfit has taken their place. This group has questionable ties to some East Coast businesses and they indicated that the transfer fees for handling gold would be twenty-five to thirty percent."

Johnny gave a low whistle. "That bites. I thought the old fees were exorbitant, but this is over the top. What do you mean by questionable ties? Organized crime, mafia, something on that order?"

"Something on that order. It turns out that some of them are banking the new casinos springing up, especially the ones at Tahoe. Big money and big names behind it. The only thing they could reassure me about was they would buy as much as we wanted to sell, no questions asked."

"Do Justin and the others know this yet?"

"No. I only found out last week and was saving it for our discussion tonight or tomorrow."

"This takes some of the wind out of Ray's sails. Even he won't appreciate a one-fourth or one-third loss of our assets."

Rod lit a cigar and sat back in his chair, the only chair in the room. Johnny was sprawled on the bed, holding the bottle.

"You watch. He'll whine about our delay in moving the stuff, not cashing in when we could have gotten a better deal." Rod took a long draw and blew the smoke out slowly.

Johnny took another sip and passed the bottle back to Rod. "What do you think we should do? Look for another outlet, sell to these guys and take our money, or wait it out a bit longer?"

"Might depend on what a bit longer means. If we wait, we can try and find another buyer. Not guaranteeing we'll find one. I suspect that moving bullion or ore happens in a limited marketplace. It might come down to what Brandy and you want to do." Rod gave him a hard look as he took the last hit from the bottle.

"What about Emma? Seems like everyone keeps forgetting she and Steve made the original discovery. She's in her sixties. She might have something to say about waiting."

Rod thought a moment. "Hard to know what she'll want to do. Justin appears to be doing okay with the hotel, so there doesn't seem to be an immediate need there, but…well, damn it Johnny, I just don't know anymore. When we first formed our little group, it was exciting to think that we had fallen into easy money. We had it assayed, we had buyers, and we could have been spending it and enjoying better times for the last ten years."

Johnny laughed. "Do you think we'd still be spending it? Not you and me, that's for sure. You'd just move up to a higher stakes card game. Maybe some better cigars and better booze. I'd squander it some way. Easy money, easy spending. Now that we are older, if not wiser, the money might last longer."

Rod glanced at his watch and stood up, throwing the bottle neatly against the wall and into the trash can beside the small table. "Almost time for dinner. I need to clean up, maybe even shave. Don't want'cha giving Brandy all the excitement. I'll see you down there."

Johnny nodded and walked out, turned right and headed for the lobby. It was after four and there was still a chance to see Brandy and determine what she thought of the coming negotiations. A quick look through the door behind the lobby desk revealed she had returned. The desk clerk nodded and Johnny knocked on the frame as he entered her office.

"Johnny, come on in. Lucy told me someone wanted to see me, but she didn't know your name. I should have guessed." She motioned to a chair in front of her desk.

He turned and closed the door before taking a seat. "Wanted a chance to chat before we get into the heavy stuff with the others. Hope you don't mind."

Brandy gave him a smile and a subtle eyelid flash. "I never mind chatting, you know that, however heavy the stuff is. It's been a long time. Forever it seems."

"Yeah, a lot of days, a lot of miles. I have to admit it's been good to get away, but I do miss those late-night games. Are they still as much fun?"

She sat back, showing a face more serious, more thoughtful. "It's still something to look forward to. Not a hell of a lot else going on in Sagebrush, as I'm sure you've discovered. But no, Johnny, it's not the same. We don't meet every week. It's down to a couple of times a month, usually on a Friday. With the Woodwards gone, we lost some of our craziness. We've lost some of our youth, our innocence, if you will. Don't laugh. I know it's hard to think of any of us as innocent, but think about who we were then. I was still a teenager, and you were in your mid-twenties. We didn't care about anything, just having fun and wiling the time away waiting. Waiting for what? When the money came, we didn't know what to do with it. We still don't."

"Yeah, Rod said something similar. I reminded him that we would have probably blown through our respective shares by now. At least I think Rod and I would have."

"Most of us stayed here. Rod and I got out on our separate missions. You were the exception, so no, the games aren't the same. I don't know if we can recapture some of that later tonight or not. I assume everyone will play, even the ones who aren't in on our secret."

"That's what I wanted to talk to you about." He pulled the chair closer and spoke in a quiet voice. "Brandy, Ray is agitating for us to cash out. You know that, but what you don't know is that Rod has some news about our disposability and the costs that go with it. The fees will be substantially higher unless we can find a different group to do business with."

"Ooh, that's too bad. I think we all hoped we could end this so-called tontine in the very near future. I think about Emma and the fact that she doesn't have as much time as we do. She's in decent health, but at some point she won't be able to travel or enjoy the money as much as we can."

"Does she still want to donate most of her share to the community?"

"I think so, but I'm sure she might also want to enjoy some of the proceeds. Since she doesn't play poker, we don't see her as often. She does some volunteer work for the school and belongs to a number of civic groups, but I believe she would like to wind up this venture."

"What about you, Miss Mature-Woman-in-Her-Twenties? Have you decided on a career in hotel management? Gonna settle down in Sagebrush or head out to greener pastures?" A tumbleweed blew down the street past the office window as if to underscore his comment.

"I've been thinking about it, Mister Man-about-the-World, but no, it won't be Sagebrush. If I go into hotel management or something similar, it'll be at a neon-lit casino resort with lots of flash, lots of action. I still occasionally hustle a few drinks at one of our local watering holes. I'm not ready for a pinstriped business suit. If I settle down, it'll be at a higher-stakes table under brighter lights." Her eyes flashed again, like in times past when a flirtatious look could mean anything from a noncommittal tease to a serious come-on.

Johnny smiled. *Perhaps we can explore more of that in the days, or nights, to come.* "I'll be around for a while after our meeting and, depending on the decision, for perhaps a while after that. If we bail and get our funds, it'll take a while to receive the cash. Maybe we can discuss options."

"Maybe, Johnny, maybe. I'm not sure when or whether to trust you, but then, you probably feel the same way about me."

He nodded and stood up. "I will admit this, dear. During all the time I've been away, you were never completely out of my mind. I would recall you at strange moments on the road, while eating alone, and, especially, during poker games. I always expected to look up and see you smiling just before you laid down your hand and raked the pot. It's a hard image to lose."

He turned, opened the door and left, leaving her to think, smile, and ponder what the evening would bring from the group and what might take place afterward. Together again—what would come of it?

THE DINNER WAS SET FOR SIX O'CLOCK, BUT THE PRE-DINNER social started at five-thirty. A bartender stood behind a small counter in the corner of the dining room, providing drinks on request. By quarter till, everyone had arrived: Emma, Ray, Rod, Brandy, Johnny, and Justin, serving again as nominal host. The drinks and dinner were ostensibly guest services of the hotel but in reality were through funds provided by the TTT. Officially, the dinner was for members of Rattlesnake Basin Enterprises, which bought the hotel. Napkins and a large wall banner sported the initials RBE in large script to provide recognition and validity.

Johnny looked casual but clean, Rod had changed from work clothes into slacks and shirt, Emma looked prim in a summer print dress, and Justin and Brandy were still in casual business clothes. Dress and manner displayed the appearance of a small-town business group gathered to discuss plans for the hotel and possible contributions to the community. The room was closed to other diners for the evening, guarded by a sign that stated:

RESERVED FOR RATTLESNAKE BASIN ENTERPRISES.

The servers were active during the dinner portion of the meeting, providing food and generous libations. Even modest tea-preferring Emma enjoyed a few glasses of wine. After dessert and the dishes were cleared, the servers disappeared and closed the kitchen doors, and the group of six was free to begin the evening discussion in earnest. Until then, comments had been confined to general news on what each person had been doing during the past ten years. Much of that centered on Johnny, the traveler. Emma gave him reassuring smiles as he gave some family-friendly highlights of his wanderings across the South and along the Atlantic Coast.

Justin took a few minutes to recall the memories of Steve and Donna Woodward. Johnny glanced a few times at Rod and Ray, noting the undisguised sour look of the former and the placid, unconcerned look of the latter. After Justin's tribute, Emma recited a brief prayer.

Justin had apparently conferred with Rod about the disposal problem, because he started the conversation. "Mr. Haas has some news that we need to consider as we begin our main topic of concern."

Rod took a hasty sip of whiskey and cleared his throat. "In preparation for our get-together, I spent several days in Reno a week ago. I visited some of the places I used ten years ago when we made the first sales of our property and five years ago when I checked on them again. I was surprised to find that the places were still there but not the people I had dealt with for the past fifteen-plus years. I knew those people, trusted them, and they provided us, as you know, with the cash to purchase this hotel and maintain our assets." He took another sip and continued. "The new people perform some of the same services, but at a steeper price, a much steeper price." He looked around at the group. "They want between twenty-five and thirty percent of the assets' value per transaction. There are no volume discounts. They promise discretion and a quick cash settlement. I didn't indicate how much we had, but they said they could purchase any amount. Considering who they probably represent, I don't doubt that they have the capability."

Johnny had to admire the way Rod presented the news, almost as if he had metamorphosed into a business executive. His language, smoothness, and precise manner belied his blue-collar background, the gruffness of his everyday speech. He could have been lecturing in a boardroom or classroom.

Rod looked at Ray as he continued. "The value of our holdings has not increased or decreased, inflation aside, but the cost of transfer has almost doubled from what we were facing earlier. I know that many if not most of you want to sell it and get rid of the agreement. I don't know if this will cause us to think differently, but that's the way it stands. Sorry to have to report this." He reached for his glass, downed the last drops, and headed toward the corner bar to serve himself a refill.

Justin looked around the table. "Not what we wanted to hear, folks, I know. I think we were all looking forward to resolving the issue tonight or within the next few days. Comments?"

Ray sat straight in his seat and stated the predictable. "I was afraid this would happen. We lose what, ten, fifteen percent of our total value while it sits here gathering dust? It is the same as if gold dropped in price. Complete discretion? Hell, I guess it should be complete for what they want to charge us." He glared at everyone but saved his longest stare down for Justin, daring him to save the day.

Rod had just returned to the table, but he heard Ray's clear voice.

Johnny hoped that the kitchen was clear of staff. "It seems we can take one of three tacks. We can go ahead and sell, grabbing what we can and be done with it. As Ray correctly tells us, in a louder voice than necessary, it will mean less for each of us, but we'll have it and be free to go our separate ways." He glanced at Brandy as she gave him a brief smile of encouragement. "Or we can wait another five to ten years and hope that conditions are better for a more profitable return."

Ray scowled. Emma sipped quietly on her third glass of wine. Rod sat down with a full glass of booze, ready to continue his trip into blissful oblivion. He nodded at Johnny to continue.

"Rod and I briefly considered a third option. We agree to retain our current assets but aggressively seek other routes for transfer and sale. He says that there is no other avenue that he knows of at the moment, but he is willing to make the effort. Perhaps some venue besides Reno. If we can find a better deal, we can meet and decide at that time."

Justin leaned forward, hands folded on the table in front of him. "What time interval are we thinking about, Johnny? A few weeks, months, years?"

"Can't answer that. Could be days if we hit something right away. Could be never and we are stuck with the only game in town, our friends in Reno."

"Friends, huh? Whose friends, Rod's?" Ray was also drinking, his belligerence growing steadily.

"Don't need to shout it out, Ray." Justin was again stuck with the role of mediator, attempting to keep the group on course. "Johnny, how long do you plan to stick around? Will you be here if Rod can find the right business associates?"

"I plan to be here for a while. I'll try to pick up a few odd jobs and would like to retain my room here for at least a month, maybe more. Get some card time in." Another smile from Brandy.

Ray lowered his voice, changing from the enraged victim to a soothing suitor. "How about you, Miss Dodson? We haven't heard your views on this. Sell now or wait until whenever?"

Emma looked at him and then the others, one by one, taking her time. Ray waited patiently, although his fidgeting fingers revealed his internal turmoil. "Johnny's compromise makes sense. I wouldn't mind receiving some money within a reasonable time, but I don't want to proceed in a haphazard fashion. I trust Rod to find us a better business deal."

Ray turned to Brandy. "How about you? Surely you aren't satisfied with the status quo? You must want something more than you've got." Despite his attempt at diplomacy, he couldn't keep the cynicism and touch of scorn out of his voice.

"What makes you think I don't have what I want? Who are you to judge anyone else or what motivates them? I back Johnny's third idea. Let's keep things under control and see if we can find a deal that is at least as good as what we were offered earlier. If not, we can revisit the decision." Her drink was empty, but she remained sitting.

Justin cleared his throat and summarized the discussion. "Well let's have a show of hands. Who is in favor of selling now to the group in Reno?"

Ray raised his hand and glared around the table. No one joined him.

"How many want to look for other buyers and a better deal?"

All the rest affirmed the option. Justin looked around the table and slowly raised his hand. "Near unanimous. Sorry, Ray, but you'll have to give us some time and maybe you'll be rewarded by a bigger pot."

"Yeah, maybe," he grunted. "Looks like I'm outgunned. How much time are we talking about? When do we call it a no-go?"

Justin answered. "Let's give it a month at least. If we have some promising leads, we can extend it as necessary. If not, we can reconsider our options. Does that meet everyone's approval?"

All nodded or mumbled yes, except Ray. Arms folded, he stared straight ahead, pouting like a spoiled child who hadn't gotten his way.

Justin continued. "Let's not forget, we have a game tonight. Pete and Ken will also join us. Bring your money and your hopes."

As glasses were finished and chairs pushed back, Johnny stepped next to Brandy and asked her if she was up for some barhopping on Saturday.

"Just you and me?" she asked, as if considering a night out for the first time in her life.

"That would be fine with me unless you need more company."

She looked at Rod. "I doubt if he'll have other plans so let's bring him along. Looks like he could use some companionship. Whadda ya say?"

"No problem. We can help him get three sheets to the wind by eleven. Then it's just a matter of getting him home."

"We know where he lives, Johnny boy. It's a date." She walked over to Rod, invited him for the next evening's tavern sojourn, and the three left for their rooms to get ready for the game. Justin offered to escort Emma back to her house and Ray walked out of the dining room by himself, defeated but still defiant.

Ray was sullen during the game but brightened up as some of the pots came his way. By the time the night ended, he was several dollars ahead and smiling. The Hotel Three, as they were sometimes called, returned to their respective rooms. Brandy broke even, Rod won a bit, and Johnny lost more than usual. Each slept alone.

— ◆ —

There was no game on Saturday, but as planned, Rod, Brandy and Johnny went out to dinner at the small cafe up the street and then bar hopping, visiting all three of the night spots. Two were relatively busy, but one was quiet and gave them a chance to talk about Ray and his change in behavior during Friday night's game. Brandy and Johnny ordered tequila sours, and in a surprise move, Rod asked for a margarita with extra salt.

"Let Ray win a few dollars when we play and maybe we can keep the mad dog from biting," said Brandy.

Rod took a sip and growled, "There are other cures for mad dogs."

Johnny said, "How about you and I taking a ride to Willow Creek tomorrow?" He was looking at Rod, but glanced at Brandy. "Didn't mean to exclude you. If you wanna come, okay by me, but I need to talk to the man."

"Be my guest. I have some other things to do."

Rod nodded. "We still have some time before the bars close. What's next?"

"Back to the first one and rejoin the noise," answered the brunette, rising to her feet. So it went.

THE NEXT DAY, WHILE BRANDY DID "SOMETHING ELSE," ROD AND Johnny drove out to Willow Creek and the spot where Steve and Emma had recovered the gold. Little had changed at the cache site, although the highway had been repaved and some new directional signs installed along the route. The area next to the boulder was overgrown with grass from heavier-than-usual spring rains, but there was no sign of disturbance. Ray had never been told the exact location of the discovery and no members of the group had attempted to search for additional caches. The group decided to forego additional exploration until the current assets were sold and transferred from the hotel. Before Steve met his end, he had made a few discrete inquiries about possible purchase of the land, but it was confirmed as federal property and not for sale.

Rod and Johnny had dinner that night and discussed Ray's possible involvement with the Woodward accident. Johnny decided to see if he could find out more from Jay while he did some work for the Gordons or during a chance meeting in the next several days. He needed to be careful and not arouse Ray's suspicions, but he was curious about Rod's comment on Jay's behavior and especially on his memory about working on the car. He wasn't the first to indicate that Jay might not be as strange in the head as Ray let on.

Brandy took the next Thursday off and drove out of town for the night, saying she would be back and ready for the game on Friday. She didn't say where she was going and Johnny didn't want to know. What would be would be, he figured. Any promise of a hookup during the week with the brunette had not been made, but like she often reminded him, anything was possible.

CHAPTER SIX

The Trophy

It was difficult to ascertain where or to whom Brandy's wilder side was oriented. Most of her friends were convinced she had one. She had always been the flamboyant one, the girl of unknown origin since the day she came into town at age of seventeen. Her card-playing skills and ability to deal with people of all ages, genders, and persuasions were admired, if not envied, by many. She fit nicely into the independent and self-determined community of Sagebrush and particularly well in the hotel poker group, but she remained an ongoing mystery and a frequent topic of conversation among others. Where was she from, who were her parents, was she dallying around town with someone and if so, who? Things hadn't changed a lot in the past eleven years—she was still shrouded in secrets, although she was no longer the long-haired Madonna with her own apartment. Attempts by the curious to investigate, Ken Williamson especially, resulted in a dismissive smile and no comment.

After Johnny's dad and mother died, he returned to Sagebrush and made a deal with Justin for reduced room rent in exchange for part-time labor around the hotel. When he moved into Sonya's trailer, he informally retained the room for sleeping off-late night poker games. Rarely did the Sagebrush Hotel fill with guests, but on the rare occasion that it did, it was understood that Johnny would forfeit his sleeping place.

Brandy didn't move into the hotel permanently until she started working for Justin. Prior to that she also spent an occasional night there after a long game or when extra alcohol consumption was a deterrent to walking home. During the ten-year period before their reunion, she came and went from town as the mood compelled her, giving Justin enough notice to cover for her. She was rarely gone more than ten days at a time, but to where or with whom? The mystery continued.

It was a trait that she and Johnny shared although not necessarily together. Brandy once commented about anticipation being most of the satisfaction, a line her friend often quoted. Johnny knew what she meant, because poker offered the same expectations. The slow reveal of one's cards, in draw or stud, the coming out as bets deployed, the emotions or lack thereof as each player made their moves—that was the excitement that drew them. Winnings were nice, but the action was everything.

Although it amused them that they were the often the focus of speculation, bluff and deception were other aspects of poker that had a basis in the machinations of real life. "Playing the game" was the way Johnny expressed it and they were both good at it. There was always the possibility that consummation would be realized. As Brandy told him on more than one occasion, "It ain't out of the realm of reality."

That was good enough for Johnny. Their closest approach to having sex was the night she told him about the trove group and they slept together, still chaste, still innocent. Ten years later, their relationship recommenced as it had ended.

———◆·———

The Friday night game started later than usual because of the RBE dinner. Pete, Ken, Ray, Justin, Rod, Brandy, and Johnny were at the table. Ken, as usual, made no secret of his curiosity about Rattlesnake Basin Enterprises. He had felt envious and hurt that he had never been invited to join the investment group. He was also unaware, as far as anyone knew, of the identities of all of the members.

The game proceeded without rancor from Ray and a good time was evident even though the cards weren't running in his favor. At eleven-thirty, he folded his cards for the last time and stood up.

"Damned if I can get a winning hand tonight. I'm outta here. Next time, I'll be loaded for bear." He smiled at Rod and Johnny, glanced at Brandy, and started for the door.

Brandy and the boys said good night, grateful that no one of them had taken all of Ray's money. Rod, Ken, Justin, Johnny and Brandy were left at the table. Rod had been drinking steadily, losing a little but still game enough. Brandy and Johnny were clearly winning, with Ken and Justin mostly holding their own.

It was Rod's turn to deal. He shuffled the deck more than enough times and Johnny was about to tell him to deal when Rod put the deck down on the table and looked at Brandy carefully. As she often did, she ignored him and poured herself another drink. "I'd like to raise the stakes for this hand," he said, staring at each player in turn.

Brandy smiled at him, a come-on that was hard to ignore. For anyone sober and experienced with her table etiquette, it wasn't a welcome sign. "What do you have in mind, Rodney?" She used his full name when in the teasing motif, and he knew it.

"I propose that we play this hand for your hand. Actually, for a lot more than your hand. I propose that we play for a night with you, your room or the winner's."

Brandy glared at him and took a large swallow of Black Jack. She looked around the table to survey reactions.

Justin sat back in his chair. "No, Rod, deal me out of this. If Brandy permits this, and I'm not of the opinion that she should, I can't...I won't participate."

Ken quickly seconded Justin. "I can't go along with this. Even if the young lady allows," he gave her a fleeting smile, "I won't play for...well, play for the favors of another."

Rod looked at Johnny. "How about it, buddy? Shall we get crazy? Just you and me? I'm sure you've already had more than a taste, but how about letting your buddy in on some?"

Johnny hadn't taken his eyes off Brandy, directly across the table, during the proposal and responses. "What about Brandy? Will she be dealt in, and if she wins, what does she get?"

"I'll answer that." Brandy had not lost her cool. If anything, she acted as if it were her proposition and she was in control of the outcome. "If I win the hand, you both give me all the money you have in front of you. Rod, you'll need to dig in your wallet and match Johnny's stake. If one of you wins the hand, I'll spend the night in your room but I make no promises on what will happen there. It will be up to the winner to convince me, seduce me if you will, and I will determine whether I comply. In either case, I will spend the night and leave at sunrise. If that's agreed, we can let Justin shuffle and deal a hand of showdown. Make it seven cards to maintain the suspense."

It was obvious to everyone that Brandy was not dreading but actually enjoying this departure from the usual stakes. Rod didn't know what to make about the restricting qualification. Johnny didn't like any part of it, and if Brandy had refused, he would have backed her up, but her eager acceptance, even with modifications, left him puzzled and distressed. He knew she could be a wild card, but this was new ground. Was this the older, more mature Brandy? Justin seemed nervous as if the ethical fate of Sagebrush rested solely on his shoulders. Ken, despite his refusal to actively participate, was amused, relishing an event that might provide him with treasured gossip for days to come.

Justin shuffled the cards slowly, letting them slip and slide twice. Ken cut them and the hotel owner dealt them to each player face up, one at a time. Rod received a king, Brandy a four, and Johnny a seven. There was a pause as the three principles looked silently at each other. Another round showed a nine, a deuce, and a six, respectively. Too early for anyone to smile or relax. The third cards produced a pair of nines for Rod, a jack for Brandy and a pair of sevens for Johnny. Rod and Johnny stared at each other with slight smiles, as if this was something they could bluff, but there was no bluffing in showdown. The fourth cards came out. Rod had a ten, Brandy a five, and Johnny a queen. Brandy was unpaired but had three cards to a low straight.

"Where in the hell are the aces?" grumbled Rod.

Brandy sat back in her chair, still holding her glass, now almost empty.

The fifth cards showed an ace, three and deuce. Rod had a broad grin, high hand at five cards, but Brandy had four cards to an open-ended straight. No one had the makings of a flush. Justin looked at Rod and dealt. The sixth cards landed: four, eight, and six. Johnny's two small pair reigned, but everyone had an out. Like a game played out in a Hollywood movie it would come down to the last card.

Brandy told Justin to reshuffle the remaining deck for the last card. "Deal them down so we can talk." There was a mischievous look in her eye. Rod and Johnny could only guess what she was up to, but she was obviously in control and relishing every moment regardless of the outcome. Justin shuffled, Ken cut, and the last card was dealt down to each player.

Rod looked at Brandy. "What do you have in mind sweetheart?"

Brandy smiled. "Perhaps you should ask Johnny. He has the high hand so far." She looked at Johnny as if he had already won it. "I further propose that the loser, the last place among the three of us, buys breakfast for the rest of us tomorrow, including Ken and Justin. Say, at seven, an hour after sunrise." She had the weakest hand showing but could draw a pair of jacks to beat Rod. She couldn't beat Johnny unless she pulled the straight.

Rod muttered something about how breakfast was already free for four of the five at the table, but Johnny indicated the added proposal was all right with him. The loser would be a loser. Each of them had to draw out on the last card to beat him.

Brandy took charge again. "Since I seem to be the trophy of the hour, let me turn my card over first. If I have the straight, you cash-deprived men can weep and sleep with each other. If not, then I am at the mercy of one of you gracious gentlemen." No one missed the sarcasm. She slowly placed the card up. A seven.

"Too bad, so close," said Rod. "I guess you get your boyfriend or," he paused to let the word register, "me. I need some help, though, don't I buddy?" He flipped the card up suddenly, as if it was a poisonous spider. It landed on top of his spread hand. A ten. "Two pair," he yelled, both hands in the air, leering at Brandy.

Brandy looked at Johnny. "All you need is a queen, six, or seven. Reasonably fair chance, Johnny."

Johnny reached out and turned the card. It was an ace. Good card but no help. Rod won the hand and Brandy.

She wasn't exuberant but she smiled at Rod as if she expected no other outcome. Brandy stood. "Well, gentlemen. I had the lowest hand and I buy breakfast tomorrow. See all of you at seven?"

Ken and Justin nodded. Johnny slumped back in his chair and reached for the bottle instead of his glass. Justin and Ken rose from their chairs and called it a night. They talked in muffled voices as they walked down the hallway, unsure of what they had just witnessed.

Rod collected the cards, chuckling at his good luck. "Last card Charlie, huh? I've got to save this deck, maybe have it bronzed." He gazed lovingly at Brandy. "Ready whenever you are, darlin.'"

She walked around the table and planted a kiss on Johnny's forehead. "Until tomorrow." Without looking back, she followed Rod out of the room, walking down the hallway by his side.

Johnny gulped the last hit from the bottle and slowly got up, trying to decide whether to go to his room or find a bar still open. The hallway was empty. He stopped at his door, hesitated, and then entered. He heard Brandy's door open, footsteps coming down the hall, and then Rod's door open. *That's that*, he thought. *I'll never forgive that miserable bastard.* He knew it was partly his own fault for agreeing to the game. He had nothing to win and everything to lose. He let Rod pull the con even if the game itself was fair, but would Brandy have declined if he had protested? Probably not.

Brandy didn't knock. She knew the door would be open and she entered the room. She was relieved to see that Rod hadn't undressed. Maybe he wasn't as sure of himself as he had acted after the game. She had never given him any reason to think he had sexual privileges or an invitation to pursue her. Ten years ago she had spent the night with him, just like she had with Johnny, but physical sex wasn't involved. Tonight was different. By agreeing to be the ante in the last hand, she had raised his hopes and fed his ego.

He gave her his lopsided grin and motioned to the place on the bed next to him. She stood in front of him, hands on hips, seeming taller, more indomitable than ever.

"Okay, Rod. You won the hand, but conditions still apply. I agree to spend the night in your room until sunrise but only if you respect my wishes and behave like a gentleman. For your information, I would have said the same thing to Johnny. Regardless of what you and others believe, he and I are friends only, maybe a shade more than platonic but not intimate. I choose who I go all the way with and I tell you up front that we won't be doing that. We can play around, have some laughs, and sleep together, but that's it. Do we have an understanding?"

Looking up at her, his cockiness evaporated by the determination of her stance and speech, he merely nodded, like a little boy being scolded by his mother. He moved to the nightstand and picked up a bottle of cheap whiskey, poured some into a glass, started to drink, then offered it to Brandy. She took the glass and thanked him. He retrieved another glass from the bathroom and poured some for himself. They clinked glasses.

"Here's to the luck of the cards," she said, "for better or worse."

"I guess this is for the worse, huh?" He downed half of his drink.

"The best would have been if I had hit that straight, but even I can't win them all." She took a sip, sat on the bed, and smiled at him. "Look, Rod, we haven't always been the best of friends, but I don't dislike you. You aren't my ideal man, by any means, but I know you and Johnny are friends and I hope we can get along as well. Let's have a good time tonight. You forgave me ten years ago when I betrayed your trust and I will always be grateful. I'll be even more appreciative if you don't pass around a lot of lies about what we do tonight. I don't know where I am going or when, but I have no desire to leave a lot of rubbish behind. I don't want to be known as the town whore, okay?"

"Sure, Brandy. I respect you, and I don't want to do anything to ruin my relationship with Johnny. He's okay, and I think you are too, even though I don't know you as well as I might have wanted. I do know you're one hell of a poker player, and you turn a pair of jeans into something else. I'm glad I brought you into the treasure group. I'm good with that. I might tease Johnny about tonight, but I won't spread any rumors. Justin won't say diddly, but I'm not sure about Ken. He might want to blab about a lot more than what he knows."

"I'll deal with Ken, not to worry. Ready for another drink?"

Brandy and Rod spent the night, snuggled in the cheap hotel single bed and rose as the sun lit the east-facing window. He didn't get everything he wanted but received more than he expected. She accomplished her objective. She stayed in control, the leader of the orchestra, the maestro in charge of the circus representing the pulse of life in a small desert town.

Rod had a serious mission to accomplish. As agreed, he would set out the following Monday for Los Angeles, San Francisco, and other points in the great state of California to see if he could scout up a party interested in purchasing gold. He didn't have as many familiar contacts as before and needed to take as many precautions as he could, revealing nothing until he was assured that those he sought were reliable and trustworthy. Not an easy task in the darker world of smuggling and merchandising illegal possessions.

In the meantime, Johnny was facing his own moment of truth with Brandy. He didn't rise until after nine, reluctant to face the day. The events of the evening before had taken him by surprise. No, more like he had been shocked at how easily Brandy had agreed to Rod's proposal. For that matter, what had gotten into Rod? They often teased each other and Brandy about sexual liaisons while drinking together, daring each other to cross the invisible line, but other than the innocent night she had spent with each of them, Brandy never pursued a physical relationship with either of them. Johnny had always thought, incorrectly it seemed, that if he wanted to push it, she would have agreed to bed down with him on several occasions. His initial reluctance might have been due to Sonya, but that had never been a prohibitive restriction. Brandy admitted to a few encounters of her own ten years ago and while he had been away. She was not a virgin but apparently picked and chose her times carefully as well as when and with whom.

Why Rod? He did win the showdown. Justin had dealt the cards. It could have gone either way, including a win for the brunette and the loss of Rod's and Johnny's winnings. Had last night been different in some fundamental way unknown to Johnny? He needed to talk with her, to clarify what was going on, especially since they might be on the threshold of dissolving the TTT.

Brandy was not working that day, but he saw her on the street that afternoon. She smiled as he approached as if nothing unusual had happened the night before. Johnny looked at his feet when she greeted him. He shuffled back and forth a couple of times like a bashful junior high student asking a girl to his first formal dance.

"Brandy, I wonder if you'd be up for dinner tonight. Someplace nice, maybe in Alturas." He looked up at her, not sure what to expect.

"Well, Johnny. You've never taken me to Alturas, or anywhere else for that matter. All of our *dates*," she accented the word, "have been right here in Sagebrush." The flirty smile was back and directed at him.

"Well yeah, that's true, but if you'll remember, way back when, I had other people in my life and a long-distance date wouldn't cut it. This seems like our first chance to have a good talk since I came back, that is, if you'd like to do that and…"

"I'd love to Johnny." She put her hand on his arm and looked straight into his eyes. "I'm sure you have questions about last night. I won't tell you what we did or didn't do. If Rod wants to confess,

I'll leave that to him. You can probably tell by now if he speaks the truth or bullshits. I wish either you or I had won the hand. If I had won, I'd be taking both of you to dinner. Which reminds me, where in the hell were you for breakfast? Remember, I lost the hand and agreed to buy. Everyone showed but you."

"Sorry. I didn't get up in time to make it. I had a particularly painful headache this morning, just clearing now."

"Poor boy. What time do you want to leave and how formal will we be dining?"

"Casual nice, nothing real fancy. After all, it's Alturas and you can pick what kind of food. We'll leave here about five."

"Five it is. Knock on my door." Another provocative smile and she was gone. Johnny watched her walk away, marveling at her backside and the nonchalance of their conversation. It would be an interesting evening.

———— ◆ · ————

BRANDY ALSO HAD A TASK FOR THE DAY. SHE APPROACHED KEN'S barbershop, knowing it was a Saturday and that was usually kids day. She normally had Ken cut her hair. She kept it simple and short and preferred his services to those of two women who ran beauty parlors out of their homes. Ken could be relied on for the news about town. To her relief, there was only one boy in the seat and only his dad waiting for him. She said hello and took a chair. A few minutes later the boy and his dad were gone and Brandy climbed into the old-time barber chair.

Ken smiled and put a clean apron around her. "Same as always, Brandy?"

"Yep, that works for me."

"Thanks for breakfast today. A rare treat for me. I told my wife that it was part of a poker game payoff, but I didn't tell her why."

"Ken, that's one of the reasons I wanted to see you today, although it was also time for a cut. About the game. We all had a lot to drink last night and I realize it ended differently than most."

"Yes, well I must say that Justin and I were surprised, although entertained, by the outcome."

"Uh-hmm, but Ken, I think you can appreciate how that outcome might sound to someone not familiar with our group and the craziness we enjoy among ourselves. Specifically, my fate in serving as the stake for the last hand. Regardless of who won, it wouldn't sound right to others. I might not have a sterling reputation around town, but this wouldn't be good, especially for the good name of the hotel and for Justin. Follow me?"

Ken continued cutting and shaping hair, working the hair on the nape of her neck with scissors in small precise clips. "Sure, Brandy, that makes sense. I haven't said anything to anyone. I know I talk a lot. It goes with the job you know, but I respect you and Justin and everyone in the group. I'll keep it between us." He stepped forward to look at her. "None of my business and I'm not asking for any details, but are you all right? I mean, Rod had a bunch to drink and I hope he didn't hurt you…or anything." His pause was accompanied by a red face. He quickly stepped back and resumed the cut.

Brandy smiled. "No, no, nothing like that. Rod is a gentleman and we shared a few drinks and a talk. Nothing more. Nothing exciting, but I want to make sure others don't try to fill in the blanks."

"Understood. By the way, I do have some news. Emma Dodson raised some money toward building some outdoor play equipment for our park. She and the Ladies Sewing Circle started that project…" Ken began one of his customary community reports that lasted ten minutes, while Brandy sat, smiling to herself about how easy this had been. *Ken is a good guy and means well, but I'm glad I got here in time.*

THE KNOCK ON BRANDY'S DOOR CAME AT 4:45. SHE WAS NOT completely dressed yet, her blouse still unbuttoned. She opened the door, expecting to chide Johnny for being early, but she faced Rod.

"Oh, sorry Brandy, just wanted to see if you were in and might want some company later this evening, a few drinks and a bite to eat." He stood back from the door and looked like a lost puppy.

As she fastened the last buttons, she smiled. "Sorry, Rod, but Johnny asked me out for dinner earlier today. He's taking me to Alturas, but, if you want some company tonight, I happen to know that Lucy, the young woman at the front desk, has nothing on her dance card. I bet she'd be happy to be invited."

"Lucy? Is she old enough to drink?"

"She's twenty-four. She just looks like a teeny. Treat her nice, Rod, like you treat me. I'll take your invitation some other night. Okay?"

"Yeah, Brandy, that'll be fine. I'm headin' south on Monday to see if we can get a deal." He looked at her. "Are you sure that Lucy wouldn't mind if an old asshole like me asks her out?"

"Go for it. We all need company, especially on a Saturday night, but be quick. She'll be gone in a few minutes. And if I don't see you before then, good luck on your trip."

"Yeah, I'll need it. Thanks, Brandy. You're a jewel." He turned and walked to the lobby.

At precisely five, another knock announced Johnny's arrival. She opened the door and stepped out wearing a dark blue blouse, a short skirt, and a gold necklace and earrings. Johnny was wearing a sports jacket, slacks, and loafers.

"Wow, aren't we something," she said, taking his arm as they walked down the hallway and out through the lobby.

"My car's around the side." He stopped to admire her. "This actually does feel like a date. First one in a long time."

A bright-blue 1965 Pontiac GTO coupe, recently washed, waited at the curb by the side of the hotel. He opened the door and she climbed in. "Nice, real nice. You must have done well for yourself John-O."

He climbed behind the wheel and inserted the key in the ignition. The car purred, and he moved onto the main street out of town. "Can't complain. Best wheels I've ever had."

The drive to Alturas took half an hour. The time was filled with random conversation about the town, the hotel, and the plans to sell the gold. Nothing was said about Rod or the night before. As they crossed the short bridge into the south side of Alturas, Johnny turned to Brandy and asked her what she was in the mood for.

"A couple of stiff drinks and a big juicy steak, followed by a couple of stiff drinks." She laughed and put a warm hand on his arm. Two blocks ahead of them the three-story Niles Hotel loomed on their right.

"I've eaten there once," Johnny said, "but it was pretty decent food and I can testify to the power of their drinks. Old West style."

"Good enough." She leaned back, looking about as comfortable as a Cheshire cat after a canary treat.

They sat at the old wooden bar in the saloon, gazing into the mirror and at the rows of bottles. After their second drink, it was time to eat and they made their way into the adjacent dining room. The hotel was offering fresh venison for the weekend and they both ordered it with all the trimmings, followed by home-made apple pie ala mode. Their dialog was light and flirty but avoided any reference to Rod other than a shared wish for his future success. Brandy mentioned that she had sicced him on Lucy for the evening.

"Is that your good deed for the day?" he asked as they started their after-dinner rounds of alcohol.

"That and a conversation I had with Ken this afternoon."

"I noticed you had a fresh cut. Looks good."

"I told him not to broadcast the events of our Friday-night game and he assured me he wouldn't. To protect the reputation of Justin and the Sagebrush Hotel, of course."

"Of course. And how would he know what to broadcast?" asked Johnny. For the first time, she had mentioned the infamous night. He wasn't sure he wanted to know anything more, but then again, he did.

"I told him the truth. Nothing happened. We had a couple of drinks, shared the bed, and that was it." She leaned forward, looking into his eyes, waiting for his reaction. "Just like ten years ago."

That brought a smile and Johnny finished the whiskey straight on ice. "One more for the road?"

She sat back and glanced at her glass. It was almost empty. "It's a long drive back and we've both had a fair amount. No room down the hallway to walk to. Think we should stay in town, grab a room somewhere?" She stated it matter-of-factly, not what he might consider a suggestive come-on.

He looked around him. "We're already in a hotel. The car is parked, so we can walk up to a room. Let's just check-in here."

"Johnny, this isn't a crash pad. This will set us back some money."

"Us? I'm paying the tab. Since I deserted you for breakfast, I'll let you cover the tip for the bar bill, and I'll get the rest. Besides, the place has some atmosphere. Let's have another drink and while they're coming, I'll check us in. Have any particular name you want to use?" He grinned, not expecting her to answer.

She opened her purse, took out her driver's license, and handed it to him. "I'll order and you register us as Mr. and Mrs. Charlebois. Can you do that?"

He took her card, stood up, stepped back, started to ask her if she was serious, and decided that she was. "Yes ma'am." He made his way to the hotel lobby. Another drink, and they adjourned to their room on the second floor.

Satisfied that she had told the simple truth about Rod and herself, Johnny slowly undressed while Brandy took a quick shower. He hopped in next and when he came back into the bedroom with a towel wrapped around him, she was under the covers, the sheets pulled up to her neck.

"Lose the towel, cowboy. I didn't bring any night clothes so we will have to be *au naturel.*"

"Ah, my favorite wardrobe." He threw the towel on a corner chair and climbed in beside her. As their bare thighs aligned, she slid into his arms and pressed against his chest.

"Thanks, Johnny."

"Thanks for what?"

"For tonight, for dinner, the trip, and for understanding about Rod. It got weird last night. I'm not sure why. One thing led to another. Blame it on the moon, I guess."

"The moon wasn't full last night."

"Doesn't have to be. It's still to blame."

"Works for me. You realize that this is our second time in bed but the first time in the raw?"

"Stop talking and do something. Start with a kiss or something along that order."

"Yes ma'am." He did and she did. So much for orders and innocence.

JOHNNY FOUND JAY ON WEDNESDAY MORNING, LOADING A TRUCK outside of the grain dealer, about three blocks from the hotel. Johnny saw the truck go by the hotel as he was finishing a late breakfast and noted that Jay was by himself. He walked down the street and greeted Jay as he was getting the bed of the truck ready to receive several sacks.

"Making a run, Jay?"

"Yes sir, gonna deliver this barley to Susanville for Mr. Cox. Be gone all day."

"Here, I'll give you a hand so you can get on the road earlier." He walked with Jay to the loading dock of the grain store and started hauling the large sacks to the truck. As they walked back for their second load, Johnny said, "Jay, can I ask you about something that happened while I was away, something from a few years ago?"

"Sure, Johnny, what'd you wanna know?"

They paused at the dock. "It's something Rod told me after I came back. He said you and he were talking about the Woodward accident and the car they were driving. Do you remember that?"

"Oh sure. I felt really bad about what happened to them. I liked Steve and Donna and I liked their kids."

"Do you remember when Steve brought his car to you to have some brake work done?"

"He didn't bring it to me, I don't know nothing about brakes. He brought it to my brother because he can fix almost anything on a car."

"Ray fixed the brakes on Steve's car?"

"Yeah, and he made some adjustments to the steering wheel and looked under the car and made sure it was okay for the trip they were going to make."

"Did the car seem okay to Ray when he gave it back to Steve?"

"Sure. Ray wouldn't let Steve drive a car that wasn't fixed right. Steve was happy to have it fixed."

"Did you see Ray do anything unusual when he fixed it?

"What do you mean, Johnny?"

"Did he say anything about the car's condition or needing to do something different than he usually did with a car?"

Jay frowned as if thinking deeply, trying to recall. "No, Johnny, I don't think so. Steve dropped it off in the morning and took it back that afternoon. He paid Ray for the work and drove it away." He frowned again and put his head down. "That was the last time I saw Steve. Two days later, he drove out of town and we never heard from him again until we found out his whole family got killed in that accident on the mountain." When Jay looked up, there was a trace of wetness in the corners of his eyes.

They picked up two more loads of grain sacks and placed them in the truck. Jay said thanks and Johnny said goodbye. Afterward, Johnny realized he hadn't said anything to assure that Jay wouldn't repeat what had been said. It was time for an afternoon nap and he returned to the hotel.

A loud knock on his door at three o'clock woke him from a sound sleep and sweet dream of Alturas. "Johnny, open up." The voice was loud, impatient, and hostile. Johnny opened the door and viewed a red-faced Ray Gordon, fists clenched and feet spread. Realizing what must have happened, Johnny stepped back and asked him if he wanted to come in and talk.

"Talk? Talk? I'll ram a fist down that skinny throat of yours. What the hell do you think you're doing trying to interrogate my brother?"

"I wasn't…"

"You motherfucker. You and everyone else in town knows Jay ain't right in the head. He don't know shit from Shinola and you're pumping him about something that happened three years ago. What gives you the right?" Ray moved into the room as Johnny retreated to stand beside his bed.

"I'm sure we can discuss this without shouting or threats, Ray. I was simply helping Jay load some grain sacks so he could get on the road. I was curious about Steve's car, that's all."

"Then you should have asked me, dammit, I'm the one who worked on it. He only handed me some tools. He don't know nothing about mechanics or autos. What did you wanna know?"

"Just if the car was in good condition when Steve left with it. Just curious."

Ray glowered at him, fists relaxing but still poised as if ready to strike. "The car was working fine. If I repair an auto, it works fine. That's all you or anyone else needs to know."

"Seems like you're a touch overheated if that's the only issue."

"What does that mean?" The fists clenched again.

"There seems little reason to get this worked up because of a question about Steve's car. Jay remembered the repair and he said it looked good when Steve drove off. He wasn't upset so why should you be?" Johnny crossed his arms, making himself vulnerable to a sucker punch if Ray decided to throw it. If he did, it would confirm Johnny's suspicions that Ray had some terrible secret to hide.

Ray relaxed his hands and shoulders, the grimace becoming a look of contrition, as if he realized he had pushed too hard for his own good. "Dammit, Johnny, I probably shouldn't have lit into you this way, but you know I'm pretty protective about Jay. You know why. I don't want anyone thinking they can take advantage of him. Can you understand that? We need each other—the whole group does if we're ever gonna realize anything from this stuff in the basement." He looked around, realizing the hallway door was open. "Look, I'm sorry, okay? Let's let this be bygones. We'll probably be playing again this weekend."

Johnny smiled and extended his hand. "Sure, Ray. I understand about your brother. I didn't mean any harm. Let's see what Rod finds out from his trip. I don't know when he'll be back, but hopefully it will be with good news."

"Amen to that." Ray gave him an affirmative nod, turned on his heels, and stepped into the hallway, closing the door gently behind him.

Johnny sat on the bed. *Now what? Does that tell me anything? I need to talk to Rod again, as soon as he gets back.* He hadn't said anything to Brandy or anyone else about his suspicions, but that might have to change if Ray did anything further to pose a threat. Who might be the next member of the tontine to depart unexpectedly?

CHAPTER SEVEN

Unsettling News

It didn't take long for the bad news to arrive. Thursday morning, August 10, 1967, a date the TTT would like to forget. Rod returned to town about 1:30 in the morning and went directly to his room. Johnny was aware of his arrival—his room door opening, sounds of boots on the hardwood floor, toilet flushing, and finally the squeak of bedsprings. He thought about knocking on his door but dismissed the idea as unnecessary and in bad form. Rod may have driven all night and was probably in no mood for company. Whatever he had to say could wait until later or whenever the two crossed paths. A game was scheduled for Friday, but Johnny needed to talk to him before then.

His confrontation with Ray from the week before still weighed heavily. *It wasn't about his brother. A man doesn't get that angry over a question or two. He was trying to cover up something, but I can't be certain and I'll have to be if this is going to go anywhere. Where? Suspicions and circumstantial evidence prove nothing, and what would be the motive, other than to reduce the group size? The tontine isn't a public affair and hopefully will never be. Bringing in the authorities is not an option.*

Johnny decided on an early breakfast. He needed to get away from Sagebrush and the hotel for a while, clear his head in some open space. There was plenty of that around, just had to drive a few miles on any of the three roads out of town. He showered, thought about shaving but didn't, dressed and headed for the dining room. It was quarter after seven.

Johnny wasn't surprised to see Justin at a table, reading a paper and drinking coffee. Noises from the kitchen told him the staff was busy, probably fixing breakfast for the boss. He smiled and pulled up a chair opposite.

Justin put the paper aside as Stephanie, one of the newer waitresses, brought a pot and poured Johnny a cup. "You're up earlier than usual. Big day planned?"

He took a sip. Good, strong, hot. He could never fault the hotel on its coffee. "Thought I'd take a ride out of town, shake loose some cobwebs." He took another sip. "Rod's back. Came in early this morning. Hope he has something good to tell us."

Justin looked toward the door. "Speaking of the devil, here he is." Justin waved him over and Rod pulled up a chair.

The waitress returned to service Rod's mug and ask if they wanted to order breakfast.

Rod gave her one of his solicitous smiles. "Big stack, two strips of bacon, some taters, and an egg over easy on top. Oh, and a tall glass of tomato juice, iced."

Johnny shook his head. "Damn, Rod, what took you so long to make up your mind? You been dreamin' about that all night instead of your usual perverse fantasies?"

"Didn't eat last night. Drove straight from Santa Barbara, only stopped for coffee and a piece of pie in Chico."

Johnny looked at Steph and said, "Make mine a short stack, one egg fried hard on top, no meat, no juice." She nodded, turned and walked quickly to the kitchen.

Justin regarded Rod for a few seconds. "Must be really good news or really bad news. It don't look like good if your expression is any indication. I hope it's because you're tired."

"I'm that, but you've got it nailed. In a nutshell, we're screwed. If we want to sell our stuff at this time, we're gonna lose almost half its value. No one is interested in moving it unless we pay through the nose or some other body part, if you get my drift."

Johnny took another sip of coffee, regretting he didn't have something more potent to put in it. "No buyers, huh? We're stuck with it for a while longer? How much longer?"

"Can't say for sure. One guy in Frisco told me they might be able to do something in a year or two but not right now. Not sure what the problem is, but maybe the heat from the feds is up. No one wants to deal with anyone outside of their regular channels."

"Guess we're irregular, right?" Justin smiled and looked up as the waitress brought his breakfast.

"Yours will be up in a few minutes," she said to Rod and Johnny, giving the big man a glass of chilled juice.

Rod reached into his back pocket, pulled out a metal flask, and added some clear liquid to the juice. He looked up at Justin and grinned. "Needed to zip up the flavor a bit." Johnny put his index finger up. Rod looked at him and poured some of his joy juice in Johnny's coffee.

"What the hell do we do now?" Johnny asked, looking at Justin and then Rod. "We have a couple of people who are anxious to get rid of our assets and dissolve the agreement. I can't say I disagree with them. It's been ten years and I'm sure we can all find other things to spend our time and money on."

"Amen," said Rod, gulping down half of his doctored tomato juice.

Justin nodded. "Emma and I would like to proceed with some of the plans we had as well. I don't think anyone in the group will welcome this news."

"One person in particular, is going to be very unhappy." They looked at Johnny but knew who he was talking about. He wasn't sure how much to tell Justin about Ray's work on Steve's car, but Rod frowned at him as if anticipating what he might say. "Ray was agitating before Rod left on his trip, so I can only imagine what he will be like after he hears this. The question is, do we tell him right away or wait until after the game."

Justin thought, eating slowly. Before he could answer, Steph came out with the rest of the orders and they settled into eating. "We'd better do it before. If there are going to be harsh words, let's get it over with today. I can talk to him."

Rod looked up at him. "You sure about that, Justin? He isn't inclined to show much patience with you or any of us, but, if it comes down to fists, maybe Johnny or me"—he turned to his friend and grinned—"or both of us should be the messengers."

"We need to inform Emma and Brandy as well," Johnny said. "This has to be a group decision and Ray only has one share in six."

"Right you are," said Justin. "Rod, you deliver the news to Ray. Johnny, if you'll inform Brandy and get her reaction, I'll confer with Emma. Instead of a group meeting, what say the three of us sit down in my office after dinner tonight? We'll still have cards tomorrow night, but by then maybe the storm will have passed. Okay?"

Rod and Johnny mumbled an okay as they tore through their pancakes and sides. Johnny asked Rod for his flask and poured more enhancement into his coffee. As he started to return the booze, Justin held out his hand. Johnny gave it to him while Rod chuckled and shook his head. "For medicinal purposes," said Justin, who rarely drank during the day, especially during the week.

After breakfast, Johnny wished Rod luck with his mission and told him to be careful. He informed him of the confrontation between Ray and himself. Rod nodded. "Not surprised," was his first comment. The second thing he said gave Johnny the cold chills. "I'm carrying and that son of a bitch better not try to push too hard."

Johnny knew Rod kept a pistol on hand from time to time, but he didn't want to see their nasty little situation explode into anything lethal. Johnny told him so. Rod put his hand on his shoulder and reassured him he would stay in control.

Johnny went back to his room for a bathroom stop before getting into his car and heading east toward the low-lying foothills of the Warners. He had a lot of thinking to do before he discussed current affairs with Brandy. Recalling affairs, that night in Alturas was more than he had bargained for. They hadn't talked much since then, but she was friendly and seemed to accept it as a normal step in the progression of their relationship. Was it? Where to now? How did this delay in settling the tontine change anything? What would have happened if they had received the payout earlier? What then, what now?

Johnny pulled off the road near a quiet spring and creek shaded by cottonwoods. Beyond the creek, cattle grazed in a green pasture. The road had just started its climb into the hills but he had driven far enough. He walked away from the car and found a low flat stump to sit on a few yards from the road but hidden by a large clump of bushes. There was very little traffic and even less chance of being disturbed. He lit a cigarette, something he was doing less often, not actively trying to quit, but finding tobacco less satisfying than it used to be. *Maybe I should turn to pot.* He occasionally indulged, but it wasn't a regular thing, mostly for social gatherings than for the short-term high. It didn't seem to affect him as much as others, so it, like so many other vices, held little sway over his recreational choices. Except for gambling.

Living is the ultimate gamble and the ultimate payoff. Does it work with love the way that it does with cards? Don't know if I've ever been in love. Sonya was the closest thing to that, but it was more of a convenience and mutually satisfying friendship. I never felt anything deep, anything that amounted to a long-term commitment. If I had, I wouldn't have left her ten years ago. No one else has come close until Brandy. He couldn't understand, or maybe didn't want to understand, how the brunette mesmerized him. She always had, even when she was an eighteen-year old during their first poker games. She always seemed to be in charge of herself and others. Hard to get the upper hand on her, so to speak, and her smile was beguiling and disarming at the same time. She could drink with the best of them yet never seemed to lose her cool. *Our night in Alturas proved she can be all of the woman that her looks advertised. No complaints on any score.*

Three cigarettes later, more than his usual allotment, he stood and stretched. Walking to the creek, he relieved myself, stared at the cattle going about their business, and strolled to the car. Almost two hours had passed and a lot of things rumbled through his mind in that time. His recent return from the east, the promises and disappointments of the extended road trip, the reunion with the Sagebrush crowd, Brandy, friendly low-stakes card games, the treasure and the possibilities that might arise from the proceeds, yeah, all of that and more. It had been awhile since he had spent that long doing nothing but thinking. It felt good.

He turned the car west back to Sagebrush. He would wait for Brandy to get off work and invite her out for a cold one, have a bite to eat, and then meet with Rod and Justin. He could only hope things wouldn't escalate out of control between Rod and Ray. Neither one had a strong reputation for remaining calm in a tempest.

⬥

Justin advised Emma about what Rod had discovered during his trip. Her reaction was mild disappointment over the delay in funding the community projects that she and he, along with the late Woodward family, had wanted to initiate.

"It may be up to you, Justin. You might be the only one of us left when all is said and done." She sipped hot tea and sat back in her chair. "I'm not getting any younger, so I'm not sure I'll have time to realize my share of the venture."

"Nonsense, Emma. You're in better shape than most of us and will probably be spending *our* shares. From what Rod said, I don't believe this forestalls our plans indefinitely. We need to be patient and allow the right doors to open." He sat across the dining room table from her, drinking iced tea with lemon.

"Do you think so? If we sold the bars ten years ago, we would have been well off and the money would have been put to good use. I hate to agree with Ray, but he might be correct. Now the treasure takes up space in your hotel, we have to stay on the alert that someone doesn't discover our secret, and there is that legal thing hanging over our head. The gold isn't doing anyone any good where it's at, Justin. You know that as well as I do."

"Yes, I know, and I agree with everything you say."

"What about the others, Ray and Brandy?"

"Johnny will bring Brandy up to date. They seem different now, almost like a couple. I don't know what they have in mind, but I don't think Brandy will be any trouble. She has gone along with our past decisions without objection. Rod is supposed to be talking to Ray, possibly as we speak. I don't envy him that task. As much as I would also like to end our agreement and pay each person their share, I am afraid that Mr. Gordon is the one hitch in our company, the one who could precipitate additional problems."

"I'm afraid so, Justin. Let's hope that Rod can handle him and that this postponement is a short one, for all of our sakes."

IT WASN'T GOING WELL. FROM THE TIME ROD ENTERED THE home hardware shop and asked Ray if he could talk to him in private, the confrontational flag had been raised. They stepped into a small office at the rear of the shop.

Ray closed the door. He put both hands on his hips and glared at Rod, daring him to say what he already seemed to know. "Didn't get a connection did yah?"

"How do you know what I got? I haven't said anything yet and I know that no one else has had a chance." They glared at each other from two feet apart. Rod could smell the anger in the other man's breath. Ray wasn't going to cut him any slack, so he decided he wouldn't either.

"Well, what is it then?"

"Why don't we sit down Ray and try to pretend we are gentlemen. We don't have to be friends, but I don't need any scare tactics or bullying from you. I came over here to fill you in and if you want to learn what I found out, then ease off."

Ray stared at him for a few seconds, walked behind his desk and sat. He motioned for Rod to do the same.

Rod took a stiff wooden chair and pulled it in front of the desk. "So it comes as no surprise to you that I wasn't successful. There seems to be pressure from the feds about gold marketing and most of the usual outlets are lying low, trying not to be too conspicuous for a while."

"What's a while?" asked Ray, making no attempt to disguise the gruffness in his voice or his displeasure at receiving the unwelcome news.

"Could be a few months, probably not longer than a year or two. We might be able to do it now, but it would cost us big. One guy told me his fee might be half the gross."

"Shit, that's what we get for waiting ten years. We could have settled for twenty percent or something like that, and now, it's *half*?"

"You trying to broadcast this to the entire town? Isn't your brother working in the store?"

"He don't know nothing. Leave him out of it."

"He is out of it, remember? That was your decision a long time ago. This is between us and the rest of our group. We'll need to meet early next week and decide what, if anything, we are going to do. I am only telling you now as a courtesy. We are still on for a game tomorrow night and I wanted you to know what was in the air before then."

"I may or may not join your little party. I know what the odds are and who the players are. I suspect the rest of you already know what you're gonna do. Any meeting next week will be a formality, a 'let's appease Ray day' to keep me from getting too riled."

"I'd say you're pretty riled now."

"Damn right I am. For all I know, you made a deal, and now you're trying to cut me out of it. I'll wake up some morning and find you've all moved out of town, spending my money and living high on the hog."

"Doesn't come to anything like that and you know it. Justin isn't going to sell his hotel, Emma isn't going to pack up, and though I can't say for Brandy and Johnny, I ain't got any highfalutin' plans. You're gettin' yourself steamed up for nothing, Ray, and I guess I don't need to hear any more of it."

Rod stood, opened the door and walked through the store without a backward glance. Jay was fixing something in the window and greeted Rod as he reached the front door. Rod stopped, but noticed Ray standing in his office door, hands on hips. "Nice seeing you again, Jay." He smiled and walked out.

Brandy gladly accepted Johnny's Thursday evening invitation to the Rattlesnake Junction Tavern. It had better pizza and sandwiches than the other two watering holes and it was a larger room, affording them some privacy while they talked. He would meet with Rod and Justin at eight at the hotel.

She was flirty, almost like the younger version of herself from many years ago. Johnny was happy to see the carryover from their time in Alturas, wondering if it might represent more than a one-night stand. They didn't walk hand-in-hand from the hotel, but he was tempted. They sat side by side at a small table at the back of the tavern. Her arm brushed his as they hoisted glasses of beer and laughed while gobbling down a particularly messy pizza. Twice she wiped his mouth with a napkin and she let her hand occasionally rest on his knee under the table.

"What does Rod have to say for himself?" she said, between bites of pepperoni, mushrooms, and stringy cheese.

"He says we are going to be in the waiting game awhile longer." Johnny explained what Rod told him about the risks and high cost of selling the assets at the moment and that more patience would be required.

"I like my job, Justin is a decent boss, the games are still fun, and I get out of town every so often to resuscitate my life." She smiled and gave him a wink.

"Resuscitate, huh? You gonna start using a lot of big words and put me to shame are you?"

"Shit, Johnny. Why do you pretend to be some uneducated hick from a small town who has never been anywhere?" She took a last sip of her beer and looked down at the heavy glass mug. "Think I might need something a bit stronger."

"Maybe because I am an uneducated hick from a small town. Yeah, I've done a bit of traveling but nothing very sophisticated. You didn't see any postcards from London or Paris, did you?"

"I didn't see any postcards from you. But those are still to come. Maybe some fancy places after we are rich." She signaled to Marion, the barmaid-owner, for a Black Jack straight up.

As Johnny finished his beer, he signaled for the same and reflected on her last words. *After we are rich. I wonder if that means when she is rich and I am rich or when we are rich. She might be a real treasure to travel abroad with. Travel with a broad, a very desirable one. Oh yes, I can see us walking along the Seine.*

The drinks arrived and Brandy held hers up. "I can wait awhile longer and hope for a bigger payout. It's like at the table isn't it? Waiting for the right cards and the right moment?"

Johnny lifted his, and they clinked, and he took a large swallow. The train seemed to be running on the right track. He told her about the meeting at the hotel as they walked back.

She left him with a twinkle in her eye and a promise. "I'll be gunning for you tomorrow night, Johnny Templeton. I want more than that thing you carry in your pants. I want your money."

"Like everything else, my dear, you'll have to earn it."

Justin and Rod were in the hotel office when he arrived. The owner was sharing a bottle of Drambuie and poured some in a glass for Johnny as he sat down. Justin had arranged three chairs together in a tight circle in front of the desk. "More intimate and I can keep everyone's glasses filled," he said.

Rod glanced at Johnny and grinned. "If our hotel owner isn't careful, we'll have him carousing around Sagebrush like the rest of us no-good coyotes."

"Might be a step up, a civic improvement for the community's prosperity," Johnny said.

They raised their glasses and sipped. Johnny told them that Brandy had taken the news in stride and again had ambitions to make poker fools of the men. Justin mentioned Emma's comment about getting older and her concern about Ray. As if on cue, they turned to Rod for his report.

He took another sip and leaned forward. "Yeah, it didn't go well. Ray wasn't surprised we weren't going to sell. In addition to being unhappy with us, me in particular, he accused us of trying to cut him out, of selling it without his knowledge."

Johnny looked up from the drink he cradled protectively. "Think he'll be at the game?"

Justin looked at Johnny and then at Rod. "Maybe it's better if Ray skips this one. That will give us a chance to meet with him as a group and reassure him we're not working behind his back."

"Don't know if anything will convince him. The older he gets the nastier he is. Totally different from his brother," Rod said.

Mention of Jay triggered Johnny's decision to let Justin in on their suspicions about the Woodward accident. He looked at Rod and as if his friend could read his mind, Rod gave him a go-ahead nod.

"Justin, there is something you need to know about Ray, something Rod and I have discussed, but we were hesitant to bring anyone else in on it without some proof or better evidence."

Justin sat forward, all signs of playing host disappearing as Johnny filled him in on what they knew and didn't know about Ray's involvement with Steve's car before the fateful trip. Justin lifted his eyebrows when Johnny mentioned his conversation with Jay and Ray's stormy reaction when he found out. Rod gave an occasional affirmative nod and summarized his own suspicions.

Justin leaned back and poured another round. "You're right. It's only circumstantial, and we have no way of confirming any mechanical evidence at this point. Rod, how much do you trust what your mechanic friend in Alturas told you? Is he reliable?"

"Have no reason to doubt him. I've known him for several years and he isn't the kind to make statements like that without cause. Problem is, we don't have a copy of the report. We could try and locate it in some government office, but it's been awhile."

Johnny cleared his throat. "Let's hope it isn't true, that the accident occurred through no fault of Ray, but *if* it is true, then any or all of us could also be in danger. He already has his sights on Rod and me for asking his brother questions, so he may see us as a real hazard to his plans. I don't think Emma, Brandy, or you"—he looked at Justin—"are in immediate trouble, but that could change if we bring them in on this."

"Let's not then. Johnny, I can't advise you on Brandy. She's a big girl and can take care of herself, but I don't want Emma exposed to anything. Her ignorance may be her best insurance policy."

"Only if Ray knows she's ignorant," said Rod.

They ended the meeting in a somber mood. None of them were sure if Ray would play on Friday night or not, but they agreed that the TTT should meet on Saturday or Sunday.

⸻ ◆ ⸻

The Friday-night game included the usual players, minus Ray. Only Pete and Ken commented on his absence. For the others, it seemed like he was not expected or didn't exist, but they realized what the absence meant. They couldn't count on any cooperation or conciliatory gestures from the angry hardware man. Although it was believed that Ray couldn't retrieve any of the gold without their cooperation, he could still stir up a mess of trouble. Johnny decided to inform Brandy about their discussions and suspicions after the game.

It ended early for no predetermined reason, but the usual frivolity was missing and even Brandy's promise to render havoc on the other players was not realized. She left the table down a few dollars. Ken and Justin were the co-winners of the evening.

Johnny briefly consulted Rod about his intention to bring Brandy in on the news about Ray and his friend concurred. "Best we are united on this one," were his parting words.

In the first-floor hallway, Brandy held the door open for Johnny to enter her room. He did so without the flirtatious manner she might have expected.

"I lost tonight. Not what I boasted I would do earlier." She seemed almost contrite. More an observation than an admission of weakness.

He motioned for her to sit on the bed. "We might all end up losing if we don't figure some things out. There's something I need to tell you." He sat on the chair facing her, his serious look dispelling any other intentions he might have for being in her room.

"It's about Ray, isn't it? I thought there might be a reason he didn't play tonight."

"Yep. I'm afraid our treasure trove partner is unhappy with everyone, especially with Rod. He accused him, and the rest of us, of trying to strike a sale without his knowledge. He got belligerent about it with me, but that's not the worse part."

"No?"

"Nope. Ray was involved with fixing Steve's car before his family took their last trip."

"And?"

"And Rod has a friend, a mechanic in Alturas, who looked the wreck over when they hauled it back. He told Rod the hydraulic brake tubes had areas that looked as if acid or some other corrosive substance had weakened them. They were punctured in a small localized area." Johnny watched the changing expressions on Brandy's face as she contemplated the implications of what he was telling her. She nodded for him to continue.

"I talked to Jay when Ray wasn't present, asking him about the day they worked on Steve's car. Jay remembered them doing the brakes but he said the car seemed fine. When Ray found out I had talked to Jay, he went volcanic and accused me of interrogating his weak-minded and defenseless brother. His reaction was well out of proportion to what an innocent inquiry should have produced. Rod believes he sabotaged the Woodward's car, and on the face of it, I tend to agree. Ray's greed about entering the tontine, demanding equal shares for his wife and brother, and his impatience about selling don't add up to pleasant prospects for the future of our enterprise."

"Bad news indeed, Johnny. Ray was never one of my favorite fellows in town or at the table. He was always a dark figure, too serious, too intense. And, as you say, the way he gained entrance to our group has never been a point in his favor. We bought him off. If what you say is true…"

"It's only circumstantial, you know. The pieces fit, but accusing someone of murder isn't to be taken lightly."

"No, but it does mean we need to watch our backs, doesn't it?"

Johnny began unbuttoning his shirt. "I'll watch your back if you'll watch mine."

She smiled and stood. "Seems like a reasonable proposition and at the moment, it's the only one on the table."

Ray was temporarily forgotten, as were the poker table brags and outcomes, when Johnny and Brandy resumed the snuggling and lovemaking session begun in Alturas. The Saturday morning sun found them naked and intertwined, seemingly without a care in the world.

WHILE THE FRIDAY-NIGHT POKER GAME WAS UNDERWAY, RAY Gordon had some important business of his own. During the past year he had done some tractor work for a local farmer named Sanford Wallman. He lived not far from the Charles farm and about a mile from where Johnny grew up. Sanford didn't have a lot of money, but he provided Ray's family with some of his produce in exchange for labor and parts on his machinery. He rarely came to town and most of the residents of Sagebrush barely knew he existed. Sanford liked it that way. He was unmarried, had three dogs, and spent most of his evenings reading or target shooting, one of his few passions.

Ray drove out to Sanford's farm to have dinner. They couldn't be classified as friends, as that would be more than the farmer desired from anyone, but they could enjoy a business arrangement that was to their mutual benefit. Sanford had a younger brother, Alfred, who was looking for work. He hadn't been able to find anything in Alturas and was living at the farm, helping with the chores. Ray had a job in mind for him. The three of them discussed it over dinner and a couple of beers. Afterward, Alfred and Ray shook hands—Alfred now had a little more income and Ray had someone to help him if and when the time came.

Ray thought about the news Rod had brought and the probable outcome for disposal of the gold. *No doubt about it, I'm the lone wolf in this group. If I don't take measures to protect myself, I'll be cut out completely. Maybe that's already happened. Best to keep a watchful eye on Justin. He is the key to the treasure. I can't always know what Johnny, Rod, and the girl are up to or where they will be, but Mr. Gonzales ain't going nowhere and the stuff is in his basement.* He thought about trying to change the locks but couldn't figure a way to get the master key to the vault without arousing suspicion. *I'll let Alfred be my eyes and ears.* He wasn't satisfied, but at least he had a potential ally.

Justin contacted Emma and Ray and asked them to meet with him and the other TTT members on Sunday afternoon. Emma agreed to host the meeting again to avoid the inquiries of their Sagebrush neighbors.

Ray was one of the first to arrive and he attempted to win Emma to his way of thinking about selling the asset. She indicated that she had not formed an opinion and would not make a decision until she had heard from everyone. Anticipating a meeting that might be more contentious than usual, she had stocked a couple six-packs of beer, something she rarely bought. She opened and gave a bottle to Ray and he retreated to the living room, resigned to protest, but without support, the result he knew was coming.

Rod and Johnny also received cold beer, and Justin, as was his custom, shared hot tea with Emma. Brandy was the last to arrive and, when offered a choice, took a moment to consider whether to join the men in a cold one. She asked for iced tea, which Emma provided.

Her decision did not go unnoticed. Rod and Johnny looked at each other, as if to say, *Our girl seems to be going political on us, selecting the cold nonalcoholic compromise.*

Ray sat slowly sipping from his bottle, as Rod repeated his report for the benefit of the group. He emphasized the hazards of dealing with strangers who had warned him of the current diffi-culties in moving bullion and the high transfer fees that would be required. Although Emma had been apprised of Rod's trip, they turned to her for comment.

"I would like to cash in our holdings and I believe everyone else would favor that course of action." She spoke slowly as if giving it great thought, looking at each person around the table and focusing on Ray last. "It has been ten years of keeping the secret and as far as I know, it has remained within our small group, including the Gordon family."

Ray shifted in his chair and placed the empty beer bottle on the table in front of him. "Would you like another, Mr. Gordon?" Emma asked.

"Sure, but keep talking. I'll get it." He looked at Rod and Johnny. "You ready?"

They indicated yes and chugged the last drops. Ray gathered the empties, walked into the kitchen and retrieved three bottles from the fridge. As he opened them, he looked carefully about the room and took note of things on the shelves before walking back into the living room. During his absence, Emma hadn't said a word while sipping on her tea. The five exchanged glances communicating the same message. *What is he up to?* His polite response and offer to retrieve the suds seemed a ruse, the calm before a storm, but no one wanted to voice it.

Ray handed out the bottles and took his seat. Brandy sipped on her tea, her head back in the easy chair, eyes closed.

Emma looked at Ray. "This is a difficult decision, and I would like us to discuss it further before I declare my choice."

Justin asked Rod the questions to which most of them knew the answer. "When should we try again? How long should we wait and are there any other places north or east that might give us better results?"

Ray stared straight ahead as he drank slowly. His posture seemed relaxed, but Johnny read the signs of tension, a slight firmness in the jaws and tightening of arm muscles. Relaxed he wasn't. Brandy sat up and opened her eyes. Emma continued sipping but looked at Rod as he answered.

"As I told several of you, it might be a few months or a few years. I can try again in about six weeks. I can go back to Reno and also make some inquiries up north. Maybe in Seattle or Vancouver."

"BC? No one has mentioned the possibility of Canada before." Ray leaned forward, his eyes darting around the room, measuring their responses, desperately searching for the bit of hope that a different approach might offer. "What about it? Would Canada be a better place to score a deal?"

Rod hesitated then answered deliberately. "Might be, but I don't know anyone there and I would need some time to dig up someone who had the connections. We can't go shooting off and blab about what we have to just anyone. There's an additional risk of moving the stuff across an international border. Maybe you've heard about customs inspectors?" The sarcasm was not lost on anyone including Ray. "Maybe we can consider it. Possession of gold has never been illegal in Canada, or most of the rest of the world. The problem is getting a half ton of gold into Canada without being detected, and we still need to have a reliable business connection."

Johnny smiled at Rod and then at Ray. "It wouldn't hurt to investigate and who knows, maybe we'll hit pay dirt. I propose we provide Rod with additional funds to continue his inquiries, including trips to Seattle, Vancouver, and any other place he believes might be promising. Would that help ease some of your aggravation, Ray?"

"Some of it. It would be better than waiting for what, another ten years?"

"I would also support this," said Emma.

The others agreed and the crisis seemed to deflate as they nibbled on some snacks and finished a few more beers. Ray wasn't completely satisfied, but he shook Rod's hand and wished him good luck when they left Emma's.

———◆———

ROD LEFT A WEEK LATER. HE MADE SEVERAL PHONE CALLS AND attempted to line up contacts and associates of contacts. One of his former Reno traders knew someone in a Vancouver company that was legally dealing in physical transfers of gold. Gold prices in Canada were essentially the same as in the United States., but the handling fees were expected to be more reasonable. Rod decided to bypass Seattle and try the Canadian firm first.

He returned to Sagebrush the following week. His report indicated that a gold sale in Canada was possible if they could deliver the goods. That was a big if. His understanding of the potential hazards was not reassuring. If they were caught at the border by US inspectors, the gold would be confiscated—not expropriated as in a legal purchase by the government but as part of a criminal act—and they could face serious fines and up to ten years in prison. Until they could find a safe way to get it to Vancouver, the sale was problematic. Despite Ray's protests, the group voted five to one to continue seeking a way to sell the gold, in Canada or elsewhere, and agreed to a 1977 meeting, with interim updates.

At the mention of meeting in 1977, Ray let loose a string of obscenities and slammed Emma's door as he walked out. They heard his car start with a loud roar and his tires squeal as he shot onto the gravel road. The group was quiet, reflecting on what that might mean for the next several months or years.

It was late September. Johnny was getting itchy to travel again and Brandy indicated she was tired of playing hotel manager in Sagebrush. "The bright lights of Vegas are calling and I want to try my luck at the tables and get some experience in hotel management."

Johnny hoped she would be his road companion since they were still carrying on a passionate affair, but she was adamant about her next objective, and he didn't want to stay in one place for more than a week or two.

Johnny and Brandy left Sagebrush shortly thereafter, heading in different directions. The decision wasn't mutual, but Johnny had his pride to consider.

Despite their recent bouts of lovemaking, Brandy indicated she wasn't ready to settle down. She didn't rule out a future liaison and asked him to stay in touch through their link to the hotel and tontine. She said, "We'll sell the gold at some point and then we'll both be free from Sagebrush. I'm liberating myself now, and if you need me," her eyes lit with the familiar fire, "I'll probably be somewhere in Vegas. Ask around."

He smiled. "Might just do that. Anything is possible."

CHAPTER EIGHT

Surprises (1977)

False dawn seeped through the windows as Johnny snapped awake. He was lying where he had collapsed, mostly dressed and sprawled on top of the covers. Silence reigned in the room and outside. He sat up and quickly lay down again. His right knee throbbed and he turned to one side, rubbing the thigh above it, attempting vainly to urge his leg to cooperate. Too many days on the road and too many nights without relief. He reached for his bag and extracted a couple aspirins. His body hadn't responded to the comfort of a room or a bed—the protest would continue until he showered and shaved. It was a long, luxurious shower, one of those that shouldn't be rushed as long as soap and hot water were available. There were apparently few other guests to share the water, so he lathered and loitered. The helluva tomorrow had arrived, but it could damn well wait. The towels were small and cheap and he had a respectable, but not excessive, amount of body area. The clothes in his bag were rumpled but clean. Mostly work clothes: blue jeans and a denim shirt, solid-color socks and brown leather shoes. Garb for an honest man, or so he had been told.

A look in the small mirror over the single faucet sink was not encouraging. His razor was old and dull. A close shave would have been a painful one, so a compromise was in order. *Clean fingernails and a touch of aftershave and I could be a new person. Too bad I'm not. Can't do anything about the hair, but that can come later.*

Opening the door, he peered down the hallway. Morning sunrise painted the walls reddish-orange as a rooster extended its ancient greetings down the road. The smell of bacon drifted through the hotel as the door closed softly behind him. *I am as ready for this as I can be, whatever that means.*

He glanced at the door of room 19 as he passed. He almost stopped to knock but thought better of it. There was no one in the lobby as he passed through and entered the dining room. It held about a dozen tables, but only one was occupied. A man was reading a paper. The ashtray in front of him that held a burning cigar and a cup of coffee with steam rising from it were the only items on the table. Johnny walked over, pulled out a chair and sat down opposite.

"Have a good night?" A gravelly voice came from behind the paper.

"Not bad," Johnny looked around for a waitress. He was hungry and ready to order the works—anything and everything they had. Banging from the kitchen told him someone was around. He waited. *Does that make me a waiter?* He laughed silently at the thought.

The man lowered the paper slowly so that Johnny saw only the top of his head. He had lost a lot of hair since they last met, and what was left had grayed considerably. His bushy eyebrows appeared next and then an over-sized nose, thick lips, and dimpled chin. He had let his sideburns grow shaggy, contributing to the aura of neglect.

Johnny's stare was unwavering. *He doesn't look any better for the wear than me.* It afforded a measure of satisfaction. "Hello, Rodney."

"Yeah, yourself." He held the cigar with one hand and picked up the coffee with the other. A quick drag, two short sips, and the cigar and cup back on the table without his eyes leaving Johnny's. "You look like shit. Has it been that bad?"

A slim, pleasant looking girl with no makeup, in a pink-and-white plaid apron, walked out of the kitchen and approached the table with a pot of coffee and a cup.

"Thanks." Johnny reached for the cup before she could ask. She poured and waited for him to order. "Menu?" he asked.

"What'd ya need?" she stated in a crisp, confident voice. "I can get'cha just about anything you want for breakfast."

"Good girl. Let's start with a stack of cakes, slab of bacon, eggs over easy, country fries, a tall orange juice, and keep the coffee coming."

Unperturbed, she retreated to the kitchen. No tablet, no smile, no comment.

"Friendly too, just like you," Johnny said.

"Don't mean to be unfriendly, Johnny, just the times and the long waits. You know that. But I'll let you eat before we get down to business. No rush. We'll be here a while."

"Afraid so. Some things never change, do they? I didn't see your name on the register when I checked in. I assume you're staying here like before?"

Rod picked up his cigar, held it with both hands and took a leisurely draw, his eyes focused almost cross-eyed on the burning ash. It was a habit he displayed during their poker games so many years ago, a tell that most of them quickly learned. Usually it meant he had drawn more than he expected and it was time for the smart ones to fold. Saved them a lot of money.

"Where else? Yeah, same old room next to yours. You're the one who taught me to avoid signing registers, remember?"

"Uh-huh, I guess so. Something you owe me."

"Well, if that's true, old John, I guess I have a bit of news for you."

Johnny was not sure he liked the way Rod emphasized each word, like he was going to lay down a straight flush.

Rod's eyebrows raised a notch. "John?"

"Yeah?" He sipped carefully—the black stuff was good but hot.

"She's here."

"What the hell do you mean?" Johnny set the cup down.

"Brandy. She's here."

Johnny stared at him. There was no smile, no crinkling at the corner of his eyes. If he was putting someone on, he had rehearsed it well. *Let him tell it in his own way, in his own time.* Johnny didn't answer, trying to deny him an overabundance of satisfaction. They had played that game for more than twenty years. Rod must have been thinking the same way, because he was in no hurry to provide details. He took another sip of coffee but kept the cigar in front of him, a bluish haze partly obscuring his humorless face.

"You still smoking those wine-soaked pieces of crap?"

That brought a smile. Rod put it down but not out in the tray. "All I can afford. That is, unless we have a better proposal than last time."

The waitress returned with the juice and more coffee. "Your food will be out in a minute," she said to Johnny. She turned to Rod. "Sure you don't want anything?"

Rod looked at him. "If my old buddy here is buying, I might."

Johnny nodded at the girl. "Give him what he wants."

"Ham and eggs, beat up, and some juice," he ordered as if his mind had been made up for some time.

"What kind of juice?"

"Tomato. I'm in the mood for ice-cold tomato juice. Got any?"

"Yeah. Be right back." She turned on her heels and was gone, all business.

Johnny watched her disappear into the kitchen. "Not working for tips, is she?"

They sat for several minutes, sipping coffee; Rod finished his cigar. "So, you want to hear about her or not?" he said.

"Who, the waitress? I didn't think you two knew each other." Johnny could play the game, as Rod damn well knew.

"Shit, Johnny, I'm talking about Brandy. Have you lost all interest in her?"

Johnny stiffened in his chair and reached for the orange juice. Rod noticed the tension. It was hard to fool a poker player, even a mediocre one. "No I haven't. Where is she?"

Rod watched him thoughtfully as if trying to decide how much to tell in one sitting.

"Hey, I'm paying for your breakfast, aren't I?" Johnny said.

"Yeah, you are. Thanks." Rod paused. "She's here in the hotel, in her old room. She came in yesterday morning. Looking almost as tired as you but still a lot prettier."

"She say anything to you? Does she know I'm here? Is she…"

"Hold on, I'll get to it. Here comes your breakfast. You shut up and eat, and I'll do the talking."

The waitress set his plate down and departed without a word. Johnny added butter and syrup to the pancakes and Tabasco to the taters and eggs. He didn't have to feign interest in either the breakfast or Rod's news.

"As I said, she came in yesterday morning just after breakfast and checked in. I saw her from across the street. Don't think she saw me. I asked Charlie about her—oh, Charlie's the boy behind the front desk—I'll tell you about him later. He told me she hadn't signed the register but was in room 19. Things don't ever change, do they?"

He caught Johnny with a mouthful. He gave him his "please do continue" glare.

"I caught up with her at noon. She was leaving to pick up some clothes over at Jane's place. She'd obviously been traveling hot 'n hard, and I can't say she was overly delighted to see me. Probably just tired." He waited, inviting Johnny to ask, but he continued eating.

"Anyway, she asked me how long I'd been here. Told her I had been waiting three days and that she was the latest to show, not counting those living here. She looked down at the ground, kinda embarrassed-like. I don't think she wanted to ask me, but she did. She wanted to know if you were still alive. I told her I thought you was but couldn't be sure. She wanted to know if you were gonna show. If he's alive, he'll show, I told her. She nodded and got in her car. Seemed to be lost in a lot of thought. You know how she could get when she was thinking a lot."

"Yeah, I know." Johnny had finished half of his food and wasn't sure if he was still hungry. *Funny how your stomach is when you are not used to eating much. You think you want a lot, but you fill up fast.*

Rod's food came, along with more coffee.

It was Johnny's turn to talk. "You haven't seen her since yesterday noon, is that right? And she's driving?"

Rod nodded as he all but inhaled a mouthful of scrambled eggs. *Poor bastard, he's probably been hungry for a while,* Johnny thought.

"She drove in, I walked. Seems some fortunes have flipped in the last ten years. Brandy will wait until we're all here," Johnny said. "She isn't going to play her hand until she sees who's at the table. She may be cute, but she sure as hell ain't stupid."

The waitress returned. "Either of you gonna want anything else?"

Rod looked up at her. "Room 21. Check with me later, huh, honey?" He flashed his best lascivious grin, the kind that was delivered without thought or the slightest expectation of a positive answer. She was on her way back to the kitchen without a vocal response, displaying a slightly exaggerated swing to her hips.

There was no check, but Johnny had to decide whether to give her a tip. Better do it, he reminded himself. He might be staying there for a while, and there wasn't a lot of choice in eateries or waitresses.

"Damn, Rod, you must be old enough to be her grandfather. And, ugly to boot."

"No harm done, Johnny, just thought I'd lighten up her day, ya know?"

"Umm, some light."

"You ready to go?"

"Where to?" Johnny stood and dropped some money on the table. He didn't have any more small bills so he tipped about a third of the what the bill would have been. *Bet she still doesn't smile.*

"My room. I've got a bottle. We can talk there."

Rod ain't changed a hair. Can't afford breakfast but always has some booze stashed somewhere. Johnny was not in the mood to refuse—he might want some liquid courage for later in the day.

A man in a dark shirt entered the dining room, passed them and took a seat. He glanced their way and then toward the kitchen as the waitress approached.

They left the dining room and walked toward Rod's room. *What would I do if she appeared in the hallway? I'm not ready to meet her yet, need time to think. I had anticipated seeing most of the others, especially Rod, but, Brandy? I thought she would be settled, married, happy with children, or possibly dead. She was mentioned during our occasional contacts, but I have been out of touch since 1973. Anything could have happened since then to her or to me. Despite the high stakes involved, I wasn't sure she would be here, but what the hell do I know.*

Rod opened the door—like many times before, it wasn't locked—and they entered his room. Johnny sat on the bed as Rod rummaged through a clothes drawer and extracted a fifth of Old Crow.

"Your taste in whisky is almost as good as your taste in cigars, Rod."

"Shut up and drink." He gave Johnny a bathroom glass and poured each of them about three fingers.

Johnny took a sip, letting the burning brown stuff roll around in his mouth and slide down his throat. He shuddered.

Rod watched him carefully from the one chair by the door. "Doesn't look like you been drinkin' much."

He looked at the glass, still two fingers left. "Not much. I got enough things against me without being shit-faced all the time. How 'bout you?"

Rod grinned, tossed his drink down in one swallow, and refilled his glass.

"Where do you think she is now?" Johnny asked, considering whether to match his friend or try to maintain some semblance of sobriety.

"Don't know. Maybe in her room, maybe out. Haven't seen her this morning."

"Where in the hell would someone go? It's been ten years. Anyone left around here?"

"A few. Ken, the barber is still around. Gettin' old, but he remembered me. So you came back, he asked me. The others gonna come back too? The old fart probably wants some excitement. Doubt if there's been much for a while."

"He might get his wish." Johnny took another sip, determined to indulge slowly and keep his wits. *Ken was the town gossip then and he probably still is. Everyone in town with a possible interest in us will know we are back.*

"I take it Justin is still here? No change in hotel ownership?"

"He's here, hasn't changed, which is good. He's a straight shooter. Has some new assistants, but as you can see, the hotel looks older and dirtier than the last time we met. Justin is hanging on like the rest of us, waiting for the payoff. The Gordon boys and Barbara are still around. Still have their place down the road selling hardware and fixing cars like before. Haven't seen them, but Ken said they asked about us. Thought it was about time, although they weren't sure of the exact date."

"Maybe I'll get a haircut and see what else that old bastard knows. Think he's open now?"

Rod scrunched his shoulders. "Probably not until afternoon. Not much incentive to sit in your shop for a lot of hours in a town like this." He said *town* like he was doing it a favor.

"What about Emma? Is she still alive?"

"Haven't talked to Justin yet but haven't heard otherwise. Should have asked Ken, but somehow it didn't enter my mind."

Strange that Rod forgot about Emma, the now-retired schoolteacher who started their merry misadventure back in '57. She was the oldest in the group and nobody's fool. *I hope she's still around. A sensible woman with good intentions. One of the few in our group I believe I can trust. However, after this many years, I'm not sure what I believe.*

"I hope we don't have any more unpleasant surprises like we had last time," Johnny said, looking down at his empty glass.

Rod reached over and refilled it. "Nineteen sixty-seven? Yeah, that was a bummer. Of all the people in our little group, I wished the best for Steve and Donna. Although they weren't enthusiastic about the delays, they played along and we could trust them. When I received the news I was pretty upset. Why couldn't it have been Ray?"

A decisive knock at the door startled Rod. They looked at each other. Johnny nodded at him to open it and sat back against the headboard, rotating the glass in his fingers, preparing himself for whoever might step through.

Rod stood and walked across the room, but before his hand touched the knob, the door opened. He stepped back, spilling the drink in his left hand. A tall slim brunette with short hair filled most of the doorframe. She glanced at Rod before stepping into the room and turning her attention to Johnny.

He didn't get up but his eyes locked on hers. "Hello, Brandy. You're looking as sexy as ever, maybe even more so." He swallowed a large sip of the cheap whiskey, enjoying the burn in his throat as he assimilated the vision before him.

"Johnny, Johnny. You look as grungy as ever, maybe more so." She had a hand on her right hip, thrust to the side, scoring extra points in the provocative column. "I figured you'd be with Rod and a bottle, of course."

Rod remained standing. The sudden entrance and need to remind her whose room she was in prompted a less-than-smooth invitation. "Hello, Brandy. I don't have another chair, but I can get you a glass. Want some juice?"

She ignored him and moved to the bed, standing beside it. "Not to worry. I can share a bed with Johnny. Won't be the first time, don't you know." She flopped beside him and took the glass out of his hand. Half of his drink was left and she downed it in two gulps, gave a shake of her head, and held the glass out to Rod.

"More?" He reached for the bottle.

"It's rotgut but I need to catch up with you two." She held the glass steady as he filled it halfway.

Johnny watched her take a generous swallow before she handed it to him. He glanced at the glass and then at her eyes. "You've already surpassed me. I just started." He gave her a smile but didn't drink. *Someone has to keep their head on straight. Might as well be me.*

"Ray Gordon is here and ready. Saw him this morning." Brandy lifted the glass from Johnny and hit it again, hard.

"Has he been to the hotel?" Rod asked.

"I don't think so. He's at his trailer, outside town. Same place as before, but he added a shop out back and built a small store and office on the lot. I don't think he sells much hardware or fixes that many cars from the looks of it. He and Jay mostly run errands and do odd jobs. I bet they are even more anxious to conclude things this time."

Johnny's turn. "What about Barbara? Does she still figure in this?"

Brandy paused in her admirable efforts to outdrink them. "She's with him, still looking after Jay. I'm willing to bet she isn't any wiser about the plan than she was ten years ago. Ray doesn't want her or his dimwitted brother blabbing anything."

Rod had that perpetual look of puzzlement, a predictable and often deployed guise to throw off the competition whether playing poker or playing their ongoing game. "How do you know all this? Thought you just got back in town?"

Brandy smiled and rotated the glass in her hands. "Had an early breakfast with Justin this morning. As always, he is willing to share what he knows. Not a bad guy, but more than a bit naïve. Once again he threw his pitch to use the proceeds to develop the town, this time to bring it back from the edge of extinction. I told him we would discuss it."

"Did you now? You think we'll turn over our shares to the wannabe mayor so he can sink more of it into this hotel and…shit! Not gonna happen." Rod poured himself another drink.

Johnny took another sip, but it didn't go down any easier. "Since you've been doing your homework, what about Emma? Is she still alive? Has she ever said anything to anyone? How about her niece—what was her name?"

"Sally. Sally Moore. I'm not surprised you don't remember her—she was about ten when we last met." Brandy gave them one of her poker hand smiles that proclaimed, *I got you*. "The two of you met her very recently." She waited for them to snatch at the bait.

"I haven't met anyone here except the desk clerk and Rod." Johnny paused for Brandy to clarify. "And you," he added. He raised their shared glass and passed it back to her. Rod maintained his look of bewilderment, but Johnny could tell he was thinking fast and furious.

"She served you breakfast this morning an hour after she served Justin and me," Brandy said.

"The waitress? The I-don't-smile-for-anyone waitress? But she's a young woman…" *Oh yeah, ten years. Emma's niece turned out to be a looker, all right.* Johnny glanced at Rod, whose mouth was open. "Does she know what's going on and why we are gathering?"

"Don't know that. Emma was asked to say nothing, but who knows? I asked Justin what he knows about Sally. He hired her about a year ago, but she hasn't mentioned anything about our scheme. At least, not to him. He did tell me she is taking care of her grandparents in a nursing home in Alturas. She doesn't make much and usually stays with her aunt, but Justin gives her a room when she wants it. He says she is saving everything for an escape, so it doesn't sound like she is in on it."

"Escape? That sounds ominous," said Rod.

"And Emma?" Johnny asked.

"She'll be here," Brandy replied, taking another sip from their community glass.

Rod and Johnny looked at each other and spoke simultaneously. "When?" Johnny took the glass from Brandy.

"We're meeting this evening for dinner right here, like last time," Brandy said. "Everyone will gather for our grand twenty reunion at the Grand Sagebrush Hotel." She smiled.

"Pretty liberal with the word grand aren't you?" said Rod.

Brandy glanced at him. "It is what we had and what we have, grand or not, which reminds me I have some errands to run. See you boys at five in the dining room. Be there or be gone." She smiled over her shoulder as she exited the room with a coquettish flourish.

The door closed, leaving the men holding almost empty glasses. Rod refilled his and offered Johnny the bottle.

He declined and got off the bed. "Have a few errands of my own." He left Rod staring at the ceiling as he passed into the empty hallway.

Johnny was tempted to knock on the brunette's door, but she may have left the hotel and he didn't know what he would say to her in any case. *Too many years on the road for both of us. Whatever is to be said will wait.*

JOHNNY WALKED THROUGH THE EMPTY LOBBY. CHARLIE WAS not at the desk, and a glance at the open door of the dining room revealed only the lovely Sally and the man in the dark shirt.

Johnny walked out the front door, crossed the wooden porch and strolled down a mostly deserted street. The sun had been baking the pavement for a few hours, enough to discourage most foot traffic. He still had a slight limp and a twinge or two of pain, but the leg felt better. Across the street and two blocks ahead, a rotating spiral of red, white and blue marked Ken's Hair Cut Salon. *Fancy name for a one-chair barber shop, but I'll see what Ken knows. He always knows something.*

Johnny's watch read ten to twelve as he approached the door, thinking he was early and might have to wait until one o'clock or later. But the sign said Open, and Ken was inside, fussing at the sink. Johnny walked in and closed the door.

The barber turned to greet him. "Johnny, you old bastard. Thought I'd see you and some of the others. I opened an hour early today to be ready." His smile was wide, generous or greedy, take your pick. Two strides forward brought him to a handshake and a shoulder clasp as if they were long-lost best friends or close family members. They were neither, but they had numerous good times together at the table and might have a few more.

"Need to get this cleaned." Johnny pointed to his hair and face and sat in the dark leather chair. At one time it might have been state-of-the-art, but it, like all the Sagebrush residents, had seen better times. Nevertheless, it was comfortable, and he relaxed, stretching his legs.

Ken moved behind him, fitted a white apron over his chest, and tied it around the back of his neck. "Long, short, or in between?" He picked up scissors and a comb. It had been a while, but Johnny knew that the rest of the conversation would be a cheerful monologue laced with seemingly innocuous questions about the group and their plans. Johnny hoped to get some useful information without revealing anything of importance.

"Keep it long, clean the sides and back, and shave the face, all of it." Johnny closed his eyes and let Ken take over. His non-stop monologue began with the first snip. Mixed in with the inevitable gossip about everyone and everything in the rambling town of Sagebrush were probing comments designed to elicit a response about tonight's meeting.

He doesn't miss a trick. He has probably had the date marked on his calendar for years. How much does he know? Johnny answered a few of his trivial comments with a grunt, waiting for something revealing. Ken was never a member of the inner group of the Rattlesnake Basin Enterprises, but from playing poker with them he knew a clique existed and who the members were. Since most of them had remained in town, was it realistic that word had not leaked out? *So far, there's no indication he knows what we are about or what secret we share. It will be interesting to hear what the others have to say during or after dinner tonight.*

"Have you seen little Sally, Emma's niece, yet?" Ken asked the first direct pertinent question as the clippers flew and the hair fell to the floor. He was in front of Johnny and looked into his eyes. "She's the waitress at the hotel, in case you ate breakfast there this morning."

"Yep, I met her. Not so little anymore." *Tell me more, Ken. Is she a member of our group? Do you know who we are? How much has Emma talked during the past ten years?*

Ken clipped the hair over Johnny's left ear. "No, she isn't. Would make some local boy a fine wife, but she wants out of here. Greener pastures elsewhere, just needs the money to go. Unfortunately for her, most of her earnings go to help her grandparents, so she doesn't have much of her own. Not yet anyway." Ken moved around to the back, combing and cutting.

"What does that mean, not yet?" He grinned, as if it there was no deeper meaning to the girl's hopes. "Is she expecting to come into a mysterious inheritance or waiting for a knight in shining armor, a rich one, to come to her rescue?"

"Neither. Just rumors, that's all. Some folks think that her aunt Emma may not be of such modest means as she lets on. There might be wealth in the family and I believe Sally is the only known heir. Nothing for sure, but the talk is there." Ken moved to Johnny's right side.

"If that's the case, why is she working for minimum and tips in a restaurant that doesn't have enough customers to make it worthwhile?"

"Oh, Justin does okay, especially during the colder months. You and the rest of your friends are here when the only things that pass through are tumbleweeds and stray coyotes. Have you forgotten? We manage to get by most of the year. I'm still here."

Yes, you are. Probably will be when the town falls down and blows away, leaving you, the striped pole, and a lone barber chair. One more question to put to Emma tonight. Has she told Sally and if so, who has Sally told? In any case, Ken didn't answer my question.

Ken put aside his clippers and comb and got a hot towel ready for the shave while he mixed lather the old fashioned way. There was a strange comfort in that. Johnny remembered him performing the same ritual twenty years ago when he had just started shaving and ten years ago at their first reunion. *Has anything changed? I'll know more in a few hours.* The hot soap felt good and the blade was sharp. *Can't complain about Ken's technique and it beats the hell out of the dull razor in my room.*

"Hear that your group is having dinner this evening at the hotel." It was hard to tell whether it was a statement or a question and what he meant by *group.*

"Uh-huh." The blade scraped across Johnny's throat, in skilled, short swipes.

"Don't suppose there might be room for any others at the table, you know, some of us who have been party to your comings and goings all these years?"

Ah, here it is. The plea for an invite. The intrigue must be killing him. He knows we aren't meeting just to say hello and refresh a few memories. Some of us don't even like each other, and on the surface, we don't have that much in common except the trove.

"Probably need to keep it private, for now. It's for our real estate holding company and we have some business to discuss." He told him in as friendly a way as he could, mindful that he hadn't finished the shave, and a razor, even in the hands of a friendly barber, was not something to be cavalier about.

"Too bad, but, I guess I'll have a chance to see most of you before you head out again, to wherever you run off to. Maybe another poker game, like old times?" Again, a mixture of statement and question, but Johnny decided not to enlighten him further. Ken wiped the residual lather from his face, applied aftershave, and removed the apron.

Johnny looked at the aging barber and recalled the great games they used to have. Ken was always a gentleman, win or lose. "Maybe we can get a game up. I'll ask the boys."

Johnny checked himself in the mirror, turned, and handed Ken a twenty. "Keep it," he said as the barber started to retrieve change from the register. He didn't have a ton of cash on him but enough for the next week's expenses and some additional. "I'll be here a few days, and I'll tell the others to stop by and say hello." *Hopefully, that will keep him from hanging around the hotel or seeking us out.* A wave goodbye, and Johnny was out the door before Ken could think of anything else.

He walked toward the only bank in town, thinking about Brandy and whether she would soften when she saw the new, clean Johnny Templeton.

He didn't recognize the teller at the two-window counter. Most of the bank's business came from the farming community scattered around the valley. A hardware store, a tractor and feed business, the hotel, a small cafe and truck stop, two grocery stores, a general merchandise and clothing store, two gas stations, and three taverns comprised the business sector. Johnny knew the bank manager ten years ago, but that desk was empty at the moment. He glanced at the name plate. *Nope, a different person.* Although Pete Roberts had often been at the poker table, he was never part of the inner circle.

"Can I help you, sir?" She smiled, noticeably friendlier than the morning waitress. She sported a wedding band.

"I think so." He returned her smile and handed her the key and his driver's license.

She looked at the key, puzzled. "Oh, that must be for a deposit box. I don't see many of these." She looked up at him, as if examining someone who had arrived from the distant past. "Please let me check our records. It'll only take a moment." She turned from the counter to open a card file on a nearby table. Johnny could see past her shoulder—there were only a handful of cards in the box.

She came back to the window and smiled. "Mr. Templeton? I apologize. I see the last time you visited was ten years ago, but your rental is paid through next year, so you're good. If you'll step through the door to your right, I'll take you to the boxes."

I know the way and yes, I'm good, better than you'll ever know. He passed through the door and followed her down a short hallway to a small alcove. There were thirty boxes of varying sizes on the wall. His was one of the small ones. She inserted her key, he inserted his, and she left as he withdrew the inner box. He sat at a small table against the opposite wall and lifted the lid on the metal tray. Inside was a small manila envelope with a single page of text with signatures. There were also two keys: one to a safe deposit box a few rows above and one column to the right of his. The other opened one of the three locks on the hotel vault. *The time has come.* Johnny pocketed the keys and unfolded the paper. He took a few minutes to read the statement and refresh his memory. Placing the sheet back in the envelope, he returned it to the tray, slid it in the deposit box, and locked it shut. He placed both deposit box keys and the vault key in a billfold pocket. Returning to the lobby, he nodded to the girl.

"Well, that didn't take long. Anything else I can do for you, Mr. Templeton?"

"No, that will be all for now. Perhaps later." He walked out the door, feeling relatively assured for the evening ahead. Amazing how a shave and haircut could restore one's outlook on the world. Smiles came easier, and the pain in his leg was almost nonexistent.

The hotel was quiet. Charlie was at the desk as Johnny walked by, but he greeted him by name. "Mr. Templeton, I have a message for you." He reached into the box with 23 over it, pulled out a small envelope, and handed it to Johnny. It had his full name, Robert John Templeton, on the front and was sealed. Johnny thanked him and continued to his room.

Inside, he removed his boots and splashed some water in his face. It was a hot, dusty afternoon and he was seriously considering a cold beer or two before dinner, but first the letter. There was no return address but he recognized the obsessively neat printing. He tore it open and unfolded a single small sheet of paper.

Johnny:

Welcome back. I will see you tonight at dinner, but I wanted to let you know we have another member in our group: my niece, Sally Moore. I needed to tell her about our project for two reasons. First, she is the only relative I have left in town and I wanted to share our good fortune with her. I know you and the others wanted to keep our plan a secret. I told her she wasn't to reveal it to anyone. She doesn't have a boyfriend or any other close friends, so I am sure she has complied. The second reason is that I am now 76 years old. I am in reasonable health, but the days are getting shorter. At our last meeting, we said we would make a final decision about the

plan and divide the resources. That time has arrived, but I wasn't sure I would still be alive. Sally will be at dinner.
Looking forward to concluding this.
Emma

He refolded the letter, put it back in the envelope, lit a match, and let the note burn in the ashtray. *So, she told her niece! And the little snot served us breakfast as if we were aliens from a flying saucer. How should I interpret her behavior? Either she's acting out of arrogance and scorn for the rest of us or she's carrying on the pretense of knowing nothing.* He had to hope for the latter. It was three-thirty and he needed the suds more than ever.

An hour at the Pioneer Barroom brought him to a better frame of mind. Three drafts in a dark corner, watching the barmaid scurry about and four customers play slop pool, allowed him to think about the meeting and the keys in his pocket. *How do we resolve this? Who's gonna be willing to take the lead? Me? Rod? Ray Gordon? No, none of those. I'd bet any amount with anyone that it'll be Brandy. Yep, she has more balls than any of the men. Justin has his cause and Emma seems to agree with him, although that was before Sally entered the picture. Our last meeting in 1967 lasted three days. Despite the schemes and changing alliances, no decision about our property was reached. Next time, we all agreed. Twenty years of hiding and discretion will be safe. Unexpected but most important, the rules for gold possession have changed, and the value of our assets have dramatically increased. There is enough for all—don't be greedy, we said. And here it is. Now or never, time to take action.*

Johnny returned to his room, washed his hands and face, put on a clean but wrinkled shirt, and descended the stairs to the dining room at 5:10, fashionably late. A hand-lettered sign on the closed dining room door read:

PRIVATE PARTY TONIGHT

He opened it and walked in to face three tables in the center of the room, pulled together to form one, covered with a long, white cloth and settings for eight people. Rod, Ray, and Justin sat around it. *Only Ray, not Jay and Barbara. They were not at the last meeting, and Ray indicated they knew little to nothing about the group's business, but this may be the final meeting.* As far as Johnny was aware, Jay and Barbara only knew that Ray was involved in a business deal but had no knowledge of the details or conditions of the agreement.

"Hey, Johnny, good to see ya." Ray stood and extended his hand. Johnny gave it a solid grasp and a single shake. *He's grinning from ear to ear like I am his best buddy bringing home the bacon plus good news. I have neither, but I need to keep an eye on him.*

Ray could be aggressive, brash at times, but he was devoted to his non-identical twin brother. Many years ago, when they were barely teenage kids playing in a rain-filled quarry, Jay almost drowned. He was under water for more than a minute before Ray discovered the bubbles and dove in to pull him out. According to Ray, Jay didn't seem the same after recovering, unable to study or finish school, retaining a pre-adolescent outlook on the world. Later, Jay was able to help Ray at the hardware store with the physical labor, and he was always friendly to the customers, but Ray considered it his sacred duty to take care of the perpetual boy. When Ray married Barbara, his childhood sweetheart, she assumed the role of Jay's mother. Barbara never had children of her own, but she and Jay developed a friendship and understanding of which even Ray was unaware.

Justin rose from his seat and held out his hand. "Good to see you again, Johnny. I hoped you would make it."

"Wouldn't miss it for the world, would I?"

Rod snorted. "Even got himself all gussied up for the occasion." He turned to Johnny. "Ken want to come to dinner with us?"

"Yeah, there were hints along that line. I told him that everyone would drop by and give him their regards."

A young woman Johnny didn't know came out from the kitchen and knelt beside Justin to ask him if they were ready.

"Wait a few more minutes Steph, we're expecting others. When all the seats are occupied, you can start serving."

She returned to the kitchen.

He is catering our dinner like last time. That makes sense, especially since Sally will be joining us. As if on cue, the door opened and Emma preceded Sally into the dining room. Emma took the seat next to Johnny, and Sally sat on the end to her right. That left Rod at Johnny's left and Ray and Justin across from him. Brandy was the only one missing, and there was an additional set place next to Justin. *For who? Is there someone else that we, or I, haven't been told about?*

Emma greeted him in her precise manner. "How do you do, Mr. Templeton? You are looking hale and hearty." She had a prim, polite smile, her trademark. Sally looked straight ahead at an empty place, ignoring all of them.

Johnny thought, *Girl's got a problem. Hope it isn't us, or maybe she remembers what I looked like in the morning.*

Justin looked up and called out, "Charlie, right here." He pointed to the chair beside him as the young desk clerk strolled over and sat down. He glanced around the table, pausing on Johnny's face, and then looked down at his plate.

Johnny stared at Justin, not in a friendly manner. "What's going on, Justin? What's your desk clerk doing here?"

Ray and Rod looked as if Johnny was seriously uninformed. He was, it seemed.

Justin said, "Sorry Johnny, but Charlie has been brought in on our scheme. Some of the others already know. Later, I'll tell you why and I think you'll understand. Please accept it for now, okay?"

What choice do I have? So that's the eighth person. That must have been what Rod was going to tell me before he got distracted with news about Brandy.

Ray and Justin peered toward the door and Johnny turned to watch Brandy make her grand entrance. She was wearing tight, very tight, black slacks, made of a material that clung to every curve and bump. Her top was made from the same material and cut low in front. As she took her seat across from Sally, Johnny could see the back of her top was also uncovered. Her short, dark hair, neatly combed, completed the somber but sexy outfit that was adorned by a silver necklace with a tear-shaped malachite stone. The effect was not lost on the males. Ray's mouth was open, and he appeared to be a few seconds from drooling down his shirt.

Emma said, "Good evening." Sally remained silent.

Brandy must be, what, thirty-eight by now? I wasn't kidding when I told her she looked better than ever, Johnny thought.

"Time to order some pre-dinner drinks, ladies and gentlemen." Justin took charge as his server walked from the kitchen with an order pad in her hand. Justin looked at Emma. "Would you and your niece care for a glass of wine?"

Emma smiled at Justin and the waitress. "A glass of Chablis would be nice." She turned to Sally.

The girl looked at the waitress and said almost inaudibly, "I'll have water, thank you." Eyes turned toward the brunette.

"Stinger on the rocks, if you have the makings." Brandy ordered with a touch of insolence as if daring the hotel to have what she wanted.

Ray requested a beer. Charlie looked at Sally for a moment and asked for a glass of water with ice. Rod couldn't take his eyes off of the vision in black. "I'll take a double brandy." There was a noticeable leer in his voice.

"Yeah, good luck with that, Rod." Brandy's voice dripped with sarcasm approaching scorn.

"I'll just have a draft," Johnny said, not wanting to mix drinks until after he ate.

Justin ordered a glass of merlot and sat back as the waitress returned to the kitchen. "Drinks will be right up, folks. For our after-dinner discussion, the important one, we'll have an open rolling bar with beverages available." He looked at Sally and then at Charlie. "Sure you two don't want something a little stronger? We have a ways to go tonight."

Sally said nothing and Charlie shook his head but snuck a peek at Sally.

"Well, here we are. Our group has gone from the original eight to six and back to eight again. Can we observe a moment of silence for Steve and Donna Woodward, two of our original members?" He lowered his head and most of the others did likewise.

The drinks arrived and a second round followed before the preset dinner was served. The talk was light and cordial, a few jokes, some discussion about the ever-snoopy barber and a few others in town who kept guessing what the group was up to.

Justin gave a brief report on the state of the hotel, the overt reason for the RBE reunion. The report was not positive. Additional money would be needed to maintain and improve the building. Everyone at the table, with the possible exceptions of Charlie and Sally, knew the real discussion began after the dishes were cleared and the servers were no longer present. The rolling cart with wine, liquor, mixes, and an ice chest of beer was brought out. A similar cart was always available for the upstairs poker games. A tasty bread pudding with rum sauce, and with ice cream for those who preferred, finished the dinner.

The servers withdrew, the kitchen door closed, and the business for the evening was at hand. Despite the generous application of alcohol, tensions were barely under the surface at Johnny's end of the table. Rod and Ray had glared at each other most of the evening, and Justin divided his time between keeping the peace and encouraging Charlie to speak up and participate. Sally remained stoic despite Brandy's attempts to "buy" her a drink. The food and drink for each reunion meeting was provided by the hotel from group funds set aside for the occasion. Emma was on her third glass of white wine—her voice a quiet murmur, and she was visibly relaxed.

I'm glad someone is. Hard to tell with Brandy. Playing poker or playing the intrigue game, she is a hard one to read. Johnny swallowed the last of his beer, got up, and moved to the side car to pour himself a snifter half full of—you guessed it—brandy.

CHAPTER NINE

Confrontations and Decisions

Justin looked around the room, waiting for Rod and Johnny to take their seats. Rod noticed his friend's change of drink and had to comment. "Going for the brandy, I see. Just you and I." He lifted his glass as they sat.

"Just the right thing to have after dinner, Rod." Johnny cast a glance toward Brandy who watched him with analytical precision. Their eyes met and he detected a slight twinkle. *Maybe she's feeling the effects.* She had switched to Black Jack on ice during dinner, but he knew she could hold any drink better than most of the men.

One person not amused was Ray. He looked past Justin at Charlie twice but spoke directly to the hotel owner. "I know you decided to bring him in but why is he here? What's the reason?" His manner was gruff and he had no apologies for his undisguised display of resentment.

Justin, normally the grand conciliator, cut him short. "I told you I was doing it. You'll be told why later, but for now let's keep it civil, Mr. Gordon."

Emma took a leisurely sip of wine and Rod looked at Charlie for a reaction. Charlie rose, walked to the bar, and grabbed a beer from the ice chest. He popped the cap with one smooth jerk of the opener like an experienced imbiber and sat down without looking at anyone except Sally. For the first time, she smiled and said, "Would you be good enough to bring me one?" He grinned and quickly retrieved a beer and a glass for her.

The distraction didn't deter Ray for long. He looked around the table and began a speech he had obviously rehearsed. "Barbara, Jay and I make up a share of what was once a group of eight," he glared at Charlie and Sally, "and I speak for all of us…"

Rod leaned forward to interrupt. "You mean your family, right? Not the rest of us?"

"Shut your damn mouth, and let me finish," Ray snarled. "As you know, we've never been in favor of the proposal by our wannabe mayor here or the Woodwards in wanting to use the money to improve the town, whatever the hell that means."

Justin sat back and Emma lowered her head with an almost inaudible sigh. Brandy's eyes were still locked on Johnny's.

"I say it's long past time to divide up the loot. The hell with the survivor plan." Ray looked at Emma. "Some of us may not have another ten years to wait and even for those who do, we might have other ideas." He turned back to Justin. "And who appointed you in charge, anyway?"

"I'm not in charge, Ray. I'm just the host for the food and drinks. I also supervise the storage of our assets. A thank you might be more appropriate than this."

"Thanks for the arrangements, Justin, but we're paying for it, remember? Another thing. When we formed this group, this so-called tontine, there were ten of us but only eight equal shares. If you remember, you all," he looked around the table, "decided that Barbara and Jay wouldn't get their own shares. The written agreement we signed at the time was that the shares would be equally divided by survivors at a later date. First, we were gonna wait ten years, but several of you said it was too soon, and we didn't have a good plan to cash in the goods. That would have given each of us a one-sixth cut in 1967. Wait till *next* time, you said. Well, it's next time, but now, we are back to eight members? Without a discussion or vote?" Ray was red-faced and out of breath, as if the diatribe had been pent up inside of him since the last meeting and required all of his energy to expel the words and harsh feelings that accompanied them.

Rod cleared his throat. "We *are* discussing it, Ray. That's exactly what we're doing."

Ray glared at him, but Rod gave him a tight thin smile as if daring him to get physical. "Oh yeah? Well, we're not giving up any part of our one-sixth to the newcomers. If those who invited them in want to split their shares, that's none of my business." Ray stared at Justin and Emma and then at the traveling man. "What do you say, Johnny? Does what I say make sense? Are you willing to give up part of your share so the two kids can get rich without the risk or wait?"

Johnny sipped and laughed. "Risk? What risk for you, Ray? What about your wife and brother? What risks did they take? What contributions to the operation have they made? Where are they? If this is going to be decided now or in the next two days, will they have a say in it or will you make all of the decisions for your cut of the pie? If you do, that's up to you and them, but I don't think you have any claim to lecture anyone else on their decisions." He took another sip, keeping his eyes on Ray's. "We can talk about the shares later, but first let's decide if we are going to cash in now." He nodded at Justin. "Does Charlie know everything?"

Charlie spoke for the first time. "I know everything. Maybe even a few things you and the some of the others don't."

Johnny let it pass and turned toward Emma and Sally. "What about our lovely waitress? Is she in on all of it?"

Emma started to respond, but Sally quietly answered. "Yes, Mr. Templeton. My aunt told me the story of the discovery more than a year ago. She told me not to say anything to anybody, and I haven't."

Emma addressed Ray. "Mr. Gordon, your belligerence is uncalled for. We have been discreet about the whole affair, which is more than I can say for you. I understand that you told a few individuals in town that Sally and I have some hidden resources. Other than my share of our assets, that is not true. Furthermore, I have not mentioned to anyone the idea of redistributing the existing shares. An apology is in order."

Rod stood, walked to the drink stand, and poured another brandy. He was a bit shaky on his feet and mumbled something about getting drunk.

Seeing things deteriorating, Justin tried to exercise some control. "I agree with Johnny. We can settle the share distribution later. I looked into the disposal of the resources, and I have a contact in San Francisco who can move all of it in one lump sum."

"How much will he charge us?" Johnny asked.

"It's a she. She has connections in Hong Kong and will move it through private investors. She wants a five percent retainer to set it up and another ten percent when the job is finished."

Ray whistled. "Fifteen percent of the whole damn caboodle? Shit no, we can do better than that. I'll be fucked if I'll agree to an outrageous fee…"

"Mr. Gordon, that language is not appropriate. Please watch your tongue in front of me and my niece."

Ray stopped, mouth open, looking around at the rest of them for support. There wasn't any.

"Well, that's still better than the original fees we were going to be charged in 1957. Is the fee negotiable?" Johnny said. "Furthermore, what does a five percent retainer come to? We don't know the full true value of the asset yet, or am I mistaken? Is there anyone else who might serve as an agent?"

Justin folded his hands on the table and assumed his customary business manner. "A lot of questions, Johnny, but good ones. Yes, we have a total value, subject to some change with time, but we'll be able to provide a close estimate. As you all might imagine, this can be a risky transfer. We have to physically deliver the materials to the agent. Then the materials are transported to the eventual purchaser in Asia, I believe, and the funds transferred back to us. This needs to be accomplished in the most discreet manner possible at all stages. Even though gold possession is now legal, there might be difficulties surrounding where we found it and who the rightful owner might be. Although it might be possible to negotiate a small savings on fees, I haven't identified anyone else who has the resources and capabilities to do it safely and efficiently. Besides, as Johnny indicated, this is cheaper than the fees we were quoted twenty years ago in Reno and a lot better than what we were facing ten years ago."

No one was bothered by the direct referral to the metal, although a few of them glanced at the closed kitchen door.

"How long will all of this take?" asked Rod.

"After we approve it, we should have our money within thirty days, provided there are no unforeseen obstacles" Justin paused. "Thirty days after we deliver the materials."

Materials, assets, resources, deals, the plan. Mostly we talk in code, never saying out loud what we all know we have. Probably necessary—it's a small town with loose lips. A miracle that we have kept it under wraps for twenty years. Despite the rumors and suspicions of people like Ken and reckless remarks by Ray and Rod, we are still in business. But Ray is right about one thing. It's time to end it. It isn't just Emma who is aging—we all are. Keep this going and the two kids will be the only ones left. Wonder where their loyalties lie. They work in the same place. Are they in on this together or separately?

"How do we get the stuff to Frisco? We should probably use a van or small truck, and we will need to load it without inviting questions." Ray stared at each of them in turn. "Who is going to provide the labor?"

Johnny raised his hand. "No problem, Ray. You will. Four of us," he nodded at Rod, "including Jay, can have it loaded into your hardware van in less than an hour."

"What about me? I can help." Charlie leaned forward, an eager look announcing his desire to participate.

"Sure, Charlie, you can earn your share, whatever that comes to," replied Rod. He turned to Ray. "Our newest member can substitute for Jay, so you can keep him blissfully ignorant." He said it with more than a touch of malice.

Brandy glanced at Sally and Emma. "What about us? How do we justify our shares, besides looking ravenously beautiful?" She had a mischievous expression.

Sally and Emma were not laughing. Sally looked like she wanted to say something, but Emma put a hand on her arm. "While you men are performing the physical chores, Sally and I can distract our neighbors. I'm sure Barbara can help us."

Justin asked. "What do you have in mind, Emma? Nothing too elaborate, I hope. We don't want to call attention to anything unusual going on. There are already too many people watching us, waiting for us to make a move even if they don't have any idea what it might be."

"Not to worry. It's summer and we usually have at least one Sunday afternoon picnic at the church. I suggest that the women help host it. Justin, you can attend and the other men can load our treasure, slip out of town, and deliver it to your contact in the Bay Area." Emma regarded Brandy. "You are invited to help as well if you don't have anything else pressing."

Brandy shrugged. She had plans of her own.

Ray wasn't satisfied. "Who's gonna drive the van? How do we know he won't take off with the whole thing?"

Rod glared at him and then winked. "Why, Ray, we will let *you* drive the van. After all, it's *your* truck, but you'll have company, Johnny, me, and, well, maybe Charlie here. That way, all interests are represented."

"Uh-huh. You forgot three interests." All eyes turned to Brandy. "Emma's, Sally's, and mine. You seem to forget who discovered it in the first place."

"We can't all go in the van. Three at the most. Others could follow in a car, but that will look highly suspect if all or most of us leave town at the same time." Johnny made eye contact with the four people across from him. "We have some ideas that might lend themselves to collaboration. Justin, you backed the plan that Steve and Donna wanted, and Emma, you were also in favor. Would that apply to Sally as well?" He peered around Emma.

Sally was looking at him for the first time. "What plan is that?" she asked. "I have my own plans for the money."

"That's okay, but would you trust Justin, Charlie, and your aunt to be represented during transport by, say, Charlie?"

Sally looked at Charlie, and he lowered his head. "I guess so, if Aunt Emma agrees." Emma nodded.

Justin put his hand on the desk clerk's shoulder. "Okay, that's one. Ray, you can represent your family. I assume you wouldn't want Jay to go in your place."

"You got that right, but who's the third person?"

Johnny put his glass down and addressed Ray. "How about you let Rod, Brandy and me work that out between us? If we can come to an understanding, we have our transport team. Can we agree on that?"

Rod mumbled under his breath and Brandy gave Johnny a smile to rival the Pillsbury Doughboy.

"Why, Johnny," she purred. "Are you proposing that we become partners?"

"Not exactly, but all of us will need to make a leap of faith. We don't have to trust each other, but we will have to work together, or none of this happens."

"Faith? That's asking a hell of a lot," said Ray.

Rod was about to agree with him, but thought better of it.

Brandy sat back and assumed the role of adult. "Rod, Ray, Johnny, aren't you are all forgetting something? No one is going to take off with anything. What would someone do with hundreds of pounds of our stuff? We've agreed that we can't pocket our shares and go our separate ways. We have to cooperate if we want anything. I'd love to be greedy and take it all, but if we don't work together, we end up with nada. Let Justin work out the transfer details and how we get paid. I'm ready to roll. As Johnny said, he, Rod, or I can be the third party for transporting the shipment. The main thing is that we keep our cool and make sure that none of this gets out." She looked at Sally and Charlie. "I assume our newest members are in accord with that?"

Sally glanced at Emma and nodded. Charlie looked around the table and said that he was in and would offer whatever help was needed. All eyes turned to Justin.

"As I said, it will take about thirty days, possibly less, to finalize the transfer and receive the payments. Cashier's checks will be drawn by our agent on a San Francisco bank account as if she had purchased a business. I gave her the name of our holding company. The ledger will show that the checks were distributed to the shareholders of Rattlesnake Basin Enterprises—that is, us."

"How much does that come to, for each share?" Ray had a pencil and a sheet of paper in front of him.

"We don't know the *exact* amount yet. We never accurately weighed the total asset. We can do that as we load it for transport. We know the purity of the few bars we sold but not how much it might vary for the whole lot. The prevailing price will be the market value. I propose we figure the retainer fee on the basis of our assay twenty years ago. However, I am going to seek the services of an analyst to represent our interests when the bars are delivered. He will be at the site when the ore is smelted, the impurities removed, and the amounts of gold and silver determined. It will be worth several hundred dollars to have someone representing us when the final value is determined. There will also be an ore processing fee and a modest transfer fee, a few hundred dollars, for the open and legal business procedures of selling the company plus the fifteen percent for the agent and purchaser's fees. With the current market price, there should still be plenty left. I should also point out that we would have a lot more difficulty if we had tried to do this at our last meeting."

The group members nodded and smiled in agreement. It had been a point of discussion during the 1967 reunion and the major factor in deciding to postpone the sale. Ray and Rod raised no further objections and the meeting ended as they dispersed for the evening.

Justin watched Charlie leave with Sally and Emma. He turned to Johnny. "I need to talk to you, no later than tomorrow. Maybe over breakfast?" He left no doubt that he had something serious on his mind that was intended for Johnny's ears only.

"Do we need to meet now?" Johnny figured he might as well offer even though he had some other plans for the evening.

"No, tomorrow morning is fine. How about seven, here?"

Johnny agreed. He followed Brandy and Rod to the door, leaving Ray scribbling on his ledger pad and Justin moving toward the kitchen to finish clearing the dining room. Johnny looked back at Ray before he walked through the exit. "Don't leave any notes laying around, Ray."

Ray glared at him, but picked up his ledger and stood.

Johnny caught up with Brandy and Rod. "Where to guys and who is buying?"

Brandy turned and gave him one of her special come-ons. "Why, you are, darling. We wouldn't think of going without you." She put her arm through his as if they were long-time lovers.

Rod rolled his eyes as if to say *what else did you expect*? It was exactly what Johnny expected, but it was dealing time, and the game was ready to start. They walked out the front door and made their way to the quieter of the three bars, coincidentally named the Rattlesnake Junction Tavern.

<hr>

A MAN IN A DARK SHIRT AND JEANS WALKED DOWN THE STREET behind the two men and woman leaving the hotel. He remained inconspicuous as he strolled along the opposite side in the late-evening shadows. He followed them to a cocktail bar. A one-block park nearby consisted of dried, pathetic bushes and trees, and random tufts of grass that were about to yield to the summer heat. He sat down on a weathered, wooden park bench and could see the door to the bar as he mentally noted who came and went. After a few minutes, he pulled out a hip flask, took a swig, and settled in for the wait. A dog wandered by, stopped to sniff the man and give him a token tail wag, but the man ignored him. The dog ambled on.

It was a Thursday night crowd at the seen-better-days watering hole, which is to say not a crowd at all. A few men sat at the bar in pairs and singles, talking to Marion, the owner and barmaid. Some stared at themselves in the large mirror, nursing their drinks against the loneliness that seemed to infuse taverns in towns like Sagebrush. No one else was in the table area.

Brandy, Johnny, and Rod grabbed a table near the back wall, away from the bar and the juke box, which was hammering out typical country and western blues. Marion walked up and took their orders.

"I'm in a margarita mood," said Brandy. "Make it a double-shot grande but skip the salt."

"How ya doing, Brandy? Heard you was back in town. Been ten years, has it?"

Marion looked at Johnny. She had owned the bar for most of her adult life. She knew the three of them, but Johnny was surprised that she remembered their names. *There's been talk around town to remind her and others. They aren't surprised we are here again.*

"I'll have the same, Marion, but with the salt."

Rod gave Johnny a look of disgust, and Brandy flashed that I-got-you-babe smile.

"Sure, Johnny. What about you Rod?"

"I'll stick with beer. Whatever you got on tap that isn't light." He lit a cigarette and offered the pack to his tablemates. They declined. "Who is it going to be?" he asked, looking at each of them in turn.

Brandy was sitting between them and leaned back against the upholstered lounge seat so she could view them without turning her head. It also allowed them a full frontal view of her. "It'll be all of us, Rodney, but I suggest you go in the truck with Ray and Charlie. Johnny and I can discreetly follow in my car."

"The day the two of you are discreet is the day pigs fly out of my ass."

"Better invest in toilet paper, Rod. You're gonna need a trainload." Brandy was as biting as ever, never taking crap from anyone. She turned to Johnny. "He hasn't gotten any mellower with age, has he?"

"I guess that means you won't be playing social hostess with the women in Sagebrush," he said.

"Guess not. I'm sure the three can handle it."

Rod took a long drag and squinted at them, although there were no bright lights in their corner of the room. "What the hell are you two up to anyway?"

"I don't know any more than you do," Johnny answered. "I'll take one of those fags, after all."

Rod pulled the pack out, and Johnny lit up. Marion returned with the drinks and they dove in, putting a pause on the accusations for a few delicious moments.

"Not a bad dinner tonight," said Brandy. "It seems Justin is trying to get us organized."

"Someone had to," Johnny said. "Our last get-together was an unqualified disaster. I wasn't sure we'd ever reconvene."

Ten years ago, the shares were redistributed and new receipts issued. That was as far as cooperation and consent went. Ray tried again to negotiate for a distribution of three shares to his family, pleading and demanding, but the others refused. The rest of the reunion was marked by suspicion and undisguised hostility, especially between Ray and Rod. Some of the acrimony carried over to the present, with the exceptions of Justin and Emma.

Now we have two new faces, but where their allegiances lie is yet to be determined, Johnny thought. *Presumably, Sally is aligned with her aunt, but she apparently has her own plans for whatever share is apportioned. Charlie is an unknown, even though he works for Justin. Guess we'll find out in the next few days.*

Brandy sipped her drink. "We'll be a tight group for a while longer this time. Our last meeting broke up after two and a half days, and nobody parted with fond farewells." She looked at Johnny as if sorry she had reminded him of their sudden split and lack of communication. "Like I said at dinner, we need to do this together." She gave Rod the hard stare. "You and Ray have got to pitch in. If you want to kill each other after you receive the funds, don't let the rest of us get in your way. Until then, please work with us." It was half plea, half demand, but neither man doubted her sincerity or determination. Brandy didn't tolerate fools.

Rod sat back and enjoyed a long chug from his mug. It left a trace of foam on his upper lip, which he ignored. "Okay, okay, I got the message. I'll be cool, but, I'm not gonna take any crap from Ray. His brother and wife are fine—no hassle with them—but I don't trust that son of a bitch, and they have one share. I'm sure he wants it all."

"I'm sure we all do, but greed will kill this deal." Brandy the reasonable one, the queen of the poker table who was rarely satisfied with splitting a pot or coming out on the night second best. When she said she was all in, she meant exactly that. It was strange to watch her negotiating for a reasonable compromise.

It was Johnny's turn to air a thorny challenges posed earlier. "What do you think about Charlie and Sally receiving shares? Should Justin and Emma provide part of theirs and leave everyone else as is, or do we divide the pot eight ways?"

Rod answered immediately. "Hell no, I'm not throwing any of my share back into the pot. Hate to agree to anything with Ray, but he's right. Let their sponsors provide a split. It's the same deal we made with the Gordons. I don't care how much they give them, but it don't come from us." He looked at them to see if they agreed.

Brandy had a puzzled look. "I know who Sally is. She was a little girl when we met before, but who is Charlie? I know he's the desk clerk and he seems like a nice kid, a bit nervous at times, but why is he in on this?"

"Justin wants to see me tomorrow for breakfast. I don't know what it's about, but I'll ask him about his clerk. I'm curious myself." His drink was half gone and Brandy was sucking ice cubes. He raised his hand and caught Marion's eye. "Another round," he called out.

Two guys at the bar turned around to look at them, but Johnny didn't recognize any faces.

"Damn decent of you, Johnny, I must say. This and breakfast. I guess I owe you again."

"Not to worry, Rod. I'll let you buy me a grand meal after you get your check." He turned to Brandy. "Should we leave the kids out of the main pot and keep the number of shares as is?"

"As is." The last ice cube disappeared from her glass.

Since Rod had already weighed in, Johnny confirmed it. "As is. I'm sure that the Gordons will vote likewise and that's a majority any way you cut it. By the way, I was never in favor of the Gordons getting three of the remaining shares after the Woodwards were" he paused, not sure how to phrase it, "eliminated. Neither Jay nor Barbara played a role and we gave into Ray in '57 only because he pushed his way into our group. There will be no more pushing."

Rod picked up his beer, gave a cursory nod, and drank the rest of it down.

Brandy smiled at Rod and then Johnny. "See, that wasn't so bad was it? We've only started down the road to tying one on and already we've made a crucial decision. I'm impressed."

Rod grimaced. "Don't be. We still have to decide who is going to sleep with you."

Johnny was taking the last good swallow of his margarita and sprayed it across the table.

Brandy, who otherwise would have rendered a caustic retort, laughed out loud as he wiped the salty liquid from his shirt and off the table. "Well gentlemen, either all three of us sleep together and we all have sex with each other" She stared at them, "or we all sleep alone and innocent, as God intended."

The next round of drinks arrived. The conversation turned to the where-have-you-been and what-have-you-been doing variety, punctuated by laughter and an occasional toast. It could have been a week rather than ten years since they last shared a drink.

◆

Sally and Charlie sat in silence on the big striped sofa in Emma's living room. She was busy in the kitchen, making iced tea, and leaving the young man and woman to talk. He was at one end and she on the other, maintaining at least three feet of space between them. He clutched his hands to his knees, as if trying to keep them from running out of the house.

She was more relaxed but wasn't going to cut him any slack. *Let him prove himself*, she thought. If he was going to be a player like her aunt suggested, he needed to show some fortitude and not be wilting on the couch like some fourteen-year-old on his first date.

Emma was aware of his discomfort and took her time, hoping the stalemate would break of its own accord. She could lead the boy to the girl but she couldn't make him a man.

Sally made the first move. "Willing to ride with Ray and someone else to deliver the stuff to the Bay Area?"

He looked at her sat up straighter. "Yes, that shouldn't be difficult. I just wonder who the third person will be."

"Who would you like it to be?"

"Brandy or Johnny. I don't think I want to be with Ray and Rod together."

"I can't blame you. I hope it's Brandy. She seems okay, but I can't read Johnny. I'm not sure if he can be trusted or not."

Emma entered the room and set down the pitcher of tea and three glasses filled with ice. "Help yourself," she said and poured herself a drink.

After they had drinks in their hands, Emma broached the discussion about shares. "You know that the others will probably not approve giving you equal shares. I know the Gordons won't. I've known that family for more than fifty years. Barbara is a nice enough person, but she won't do anything against her husband. Jay is a strange one, nice in his own way, but not right in the head since that near drowning when he was a child. Ray manages him and makes all the decisions for him, so he will also do whatever Ray decides. Funny thing though."

"What's that?" asked Charlie, sitting forward on the couch.

"Well, Ray has claimed for years that Jay doesn't have much upstairs. He is strong and likeable and has always helped Ray with his hardware and auto repair business, but Ray says he has a poor memory and can't figure things out for himself. I don't know about that. On several occasions I talked to Jay in the shop and a couple of times here at the house when I hired him to do some repairs. When he is not with Ray, Jay seems almost normal. He can manipulate numbers and he remembers things we talked about years before. I asked Barbara about it once and she just gave me a strange look, but she didn't confirm or deny what I said."

"Do you think he is pretending to be retarded, maybe playing Ray so he will feel guilty about the near drowning?" Sally sat forward.

Emma shook her head and put down her glass. "I don't know, but there's something there that doesn't meet the eye. If Jay is normal or nearly so, there must be some reason that Ray and Barbara want it to be known otherwise. Each share of our assets is now worth a fair amount of money according to Justin, and that would make them well off in a town like Sagebrush."

Charlie glanced at Sally, who had moved a few inches closer on the sofa. He looked directly at Emma. "I don't mind not getting a full share. We weren't in on it to start, so anything would be great." He turned back to Sally. "What about you? What will you do with some of it?"

Sally's eyes were on her aunt. "I would leave enough money to cover the medical expenses and provide for whatever Grandma and Grandpa Moore need. It shouldn't be a lot, but it will keep them comfortable for the few years they have left. She hesitated. "Then I want to travel. Before last year, I wanted to go to college, perhaps in Seattle or Eugene, but now I'm thinking of London or Edinburgh. I don't know." She finished by giving Charlie a focused stare, encouraging him to reveal his plans.

"I haven't had time to think about it. I had hoped to go to school, maybe community college. I have never lived anywhere but here and the biggest city I have ever been to is Reno. That was when I was almost eighteen and I wasn't old enough to drink or gamble or…anything."

Emma watched in silence, sipping her iced tea, letting the scene play out. As she observed Sally warming up to Charlie and the boy overcoming the worst of his shyness, she thought about her decision to bring Sally in on the plan. Justin must have thought likewise for Charlie, but she still didn't understand the relationship between the hotel owner and his desk clerk. He was a mystery, but if Justin fulfilled his promise, Charlie would be a mystery with money.

⸺ ◆ ⸺

As the midnight hour approached, the three at the back table were the only customers remaining in the bar. Marion wasn't in a hurry to close, so she sat behind the counter, glancing at a late-night movie on the overhead television and waiting for additional drink orders.

Rod was withdrawn, sipping beer and smoking, a silent observer of the exclusive party as Brandy and Johnny became increasingly raucous and unresponsive to anyone else. Only when their glasses were empty did they interrupt their festivities to signal to the bartender.

Rod quietly lifted his glass for a refill, leaving the table occasionally for the men's room, but returning quickly. Despite his friendship with Johnny and past encounters with Brandy, he trusted neither of them and wanted to stay in their presence as much as possible. Brandy's earlier admonition about sex might no longer apply, and Rod had every reason to believe that the night would end differently but not necessarily to his advantage.

The conversation between the brunette and Johnny was a seemingly random mixture of recalling old times, good and bad, and not-so-subtle flirtations. Despite their earlier reticence and suspicions, alcohol had freed their tongues and heightened former passions. They didn't kiss or touch, but Brandy leaned forward on the table, nearly exposing her breasts. Johnny made no attempt to disguise his interest. He sat back, smiling, laughing, and twirling his glass. They had lost count of the margaritas consumed and both were shaky when they rose to use the facilities.

Brandy laughed as she pushed back from the table. "Johnny, I might need your help finding the john. The other john," she added. She held out her hand and he stood to help her across the floor to the women's room.

Marion looked on with amusement, not sure if she should help Brandy or if Johnny had it under control. Johnny almost fell and she realized he didn't, but by that time Brandy made it through the door.

He steadied himself against the wall. "Do you need some help in there, darlin'?"

Brandy answered from behind the door. "Up to you. Ain't a pretty sight, though."

He laughed and stumbled back to the table. Marion sauntered over and asked if they wanted another round. Rod scowled at Johnny but he shook his head no.

"I think that'll be it, dear. With Rod's help here," he glanced at the sullen one, "we might even make it back to the hotel. Might even find our own rooms, right buddy?" Another scowl.

Johnny removed four twenties from his wallet. "Keep the change and thanks for indulging us. It's been a while, don'cha know?"

Marion thanked him and asked Rod if they could make it back to the hotel in one piece.

"Might be three pieces," he said, but there was little evidence of humor.

Johnny ignored him as Brandy returned to the table. Her tight black pants were partly zipped in back, so he reached behind her to finish the closure. She hardly noticed.

"That's it for the night, is it?" She had a crazy gleam in her eye, the same kind she often sported when ahead in a poker game that was about to end.

"Yeah, we need to allow Marion to get home and let Rod get some sleep." His implication was clear, and this drew another sneer from Rod. They filed out of the Rattlesnake Junction Tavern and started down the street.

Across the street was an empty park. The silent observer in the black shirt had given up two hours earlier and returned to his hotel room. He would stay awake and listen for their return.

Brandy put an arm through Rod's on her left and the other through Johnny's on her right. She mumbled a half apology to Rod for ignoring him most of the evening. "I'll make it up to you, Rod." He looked at her with new hope, but she put that to rest. "Not tonight, however. I'm beat and you know what they say about girls and beauty rests."

Rod looked away. They walked into the hotel and, with a quiet farewell, each entered their own rooms. Johnny's thoughts turned to what almost was and what might have been, but nothing diminished his fond memories of what she and he had shared in the distant past.

Rod undressed quickly, hoping he wouldn't hear hallway doors opening and closing before he fell asleep. Brandy slipped under her covers, satisfied that she was still in control. The first-floor hotel wing was quiet.

⁕

THE MORNING ARRIVED MUCH EARLIER THAN JOHNNY WANTED or expected. A knock on the door—a soft rap, then a louder bang—woke him. In a fog, his head pounding like tomorrow shouldn't have arrived, he stumbled out of bed, almost fell on his way to the door, remembered it wasn't locked, and croaked, "Enter." He was wearing only his briefs but didn't care who it was.

Justin opened the door and peaked around the corner. "Good, you're alone. And late." He looked at his watch. "Dining room, seven, remember?"

Johnny sat on the bed and it came back to him. "What time is it?" he mumbled.

"Almost seven-thirty. I have something to discuss with you before the others stir, so get dressed and I'll see you in the dining room." He closed the door and his footsteps echoed down the hall.

Johnny entered the bathroom, peed, washed his face in cold water, grabbed two aspirins from a bottle in his bag, and hurriedly dressed. *What in the hell is this all about? Why couldn't he say what he needed to say here? Need a few more hours shut-eye. Shit!*

The lobby was vacant and only Justin was sitting in the dining room. Johnny joined him at the table as Sally walked up with a coffee pot and gave him a brief smile. He returned it, turned his cup over for her to pour, and asked for two eggs scrambled and orange juice.

Justin looked at him, smiling at his disarray. "No meat, huh? Hungover and dried out is never beautiful, is it?"

Johnny took a sip of coffee and glared at him. "I hope this is worth you waking me up from whatever erotic stuff I was dreaming about."

"I think it will be, or to put it another way, it should be. Think back twenty years ago, Johnny, before Emma and Steve made their discovery and before life changed for all of us."

"Yeah, so? Life was peaceful then. No cares, no worries, play some poker, get drunk once in a while, and I was a whole bunch younger, friskier, and prettier."

"Do you remember who some of that friskiness was with? Remember a woman named Sonya, a lady you were seeing about that time?"

"Yeah, of course I remember her. I wasn't just seeing her, I lived with her. We were good friends. She was a couple of years older and knew a lot more about some things than I did. She was a good mentor, a good partner." He paused as if lost in fond memories. "I think she wanted to settle down, but she underestimated my need to get out and away. She wasn't the most beautiful woman in the world, but she had soul. I always wondered what happened to her. Do you know?"

"Yes, I do. Shortly after our big discovery and the formation of our agreement, you left town. About seven months later, Sonya gave birth to a baby boy. Did you know that?"

Johnny looked down at the table and then back up at Justin. His headache had receded, whether due to the aspirin or the topic they were discussing, he wasn't sure. "I heard something to that effect, that she had a kid, but I heard she had already left town and it was unknown who the father was. Where did they go?"

"They didn't go anywhere. She gave birth in Alturas in July 1958. That would be nineteen years ago, plus a few days. She and her newborn son returned here but she came down with a terrible case of pneumonia. The doctor said she was weak from the delivery, apparently her first. Johnny, she died a week later, leaving her son an orphan. He was adopted by Mr. and Mrs. Charles, just out of town."

"How come I am just learning this? Nothing was said about this at our last meeting."

"We, or I should say I, never made the connection until a year ago when a young man from the Charles farm came to me for a job. He had graduated from high school and wanted to do something besides farming. His given name was Dean, but he said everyone called him Charlie. I hired him as a desk clerk parttime, but now he's fulltime."

"Not only did you hire him, but you brought him in on the tontine. And all of this has what to do with Sonya and me?" A growing suspicion blossomed into solid realization. "Oh, shit. Justin, are you telling me that Charlie is my boy? That all this time I've had a son and didn't know?"

"Seems that way."

Johnny was stunned, lost in a maelstrom of swirling thoughts.

Sally brought their breakfast plates, poured coffee and returned to the kitchen. Justin began eating, letting the news sink in. He didn't envy the emotional storm he had unleashed, but he knew that Johnny had to reconcile his parentage with the new group member, and the sooner, the better.

"Does Charlie know I'm his father?"

"He knows nothing for sure, uh, I think. Mr. Charles told him who his mother was and he has gathered information from a few of the gobble gossips in town, enough to know that she and you were once more than friends. He may suspect that you are his dad, but he has never asked me. I'm not sure myself. What do you think?"

Johnny pondered the facts, running a mental calendar through his head. "If she gave birth seven months after I left, Charlie is probably mine. I am pretty sure she wasn't messin' around with anyone else. For that matter, neither was I. We were pretty straight with each other." He took another bite of eggs and a sip of juice. "Yeah, I'd say the odds are good that Charlie and I share a bunch of genes. He seems a lot different from me, at least in behavior, but I noticed a haunting look to his eyes and his nose…, well, I had a strange feeling when I first saw him, but at the time I didn't have any reason to believe I had left a son behind. Hell's fire, wish I'd known this ten years ago."

"Maybe just as well you didn't. Would you have changed your life around in '67, stayed here, settled down?"

"Don't know. I remember that when I left, I was happy to go, no lookin' back, no regrets. Only wanted to get my share of the haul and get away again, as fast and far as possible." A thought occurred to him. "Justin, that doesn't explain why *you* brought him into the group. You didn't know for sure he was my son."

"I was about as sure as one can get. If you decided not to acknowledge him or, for whatever reason you didn't return, I planned to give him part of my share."

"Shit, Justin. I have to thank you for looking after him. I sure as hell didn't. Hmm, I wonder what Charlie will say when he learns the truth."

"I'll leave that up to you, Johnny. I encourage you to tell him as soon as possible in case that changes the dynamic or outcome within the group. He might be taking an interest in our young waitress, but I have to admit that they have kept it discreet. If Ray suspected they were in league, it would probably infuriate him further. By the way, did the three of you decide who the third person in the van would be?"

"Yeah. We appointed Rod to represent our interests, but Brandy and I might tag along behind the van to make sure Rod and Ray don't go ballistic on us."

"Good idea, especially if Charlie has to sit between them. Well, as always, breakfast is on me. I need to find us an expert in gold smelting and analyses. Rod gave me a couple of names in Reno and I will head there this morning. Hopefully I can locate someone discreet and willing to take part in the transfer of our assets. Should be back late tonight or early tomorrow. Take your time, Johnny. You probably need the extra coffee."

Justin stood and walked from the dining room. Sally poked her head around the corner and Johnny lifted his cup. With another smile, she refilled it. Johnny retreated to the inner workings of his mind, replaying the disk labelled 1957, recalling pleasant memories of a trailer and a Russian woman.

CHAPTER TEN

Family Affairs

L ost in remembrances of ten and twenty years ago, Johnny finished his coffee, dropped a generous tip for Sally on the table, and returned to his room. Justin's revelations about his desk clerk had given new meaning to the phrase, "complications of the personal kind."

A son! For the past two days, he has been in plain sight, signing me in on Wednesday and attending our reunion dinner last night. Furthermore, he and our lovely waitress are now members of the tontine. The elephant in the room, the mountain he needed to climb without delay, was to sit down with Mr. Dean Charles and to come to grips with his recently discovered parentage.

How much does Charlie know or suspect? He seems like a bright kid and capable of putting the story together, yet he hasn't said anything directly to me. Oh, yeah, there was that deer-in-the headlights look he gave me on that first day at the desk, when he asked if he knew me. Was that it? Was he reaching out and I didn't have the brights to know what might be in the wind?

Johnny thought back to 1959 when he learned from Justin that Sonya had left town. He didn't think it that unusual and didn't follow-up with anyone else. Brandy might have known more, but the truth was that Sonya didn't interact with the Sagebrush Hotel group. *No, the real truth is, I didn't care enough to pursue it, and now, after almost twenty years, I learn that she died here in town after having my baby. Raised as an orphan by two people I don't know, and now I have to present myself as his father. Back from wandering around the South, playing poker, playing roustabout Romeo, not giving a damn about anything but myself. What will Charlie think, say, do?*

He knew Charlie reported to work by nine o'clock, and Johnny hoped to catch him before he started. They needed to have a preliminary chat and set a time for a lengthy discussion. He felt at a complete loss on how to handle the moment when it came. A lot would depend on Charlie. *Will he be happy to greet his long-lost dad or be resentful of the years that can't be reclaimed? How were his adopted parents? Was he well treated?* According to Justin, they were childless and took him in because they wanted a child and he was in need of a home.

There was another matter. As far as he knew, there was no legal documentation of himself as the father. If Sonya put his name on the birth certificate, Charlie would have known who he was. Something else to inquire about. What *did* the birth certificate indicate—father unknown? As much as he could use a strong hit of something alcoholic, he had to keep his head clear for the rest of the day. A game was on for the evening and he wanted to have their talk before then, preferably after five when Charlie got off work. Invite him to dinner, just the two of them in the hotel dining room. His son might feel comfortable there, a place he knew well.

Johnny needed to discuss matters with Rod without Brandy present. Although the relationship between the brunette and Johnny had changed ten years ago and was still percolating, he didn't want any misunderstandings about last night. Even though Brandy and he had played nice and didn't sleep together when they returned to the hotel, he knew Rod wasn't happy. In many ways, Rod was justified in thinking that the threesome had become two plus one and he was the outsider looking in.

Johnny knocked on Rod's door and was answered by a growly "what?" He poked his head in, told Rod he was going out, and asked him to meet him in front of the hotel in twenty minutes. He heard a muffled "yeah" and had to trust the surly one would wake up, get dressed, and be on the street sometime before noon.

At quarter to nine, Johnny left his room and walked into the lobby. Charlie was coming through the front door, looking cheerful as if either expecting good news or having just created something wonderful. Johnny approached him at the desk.

The clerk greeted him in a formal, business-like manner. "Good morning, Mr. Templeton. How is the day going for you so far?"

Johnny looked at him, trying to find some trace of guile or sarcasm, but there was none. He seemed open and innocent, unaware of what Johnny had to tell him. "Hello, Charlie. I know you need to be at work in a few minutes, but I think it's important that you and I have a private talk. There are some things I need to ask you about and some things I think you should know."

"Sure thing, Mr. Templeton. When would you like to do that?"

Johnny started to correct him on the name but stopped. *Should he call me Johnny? What about Dad? No, not yet. That can come after dinner if it comes at all.* "Let's meet for dinner here about five-thirty, unless you'd rather get away from the hotel and eat someplace else."

"No, here is all right. I like the food and I can be ready a few minutes after five, if you'd like."

"Okay," he said, relieved that things were going smoother than he had any right to expect. "I'll see you in the dining room about quarter after."

Charlie smiled and moved behind the desk as Johnny strolled out the front door. *So far so good, but I still need to prepare for the evening. How do you become a parent in one day?* The simple answer was, you didn't.

A small wood bench ran along the hotel front balcony, well lit by the morning sun. Johnny walked over and sat down, stretching his legs out in front. He had almost forgotten how bad they felt only two days ago when he walked into town. *Ten years ago I had a slick GTO to cruise around in. Now I'm a hitchhiker and not a successful one at that. Rod still has a car. Maybe we can take a ride somewhere and have our man-to-man. Grab a bottle or take a few beers with us.*

The front door squeaked open. Johnny remembered the old rusty hinges from the fifties, ones that had been replaced in the sixties and were again displaying signs of a depreciating business property. *Justin will need another cash infusion soon.* Rod walked out, glanced at Johnny, and stepped up beside the bench. He stood with his hands on hips, feet far enough apart to exhibit mild aggression.

Johnny got to his feet. "Wanna go for a drive?" He gave Rod his "old buddy" smile.

"What's this all about? Thought you'd still be under the covers with your lady friend." There was no smile, nothing to indicate friendly envy.

"We need to talk about that, Rod. She and I didn't share a room last night. Sorry we left you out of things at the bar. We hadn't intended to do that, just got carried away with the moment and the sauce."

"Yeah, you did, and you made sure I was stuck with Ray and the kid in the truck, while you and the broad conveniently tail along. Maybe."

"You didn't protest when we agreed on it."

"*You* agreed on it. You and her. I was outvoted before the decision, such as it was, came up."

"Okay, I apologize for both of us. Do you want one of us to go with Ray and Charlie and if so, which one?"

Rod processed the permutations and possible outcomes. "Charlie can't handle Ray if he decides to try anything slick. Brandy probably could, but I'm not sure I completely trust her. I should trust you, but now I'm not so sure."

"What do you want to do?" Johnny was losing patience with his old friend and Rod knew it.

"Doesn't look like I've got a whole lotta choice, does it? I'll go in the truck, but I'm not promising I won't strangle that son of a bitch if he steps out of line."

"Who, Charlie? I don't think he'll be any trouble." Johnny smiled, but Rod wasn't in the mood for humor. "Let's head out of town, maybe grab lunch and a drinks somewhere." He looked at Rod expectantly. "We still need to clear the air on the brunette and we need to have some things planned in case our worst fears about Ray come true."

They started walking toward his car. Rod had his hands in his pockets and his head lowered, as if he was trying to resolve questions that had been weighing him down.

"Yeah, I guess so, Johnny. As far as Brandy is concerned, there is no contest. Never was. I figured it was only a matter of time before the two of you hooked up. My only surprise was that you didn't do it ten years ago when the two of you left town." He looked up at Johnny as they neared the car. "What did happen during that time? Did you stay in touch? None of my business but I admit that I'm curious."

They got into his car and Rod drove east to the highway and south, in the general direction of Susanville and Honey Lake, without discussing where they were going.

Johnny picked up the conversation. "We meant to stay in touch. I called her twice, I think. Never did get into Sin City so I let her make her play for the big time. That was the first two years, and then we lost contact. I was distracted and she was changing jobs at various hotels, but I think her real interest was the tables, and she starting playing professionally or semiprofessionally. I don't know the difference."

"The difference is whether you are making enough money so that's all you have to do. If I was any good at it, that's what I would do." Rod settled back and drove on steadily, visibly relaxed, the earlier hostility no longer apparent. "What you're saying is, that for about eight years you two didn't write, call or see each other?"

"Yeah, that's pretty much it. Like I told you, I wasn't sure she would come back this time. She apparently thought the same for me."

"Too much money. Even if both of you hit it big somewhere, the price of gold shot up, and you knew that your share would be five to six figures. That'll draw anyone back, even to Sagebrush. Besides, you both miss my ugly mug." He was grinning, the old Rod that Johnny knew and loved.

They ended up in Litchfield, fifteen miles east of Susanville, near the northwestern shore of Honey Lake. After sandwiches in a small restaurant, they grabbed a couple of drafts in a local watering hole. They turned the discussion to Ray and his sporadic hostility and attempts to influence the group to his wishes. They had no doubt that he would try to do the same to Charlie and Sally even though they didn't have full shares of their own.

"What about Charlie? How does he figure in this?" Rod was picking his teeth and they were about to finish the last glass and head back to Sagebrush.

"Justin believes Charlie is my son. His mother was Sonya, the gal I was living with twenty years ago. Remember her?"

"I remember her but just barely. We only met a couple of times and I only knew what you said about her, which wasn't much. When did she have the kid?"

"Apparently several months after I left. July 1958. He turned nineteen a few days ago. Sonya died shortly after his birth and he was unofficially orphaned out to the Charles family just out of town. Did you know them?"

"Sorta. We ran across each other a few times. Seemed like okay folks. After I left the farm, I didn't have a lot to do with most of the hayseeds unless I trucked for them."

"Charlie's real name is Dean. He grew up a Charles and eventually got a job with the hotel. Justin put two and two together and told me what he knew this morning at breakfast."

"And now what? Does the kid know you're his dad?"

"Justin didn't know for sure but thought Charlie might be smart enough to suspect. I'm going to tell him over dinner this evening before the game."

"Who-whee. That should be something. All this time a dad and not knowing. What do you think Brandy will say about that?"

"I don't know. Might not make any difference, because nothing is decided between her and me anyway. Rod, I don't have a fucking idea where I stand. I'm not sure I'm gonna tell her."

"Oh, she'll find out. Bet your last stack on that. Once Charlie knows, Sally will know, Emma will know, and everyone in town will know. Nothing like a bit of scandal to get everyone's blood up, and don't forget Ken. He'll broadcast it all over."

Johnny paid the tab, and they started their drive up a mountain pass overlooking the lake and heading north and west. It was about an hour-long drive back to Sagebrush.

It was three o'clock, and Johnny figured he had time to wash up and get ready for dinner with his newly discovered offspring. The thought of it was still amazing, and despite his efforts to focus, he was undecided about what to say or how to approach the subject. *Play it by ear like I always do. It seems to work for most things, but family affairs are a different kettle of fish.*

Brandy was in her office when Johnny returned. The door was open and he considered going in and bringing her up to date on Charlie. The boy was in the lobby, rearranging some things on a bookshelf. Johnny said hi to him and decided to wait on the talk with the brunette. *Better to measure Charlie's reaction and how our relationship unfolds before I confess my new status.* He went to his room, took an unhurried shower, and rested for a few minutes to see if any brilliant strategies came to mind. They didn't.

AL AND RAY SHARED A BOTTLE OF WHISKEY AS THEY SAT OUTside the house at Sanford's farm. The old man was mostly retired from the hardest labor and his younger brother had assumed many of the chores. Ray had provided supplemental income for Alfred to nose about town, keep his ears and eyes open, and report back to the hardware man. It had been ten years of occasional reports, but there had been little information of value. Now, with the possible sale of the assets in the near future, it was time for Ray to be alert to the comings and goings of the TTT. With Johnny and Brandy back in town, he needed Al to keep tabs on everyone including Justin and Emma. Despite his animosity toward Rod and the run-in with Johnny, Ray felt that the hotel manager and retired schoolteacher were the biggest obstacles to realizing a final disposition and payout. He might be able to reason with Brandy and Johnnie, possibly even Rod, because they must feel that the time had come and no further delay could be justified.

Accordingly, Ray paid Al to spend some of his evenings and nights at the hotel. He made Al aware that settlement of a certain property investment in Sagebrush would provide rich returns and that Al would share in the profits once the deal was concluded. In return, the farmer was to follow certain individuals about town. He would remain visible as a hotel guest but be discreet in observing the group participants. He also had a few specific jobs to perform from time to time. One important task had been completed during the RBE meeting on Thursday night.

CHARLIE WAS WAITING IN THE LOBBY FOR JOHNNY WHEN HE arrived. "Don't like to sit at a table by myself," the clerk said. They entered together and sat at a corner spot, away from any diners who might come in later. They were the first and Stephanie waited on them. Sally was off, which was a relief. Johnny needed his son's full attention for the next hour. Steph gave them each a menu, something they usually didn't see at breakfast, and asked if they wanted something to drink. Johnny looked at Charlie, remembering the beer he and Sally drank last night. "Want something stronger than milk, sport?"

Charlie grinned, looked at the waitress, and said in a clear voice, "I'll have whatever he's having."

Umm, a bit of unexpected bonding before we get started. No question about it. Some alcohol might grease the slide to wherever. Johnny looked up at Steph. "Two Seagram and sevens, with ice.

She turned to Charlie, started to say something, and left to fetch their drinks.

Charlie knew the menu and mentioned that their meat loaf was pretty good. Johnny thanked him for the suggestion, so that decision was made. *Time to see what he knows.*

"Charlie, your boss, Mr. Gonzales, told me something about you this morning. Naturally, I and some of the others are curious why Justin brought you into our little group. We would all like to know more about your background, who you are, the usual things that people in a substantial business partnership might want to share. That's especially true of this particular business, involving a lot of money and where trust is so important. Does that make sense?"

"Sure, Mr. Templeton, I understand. I was uncomfortable at dinner last night. Mr. Gonzales warned me that some of you might not be happy to see me at the table. I'm glad that I wasn't the only new one."

"What do you think of Sally?"

"She's cute and seems intelligent. She's a little older than I am, but I don't think that bothers her." He hesitated. "I'm not sure what she thinks. We work together and see each other around the hotel, but I don't know her that well. I talked to her more last night at Miss Dodson's house than in all of the time I've seen her here."

Johnny was about to ask him about his mother when Brandy appeared in the doorway. She spotted them, the menus on the table, and approached.

"I see you haven't ordered yet. Want some company?"

Johnny glanced up at her and thought quickly. "Brandy, normally I would be delighted, but this time I have to say sorry. Charlie and I have some private matters to discuss. Rod might be up for something and he should be in his room." He didn't mean to phrase it that way, but she looked at Charlie, at Johnny, and then back to Charlie. *What does she already know or suspect?*

She nodded and smiled at them. "Some other time, boys. I'll check on Rod." She turned briskly and made her exit.

"Private matters? Just you and I, Mr. Templeton?"

"We can drop the formalities, Charlie. No more Mr. Templeton, okay?"

"Sure, whatever you say." His naïve eagerness was never more on display than at that moment. That innocence was about to be tested.

"Charlie, how much do you know about your mother? What were you told about your birth and family?"

He seemed confused, not expecting this to be the topic. Steph brought their drinks and Johnny gave him a chance to sample his. A slight head shake, but he suspected that Steph had given the boy a lighter dose of whiskey. They ordered the meat loaf and she left them to continue their discussion.

Charlie kept his hand around the frosted glass while he answered. "I know I was adopted. Not officially, because there were no papers, but I had to have a birth certificate when I started school. Dad, that is, Mr. Charles, gave me a copy and told me that my mother's name was Sonya. Sonya Markova it says on the paper. I think she was Russian and lived here in town, in a trailer. My adopted mom says she died a few days after I was born." He paused. "I don't remember her, but I guess that's obvious."

"Yeah. You were lucky to have folks to adopt you, officially or not. Were they good to you?"

"Oh yeah, we got along fine. I didn't have brothers or sisters, but I learned how to do farming, bailing hay and alfalfa, raising chickens, milking a couple of cows. It was hard work, but we got along great. Mom was a great cook—she could make the best fruit pies ever."

"You decided to leave the farm?"

"Yeah, I wanted to go to college. Still do, and I hope to have enough money to get a good education. Maybe become a business man like Mr. Gonzales."

"What about your dad, your real father? Do you know anything about him?"

Again, there was a slight look of bewilderment, as if he was not sure he should answer. "I don't know anything about him. I asked my dad once, but he said he didn't have any information. I couldn't tell if he did or not, but not a lot of people knew Miss Markova, so I wasn't able to find out anything about who my father might be." He took another swallow of his drink, and Johnny did the same. "There wasn't any father listed on the birth certificate." He lowered his eyes, grasping his glass.

"Charlie, I was living with Sonya in 1957. I left town late that fall and didn't make contact again until a couple years later. At that time I was told your mother had left town and disappeared. Nothing was mentioned to me about her having a baby or that she had died here in Sagebrush. I'm not sure why the big secret. It was as if no one knew the truth or wanted to tell me what it was."

Charlie stared at Johnny, mouth slightly open. His eyes were boring through the older man's, not in a hostile fashion but as if he was trying to read his mind, attempting to discover another layer of message to help him understand what Johnny was saying. It was unnerving and Johnny was not sure whether to continue.

"Are you saying that…that you might be my real father?" He took another sip. His drink was half gone.

"I can't be one hundred percent, but it is highly probable. She and I were together about seven months before you were born and I have every reason to believe I am the only man she had, well you know, intimate relationships with. We were not married, but we were tight and pretty faithful. If I had known she was pregnant, I wouldn't have left. Please believe me, Charlie, I had no idea until this morning."

Charlie swallowed the rest of his drink as if it was Kool-Aid. He caught Steph's eye and signaled for another one. She looked at Johnny.

He nodded and raised his own glass. After last night's beer with Sally, he shouldn't have been surprised at this show of sudden maturity, but the boy seemed to have aged several years as they sat at the table. *I might have aged also, but I'm already an inveterate consumer.*

"You're my dad, Mr. Temple…uh, Johnny, I mean Dad? What should I call you?"

"Whatever you're comfortable with, but not Mr. Templeton. If you want, especially for now, call me Johnny."

"Do the others know?"

"Justin is fairly sure, and I told Rod because we will be working together, and I want a few of us to know so we can protect you when we get ready to move the assets." The room was deserted, but the habit of restraint held firm. No sense in alerting strange ears at this late date.

"Protect me? From what or who?"

"Charlie, do you understand about the tontine? That the payoff goes to the survivors of the group?"

"Yeah, but we know all of the people in the group, don't we?"

"Yes we do, but you were too young to remember Steve and Donna Woodward. They didn't survive. We want to make sure that you and Sally, along with everyone else, stays healthy and safe."

"Do you think Sally and me are in danger?"

"Not specifically. We all need to be careful and watch out for each other, even Rod and me. Unless you ask me not to, I would like to share this with Brandy. We are good friends, and she knew your mother, although not well. She was only eighteen at the time and already the best poker player in Sagebrush."

Charlie laughed. "So I've heard. Is she still the best?"

"I'll find out tonight, probably to my regret."

Steph placed the second round of drinks on the table. "Your dinners will be out in a few minutes." She looked at Charlie as he picked up the drink. "I am going to cut off our young desk clerk. I could lose my job if he gets drunk and tears up the place."

The two men regarded each other in astonishment, but the look of amusement on Steph's face indicated she might not be serious.

"We'll be good," said Charlie.

"I'll try to be, but no promises," Johnny said.

Dinner arrived. They ordered iced tea for liquid accompaniment and the evening proceeded with a discussion of where Johnny had been, what he had done, and Charlie's teen years. Johnny didn't reveal all his secrets, but he didn't try to hide the overt aspects of his lifestyle or who he thought he was. *I'm not really sure at this point who I am, so my vagueness is not faked.*

"Have you ever played poker, Charlie?"

"A few times with the kids at high school, mostly for pennies or bottle caps. Once we played for baseball cards. I guess that's the highest stakes I ever won or lost."

"What did you do, win or lose?"

"Sometimes one, sometimes the other. Depended on how my luck was running. How about you, Johnny? I've heard you win most of the time. Is that true?"

"Depends on who I'm playing against. There is always someone better or luckier or both. It's always a challenge, and the outcome is never certain."

"Do you think I could play in the hotel game sometime?"

"Maybe some time, but not now. I could teach you a few things, but the guys and Brandy have been doing this a long time. New blood in the game, unless it is very good, doesn't have a great chance against the old timers. Of everyone left, Brandy is the youngest and she is old enough to be your mother."

At the mention of his mother, Charlie frowned and sat back. "Yeah, I guess that's so. I'll stick to hearts or spades with Sally, but I'd like to have you give me some pointers."

"Sure. So, uh, Charlie, we'll do that. Maybe Brandy will be willing to give you some advice. Maybe she could give us both some help."

Charlie and Johnny said goodnight. They exchanged a handshake and a brief hug in the lobby.

Johnny watched his son as he walked toward the front door. *It went better than I expected. He is mature and ready for the truth. I hope he is ready for the rest of what is to come.*

He hoped to talk to Brandy before the game but didn't want to interfere with her and Rod if they were still together. *If not tonight, I can see her tomorrow.* He walked toward his room, but stopped and knocked on her door. No answer. He entered his room, took off his boots, and lay on the bed. A few minutes to think about the evening and the curtain rising on a new stage.

⸻ ◆ ⸻

The gang started gathering in the upstairs poker room. By eight-thirty, everyone was in place: Ken, Ray, Rod, Brandy, and Johnny. Justin was the last to arrive.

He and Johnny stepped into the hallway. Justin told him he had hired someone in Reno to represent their assay interests. "He'll be ready to go when we set our delivery date. I'll give you and the others the full details tomorrow in my office."

Johnny nodded and they stepped back into the room to fix a drink and take their places at the table.

Ken was the only outsider and if he suspected anything, he didn't let on. He was pleased to be back in the chips and a member of the poker party if not the inner clique he knew existed around him. The game was amiable, filled with the usual mix of bragging, insulting, bluffing, and outrageous comments. Even Ray seemed to be in a good mood, anticipating a settlement of the tontine affair in the near future. Justin was the early winner and no one begrudged him his turn at raking pots on last card turns.

Rod, Brandy, and Johnny were subdued, neither winning nor losing much as the money ebbed and flowed across the table. Rod and Brandy sat side by side.

Seated across from them, Johnny studied their faces as he quietly played. He reminded himself once again that it wasn't any business of his what the two had done for dinner or whenever. He was happy to have Rod talking to him again and if Brandy played a role in that, what was there to complain about? That small slip of jealousy had peeked around the corner, that uneasy feeling that he wasn't as much in control of the relationship as he hoped, but then, was he ever in control? Would Brandy permit such an intrusion? He filled an inside straight, bet big, and brought home the chips. A little satisfaction as he noted Brandy's grimace.

As the players left the room at one o'clock, Justin pulled Brandy, Ray, and Rod aside and told them to meet in his office after breakfast about nine. He said he would also notify Emma, but Charlie and Sally could get the information later.

In the hallway downstairs, Rod, Brandy, and Johnny stood in front of their respective doors. As if by telepathy and mutual consent that they had an understanding, each smiled at the others and walked into their own room. It didn't seem like the time for musical beds.

⸻◆⸻

No one was ready for the gut-wrenching news the next morning. Justin knocked on doors 19, 21, and 23 at eight o'clock. Rod was still asleep, but Brandy and Johnny were dressed and about to venture into the dining room.

"What's up?" asked Johnny. "Thought we weren't meeting for another hour."

"Get Rod up, and come down to my office. I'll tell you then." Justin left, the look on his face leaving no doubt that it wasn't anything good.

Johnny knocked once and entered Rod's room. As usual, the door was unlocked, and Rod was sprawled under the covers, providing ample evidence he planned on not having breakfast that morning. After shaking him awake, Johnny told him something had come up and they were wanted in Justin's office without delay.

"What the hell? Somebody die and go to heaven?" he mumbled as he splashed water in his face and jumped into his clothes and shoes.

He followed Johnny to the lobby and into office. Brandy was already sitting in front of Justin's desk when they arrived. Two empty chairs were in place beside hers.

"Please sit down, men. Sorry to call us together so suddenly, but something terrible has happened. I called Emma's house a few minutes ago to invite her to our meeting and Dr. Willoughby answered the phone. He told me Sally had called him. She couldn't arouse her aunt for breakfast. Seems she passed away during the night. He couldn't provide any more details, other than to say she seemed fine the day before, according to her niece.

Brandy's face was ashen, and she lowered her head. Rod and Johnny looked at each other, recalling Rod's offhand comment a few minutes earlier. There was a long pause, as if everyone wanted to speak but had nothing worth saying.

Johnny asked, "Just like that? Full of life and vigor the night before last, and now…now, she's gone. What the hell."

Rod raised his head and said in a loud voice, "Another one of us? Is that what's happening? I hope they are going to do an autopsy. She wasn't a spring chicken, but she looked in good health to me on Thursday." He was angry and his hands were clenching and relaxing as if he was mentally strangling someone or something.

Brandy's voice was quiet and husky. "What about Sally? She must be devastated. Emma and her were close and neither had anyone else, unless you count Charlie for Sally. I should go to her and see if I can help." Brandy seemed to be the only one with a positive plan of action.

Justin said. "Find out if there's anything you can do. Unless there are things she needs to take care of at the house, invite her back here. I'll get her a room and she can stay here until we sort this out. Charlie should be here in a few minutes. He probably doesn't know anything about this yet." He looked at Johnny.

"I'll tell him. I don't know how close he was to Emma, but I'm sure he will want to help comfort Sally. It seems we are all involved in some way."

Rod cleared his throat. "I bet we are." He didn't have to say everything he was thinking. The other player, the other member of the tontine was Ray. No one wanted to charge ahead with reckless accusations, but the thought hung in the air like a shimmery curtain, an oppressive blanket of past allegations and suspicion.

Justin stood. "I'm sorry to be the bearer of this, but I thought you should know right away. Ray will be here at nine, but I advise everyone to say as little as possible other than to acknowledge that we lost one of our members. Not just a member but the only surviving discoverer of the trove."

Rod asked, "With Emma gone, shouldn't we consider letting Sally have Emma's full share? It doesn't make sense to redistribute everything."

Johnny shrugged. "We can decide that later, and I'm pretty sure that won't be the first concern for Sally."

"It might be for Ray, however." Brandy fixed each of the others with a cold hard stare. She had realized that this change in membership could ignite another bout of aggression whether Ray had anything to do with Emma's departure or not.

Brandy left the office to retrieve Sally just as Charlie arrived in the lobby. Ray followed him in the front door, entered and took a seat in the office, next to Rod.

Johnny excused himself to confer with Charlie, stepping outside, and gave him the news. Charlie's mouth dropped open, and tears creeped from the corners of his eyes. "We had tea together the night before last, right after our dinner here. She was so nice, and she didn't seem sick. Why did she die?"

"Charlie, we don't know. The doctor only reported that she had passed away sometime last night or early this morning. No details yet. Brandy is going to bring Sally back here, so you might want to spend some time with her, if she needs someone."

"Sure, I can do that. I'll help her anyway I can, mister, uh, uh, Johnny." He smiled as if having arrived at a final decision on how to address his father.

Johnny squeezed his shoulder. "You do that. We'll be having another meeting to discuss what to do about everything." He turned and went back inside, joining the other three men in the office.

Justin was bringing Ray up to date. Ray's hands clutched between his knees as he leaned forward, an anxious look on his face, nodding as Justin told him what he knew. Rod slouched in his chair, legs extended, looking at Ray and then at the floor. Johnny took his seat but gave Rod a hard stare, a silent warning to say nothing and not provoke the mechanic in any way.

Ray asked, "Where is Brandy and our young friends?" It was hard to detect if it was said with sarcasm, but Rod gave a small grimace.

Johnny leaned forward to face Ray. "She's gone to Emma's place to pick up Sally and help Dr. Willoughby with arrangements. Charlie is working the front desk."

"This is a terrible moment, but we still need to conduct business," said Justin. "I hired an assayist to be in San Francisco when we deliver the shipment. They will process the ore immediately at a small private smelter in San Pablo. He'll be on hand to witness weighing and oversee the purity determinations. It will cost us five hundred dollars for his services, plus his travel and lodging expenses. We have a quorum here, so can we agree to proceed on this?" He looked around the room and everyone indicated assent.

"Good. When everyone is here, we'll meet again and plan for the delivery. As I understand it, Ray and Rod will be going in the truck with the stuff, and Charlie will also go along." Justin looked at Rod and Ray, but neither objected. "I understand that Brandy and Johnny will be tagging along in a separate car. Everyone's interests should be represented as we agreed the other night. I will stay here but be in touch in case any business questions arise. I presume Sally will also remain here at the hotel, but she may also need to take care of Emma's personal property."

At the mention of Sally, Ray shifted in his chair. It was obvious that he wanted to ask about her and her continuing participation but thought better of it. He was well aware that Rod and Johnny were ready to pounce if he raised objections.

Justin looked around the room and sighed. "Not much more we can do until Brandy returns. Let's plan on meeting at five. Charlie and Brandy will be off work, and we can proceed, over dinner, if that's agreeable."

"Don't know about dinner," said Ray, "but I'll be here. How about I come at six and you don't discuss business until then?"

"Agreed. We'll meet back here at six." Justin stood and the others got up, opened the door, and walked through the lobby. Johnny gave Charlie a smile and told him about dinner and the meeting.

Rod grabbed Johnny's elbow. "I know it's still morning, but let's get down to the Rattlesnake. I need a cold one and I bet you do too." Ray was disappearing through the front door.

Johnny nodded. With a glance at Charlie, the two stepped out of the hotel and began the three-block walk to the only tavern open before noon.

Brandy and Sally arrived at the hotel at three-thirty. Sally's eyes were red and swollen, and despite Brandy's best efforts to play mother, Sally seemed inconsolable. Charlie recognized his obligation and walked Sally into the dining room to get her something to drink.

Justin motioned Brandy into his office and they closed the door. "Ray will be back at six. Rod and Johnny are somewhere in town, probably at one of the bars." He scratched his head as they sat down. "Just when we were on the verge of getting everything together, shipping the stuff and paying everyone off, this happens."

Brandy was back in charge and sat straight in her chair, the color back in her cheeks, her voice steady. "Willoughby called for medical transport and they are taking Emma to Alturas. I suggested that he order an autopsy. When he hesitated, I explained that she looked and acted fine on Thursday. I asked him if there was any condition she had that might have led to her sudden death, but he said he didn't know of any. Her only medication was a minor pain reliever for arthritis, and her last physical was fine. He agreed to the autopsy, but we won't know the results for several days. By the way, Emma didn't look like she had passed peacefully. The bed was a mess as if she had been rolling around in pain. It looked like she threw up. The doctor thought she might have had a heart attack, and he could see signs of muscle constriction as if she had convulsions. Apparently, she didn't cry out, because Sally was sleeping in the next room and unaware of what had happened until she rose for breakfast and Emma wasn't up."

"Umm, sounds horrible. Poor Sally. That means we might be sending our shipment to the Bay Area before we have word on Emma. Brandy, when Rod suggested we transfer Emma's share to Sally, you had a pretty strong reaction about Ray and his probable objection. Would you still favor giving Sally a full share?"

"Might not have a choice in that, for two reasons. On the way back, Sally confided in me that Emma's will names her as the sole heir to her property. I don't see why that wouldn't include Emma's share of the treasure. Remember, she and Steve were the ones that found it."

"I haven't forgotten, and I'm in agreement, but I predict it's only a matter of time before Ray lobbies for expanding his family's share or keeping Sally and Charlie at partial shares."

Brandy folded her arms. "That's the second reason. We have a tontine, remember? A survivor's club. No one brought up the Woodward's heirs when they passed away. Ray might rightly object to Sally taking the place of an original member since there is no provision for it."

"You're right, and we would need a formal vote—or maybe not. If I draw up the papers naming Sally as Emma's replacement, it would be Ray against everyone else."

"We should decide on this before we send the assets to the Bay Area. Once the money is available, the battle lines will be harder to reconcile, don't you think?"

Justin looked at her carefully, admiring the way she grasped situations and understood the hazards of business deals and personal relationships. "Yeah, I do, Brandy. Maybe we get it over with tonight with the kids present. Has Johnny told you about Charlie yet?"

"No. What about Charlie?"

"I know he planned to, but all of this must have kept him from talking to you, so I'll let you know. It's highly likely that Charlie is the son of Sonya and Johnny. His birthdate and history, along with the dates of Johnny's travels coincide. Johnny has accepted the fact, and apparently so has Charlie. If Emma's share goes to Sally, the decision should be straightforward. I'll let Johnny and Charlie work their shares out."

"I agree, although Mr. Gordon might have other ideas about it."

"He's outnumbered. I'll draw up a new set of papers and have them ready for signatures this evening."

"Okay, Justin, but let's keep everyone on alert. I don't know if Emma's death is natural or not, but let's not take any chances. I don't trust that son of a bitch and don't think anyone else should either."

"Fair enough."

"I take it Charlie is looking after Sally?"

"Yes, he'll check her into the room next to yours."

"Good, I'll be able to help keep an eye on her and on Charlie, too. I never imagined that Johnny might have a son, not in Sagebrush anyway. Who knows about the rest of the big wide world?" She gave a short laugh and went back to her office while Justin started preparing new agreements for the treasure trove tontine.

ROD AND JOHNNY SPENT MOST OF THE AFTERNOON DISCUSSING precautions about the shipment and how to deal with Ray. Neither one wanted to get soused, so they ate and nursed their drinks.

"Still packing?" Johnny asked.

"I wasn't, but I will now. I have a compact .38 that won't be conspicuous but can do whatever is required. I'll have it on me when we're in the truck."

"Be careful, Rod. Ray might also be carrying and Charlie will be between you two. I don't want him in the middle of a shootout."

"There won't be a shootout. One shot, maybe, but that's all we'll hear from Mr. Gordon." He grinned and then donned his sober face. "Look, Johnny, I don't think it will come to that, and I won't do anything to put the boy in harm's way. If I think there's any possibility of that, we can have him ride with you and Brandy. I take it you two are still gonna follow along?"

"I think so, especially after what we learned today. We'll see how things go after dinner and whether we need to make different arrangements."

"Yeah, those arrangements are changing all of the time, aren't they? One more and then we head back?"

"Yep. Your turn to buy, buddy."

———————

Sally sat straight in the chair, hands in her lap. Charlie sat beside her, undecided whether to take her hand, put an arm around her shoulder, or keep his distance. He felt awkward and useless and didn't have the words to comfort either her or himself. They were alone in the dining room.

She picked up a glass of Coke, sipped, and put the glass down carefully. "Brandy told me you were an orphan, that you never knew your mother or father, so I guess you know all about feeling alone, not having a close family. I didn't know mine, either. They died when I was six. My grandparents raised me, and now they are old and in a nursing home." She reached out and wrapped her hand around his.

He gave her a half smile, still not sure what to say. He was supposed to be helping her and now she was trying to make him feel better. "I was okay growing up. My adopted folks were good to me, and I didn't know they weren't my real parents until I was nine. Odd thing though. I found out who my mother was and that she died right after I was born, but I never knew who my father was until last night."

"Last night? You found out about your father last night?"

"Uh huh. Johnny took me to dinner and explained what happened twenty years ago. He was living with my mother in a trailer and left about seven months before I was born. He says he didn't know my mom was pregnant or he would have stayed."

"How do you feel about that? It must be a shock to find this out all of a sudden. Do you believe him?"

"That I'm his son? Yeah, the facts fit and, it would be a lot easier for him, if he wanted, to ignore it and move on. Apparently Mr. Gonzales told him, and he wasted no time in letting me know. I think he actually likes the idea of having a son."

"Well, he didn't have to do any of the work of raising you, kinda like having you presented as a fully grown present without the toil." She took a sip and gave him a look as if appraising him seriously for the first time.

"I guess that's true and I don't know what will happen now with the money and everything, but at least I have a real living dad." He paused. "It's so strange because I'm still not sure what to call him. He seems okay with Johnny, and it feels natural, and yet…well, I always called Mr. Charles dad. It's weird to call somebody else that."

"A few weeks ago, Aunt Emma told me she had rewritten her will, naming me as sole heir. I think that means I get her share of the treasure, but Brandy cautioned me to not say anything until we all meet. She also warned me to be careful what I say around Mr. Gordon and not to be alone with him. What's going on? Should I be afraid of him?"

This time, Charlie reached out and took her hand. He knew she was older and less naïve, but she was in distress about her aunt and frightened about Ray and what might occur over the next few days. "From what I know, and that's not a lot, the others in the group can handle Ray Gordon. I've heard a few rumors, not good ones, but Rod will be with me when we take the gold to San Francisco. I think Johnny and Brandy will be on the trip in a different car." He looked at her and lowered his head. "I wish you could come along too, Sally."

She squeezed his hand. "I didn't know what I wanted to do before today, and now I'm even less sure. I need time to think all of this over. Brandy seems like someone I can talk to. You know, Brandy, my aunt, and Mrs. Gordon—Barbara—we were going to divert attention while you drove to the Bay Area. I don't think that's gonna happen now with just Barbara and me."

"No, I guess not. Brandy will be with us. She seems to be a woman of the world. Will she be your role model?"

"Role model? C'mon Charlie, what would you know about women role models?" She immediately saw the hurt look in his eyes. "I'm sorry, I didn't mean that, Charlie. Brandy is clever and I can learn a lot from her, but no, I don't want to be like her. I want to go to college and have a career in writing or editing, working for a big magazine like *Harper's Bazaar* or *Cosmopolitan*. That's what I would use my share of the money for. Like I said the other night, I would leave enough to take care of my grandparents."

"And travel? You said you wanted to go to Europe, maybe go to school there."

"Maybe. It might depend on a lot of things. You said you wanted to go to school. What do you want to be when you grow up?" She said it while giggling and stroking his wrist, but it wasn't condescending.

He laughed, realizing that there was some truth in her referral to his age. "I guess I do need to grow up some. Maybe a lot. I've been protected here, first by my parents on the farm and then the job here at the hotel. Maybe I'm the one who needs some time on the road."

"With Johnny, your dad?"

"Maybe. Maybe just me. Maybe with someone else." He didn't look at her, but felt the squeeze on his arm. When he looked at her face again, she was studying him. It was unnerving but pleasing in a strange and unfamiliar way. He had rarely experienced the attraction toward girls in high school that he was feeling at the moment.

"It's almost time for dinner. I need to go to my room and clean up." She pushed her chair back and stood.

Charlie did the same. "You're next to Brandy, in room 17. I checked you in."

"You know where I live, Charlie. Don't be a stranger." With a smile and an eye bat, she was gone. He couldn't help but notice the extra swing of her hips as she walked out of the dining room.

CHAPTER ELEVEN

Disposing of the Trove

As planned, Brandy, Johnny, Rod, Justin, Sally, and Charlie ate dinner in the hotel dining room. Sally seemed partially recovered from the morning turmoil and it was obvious that Charlie had done his part to comfort her. The two sat side by side and glanced at each other every few minutes, smiling and making small talk as if they were the only ones at the table. By agreement, the other four refrained from discussing anything serious. There were a few other diners in the room, so no mention of gold, treasure, or the upcoming transport was made.

It was a simple meal of soup, salad, and open-faced sandwiches served without alcohol. Rod mentioned once that it would go better with a beer, but Johnny and Brandy indicated there might be time for that after the business meeting with Ray.

Sally looked toward Justin. "Charlie and I are invited to the meeting?"

Justin smiled. "You are now shareholders in our little real estate company, and we will be discussing the disposal of our assets, so your opinions and votes will be as important as anyone else's."

"That reminds me, Justin." Johnny leaned back in his chair after dabbing at his mouth with a napkin. "You offered to split your share with Charlie, but I think we can transfer that offer to me. Charlie and I will split my share."

Sally smiled at Charlie.

Justin started to protest but then nodded. "Yes, that makes sense. You both get half a vote if it comes to that." Murmurs of assent from Rod and Brandy followed. Johnny smiled at his son not only because of the proposal but because he could see that Charlie and Sally were getting along well.

When Ray arrived at the hotel, the rest of the group was leaving the restaurant. They walked into Justin's office and took seats that had been transferred from the dining room.

"Sorry we don't have executive leather for you, but we shouldn't be here too long." Justin looked at Ray. "Our main item tonight is to finalize plans for the shipment on Wednesday. I called our agent in Frisco, told her about the analyst we hired and to expect delivery on Thursday. The second item is to confirm the redistribution of shares occasioned by the passing of Emma Dodson. Before we begin, I would like to have a moment of silence in her memory."

Everyone bowed their heads for fifteen seconds, then Justin asked, "Are there any other things on the agenda for this evening?"

Everyone looked at Ray. He wasn't at the dinner, and if anything new was forthcoming, it would probably originate with him. They were not disappointed.

"I assume Miss Dodson will be buried here in Sagebrush. Do we know when the funeral service will be?" Ray asked in a low, mild voice, absent the typical gruffness and volume.

Justin answered. "Emma has been transported to Alturas for medical examination. She will be returned here for services when the exam is completed."

Sally kept her head down and Charlie reached out to hold her hand.

"Exam, what kind of an exam?" asked Ray. "Do you mean an autopsy? Why?"

"You're asking the wrong person, Ray. Dr. Willoughby requested one. In his judgement he might have thought the reason for her passing was not clear and he wanted to determine if there was an underlying condition."

Ray sat back and softly said, "Oh." Brandy stared at him, but he had his head down and didn't notice.

Justin took charge and wrote on a legal pad as he asked questions and confirmed commitments. "Ray, we're using your hardware van, the closed panel one, right?"

"Yes. It will be clean and I'll have tarps to cover our stuff."

"Rod and Charlie, you'll be in the van with Ray, right?"

"Right" from Charlie and "Yep" from Rod.

"Brandy and Johnny, you'll be following along, keeping some distance, but as a backup if needed?"

Ray interrupted. "Needed? For what? The van is in great shape and we'll make good time there and back. We probably won't even see them until we return." He spoke with a sneer, not aware that Charlie had a newly discovered relationship with Johnny.

Justin knew a bigger issue with Ray was yet to come. "I suggest we begin loading the van off the back dock at eight. It won't be dark yet, but there should be little activity on the street, and most of the hotel guests will have eaten and be out of the way. We will bring the bars up like we placed them, two at a time in gunny sacks. Our transfer crew will be myself in the inner chamber, Charlie and Johnny on the stairs and dock, and Brandy in the van with Rod to stack them neatly. They need to be secure and not roll around. We'll layer them across the floor, place a tarp over the layer, and repeat the process until we have all aboard. I figure we can have everything ready to go before nine. Be ready to travel immediately after. Does that sound right?"

"Right again," said Johnny. "I also have a job for Sally." Everyone turned to look at him as he glanced at her. "She can stand at the end of the alley and give us a signal if anyone is wandering by."

"I can do that. I want to earn my share."

Ray glowered but kept his mouth shut.

"Ray, select a few light hardware items to place on the top tarp in case someone gets curious about what you're hauling. I'll have travel money for all of you for lodging, meals, and gas. When you're finished with the delivery and get a signed receipt from Wei Li Chan, you can drive back right away. At that point, our assayist will take over and be responsible for the shipment processing."

"How do we know we can trust him?" asked Ray.

"Because I recommended him," answered Rod.

"And because I met him. He has professional credentials and good references from others in Reno," said Justin. Ray shrugged, conceding the point. "If that is settled, then we have one other minor task to complete." Justin stood, opened his desk drawer, and withdrew several copies of an official-looking document. Everyone but Sally and Charlie recognized the latest version of the tontine agreement. Justin passed a copy to each person.

"This is for your visual inspection. I had hoped to have them signed tonight and notarized on Monday, but a small change was made tonight over dinner. Ray, it has been suggested that Sally receive Emma's full share of the proceeds. It turns out she is Emma's sole legal heir to her property. I was asked at dinner tonight to transfer Charlie's share, the one I was going to split with him, to Johnny." He looked at Johnny. "Should I tell him?"

Johnny waved him off. "I'll tell him. Ray, it turns out Charlie is actually my son, so I will split my share with him. The total number of shares will stand at six, just as before."

Ray looked first at Johnny and then at Charlie. "I guess congratulations are in order, or consolations, depending on your point of view. At least that explains the boy's inclusion."

"If we all agree, I'll have the changes added to the document. This should be our final edition of the treasure trove tontine agreement if everything goes well this week."

Everyone but Ray gave the document a cursory glance and returned it to Justin. Ray took longer and they could see he was struggling with the urge to say something about Sally's share. He gave a low grunt and passed the paper back to Justin. The time was 6:45 and there didn't seem to be any reason to meet longer.

Rod looked at Brandy and Johnny, indicating the Saturday-night expectation of a few rounds down the street. No poker game was scheduled. Justin wanted to get home, and Sally and Charlie walked out of the office together, not sure what, if anything, they were going to do. Brandy recognized their plight and turned to Johnny.

"Should we invite them to go with us? They can't drink what we're having, but they can be with us, and I think Sally could still use some company."

Johnny looked at Charlie looking at Sally. "Sure she doesn't have the company she needs?"

"They can always say no, but I think we should ask."

Rod was standing next to them, and he nodded.

Johnny shrugged. "Okay, Miss Matchmaker, invite away."

As Johnny and Rod started for the door, Brandy approached the two young ones and asked them if they'd like to tag along. Sally hesitated, looking at Charlie.

An expression of enthusiasm poured from Johnny's boy. With a wide grin, he turned to Sally and said, "Yeah, that'd be great. Let's go. We're part of the enterprise, the real estate company. I bet they have pool or darts or some other games there."

She smiled and they followed Brandy out the door, a few steps behind Rod and Johnny.

A BLOCK AWAY, A MAN IN A DARK SHIRT WATCHED THE FIVE leave the hotel from a car parked down the street. He noted the newest members of their group and waited until they were a block away before starting his car. They entered the Rattlesnake Junction Tavern.

The man pulled his car to the curb, a block away. Comfortable in the front seat with a bottle of gin, he slouched down, almost out of sight. He reasoned it would be dark by the time they emerged from the bar, and they would be too distracted to notice him or his car. Unlike the last time when he waited in the park, he wouldn't leave until he saw them return to the hotel. He knew what was about to happen, but he hadn't been alerted about the desk clerk and hotel waitress. What did they have to do with it? He needed to talk with his associate.

———— ◆ ◆ ————

Justin wasted no time in seeking the help of the county sheriff, a former school colleague and current friend. After Mass on Sunday, Justin called Jeff Courtney in Alturas. He was at home and off duty but answered the call and listened carefully to Justin, whom he still called by his school days nickname, Just-Go.

Justin apprised him of the death of Emma Dodson, a teacher Jeff remembered from growing up in Sagebrush. There was no mention of the tontine or a connection to anyone specific, but Justin told him what the doctor said about her general good health, recent dinner with a group at the hotel, and her physical appearance when Sally found her on Saturday morning.

"Well, Just-Go, she was seventy-six. Not really ancient, but things like heart attacks happen even in much younger people."

"I know, Jeff, but I have reason to suspect possible foul play. I can't give you any more than that, but an autopsy has been requested, and Emma is now in Alturas awaiting examination by the coroner."

"What would you like me to do, Justin?"

"Seal off her house and inspect it thoroughly, especially the bathroom, kitchen, and her food supplies. I don't know what you might find or even be looking for, but get someone down here who can investigate, take samples, and get them to the right people. Can you do that?"

"Um, that's a tall order for our quiet spot on the plains. We don't have any specialists here. Our routine investigations usually concern DUIs, bar fights, and someone firing a gun in the wrong place. Murder investigations are usually handled by the state, but I do have a new hire, a young woman out of college on her first law enforcement job. Maria Elena Santiago has a fresh face and a sharp mind. I think this is the sort of thing she'd be interested in, but she doesn't have a whole lot of experience. Suppose I send her to you? Can you help her in poking around Emma's place? I'd come down myself, but I have a couple of court dates coming up."

"That would be great, Jeff. Thanks a bunch. I hope this doesn't come to anything, but I want to make sure that nothing at her house changes or disappears before we get the autopsy report. When can she arrive?"

"I'll put Maria on special assignment and have her there this evening. Be good to her, Justin. She may be one of my brighter rising stars."

"No problem. I take it there will be a place to send any suspicious samples?"

"Yep, they go to the labs in Sacramento. They've got the equipment and expertise to ferret out anything unusual."

"Thanks again, Jeff. I owe you a big one."

"Yeah, maybe dinner and a room when I'm off duty, Mr. Hotel Businessman."

"You got it." Justin hung up and decided to take a ride out to Emma's to make sure the doors were locked. At the last minute, he asked Sally to go with him. She still had clothes and personal belongings in the house and would be a better judge of anything that looked rearranged or missing.

They returned at four o'clock, Sally with extra clothes, toiletries, and files of legal papers, including Emma's last will and testament. At six o'clock, Maria arrived at the hotel. Justin invited her to eat in the dining room and brought her up to date on Emma, her last days, and the relationship between her, Sally, and some of the other people in Sagebrush. Ray was not mentioned.

Maria rode out with Justin to the house and searched the rooms for anything unusual. She had a number of plastic bags with her. She asked Justin what kinds of things Emma usually ate or drank. He pointed out some vegetables and fruits and remarked that tea was her favorite beverage, hot or iced.

One of the tea jars, containing ground loose leaf, sat prominently on the shelf. The lid was loose and bits of leaf were scattered around the jar. Maria opened it, sniffed, and frowned. "She must have been into some strong or exotic herbal teas. I like them myself, but I've never smelled one like this." She looked at it closer, tumbling the grounded tea and noticed a few larger clumps. "I'll take a sample of this." She poured several grams into a plastic bag, sealed, and labelled it.

She also sampled some of the fruit and vegetables. As Justin watched, she asked, "Are you suspicious that she might have been poisoned?"

"I'm not sure what I think, to tell you the truth. Her death was unexpected. Her heart had not been an issue, and she and her niece were partners in a substantial business deal that was about to be concluded."

"And her niece was here at the time of her death?"

"Yes, as I told you at dinner, Sally is the one who called the doctor. They were very close, the nearest relative each had. Sally has grandparents in Alturas."

"I will need to talk to Sally before I leave tomorrow."

"No problem. She is staying at the hotel, in room 17."

"I'll send the samples to the lab later tomorrow and hopefully have a report by the end of the week."

After another walk-through, they got into Maria's car and drove back into Sagebrush, parking alongside the hotel. Their arrival in the lobby was witnessed by a man in a dark shirt, eating in the dining room.

Maria interviewed Sally for more than an hour that evening in Sally's room. Maria took a room on the second floor for the night and left after breakfast on Monday morning.

Sally indicated to Charlie, and later to Brandy, that the questions had been thorough, focusing on what Emma had done Thursday and Friday. Maria had taken down the names of everyone Emma had been around for the past several days. Sally didn't believe anyone had been to the house after Charlie visited on Thursday.

———— ◆ ————

ON MONDAY, JUSTIN DREW UP THE NEW TONTINE DOCUMENTS and had each sign their copy. They were notarized at the bank, and he returned a copy to each, keeping one for the hotel safe. Justin, Ray, and Johnny went to the bank and removed the master lock key from the deposit box. Justin retained it for use on Wednesday evening. Ray provided several extra gunny sacks for carrying the gold bars out of the hotel cellar.

Johnny didn't see a lot of Charlie. When he wasn't working, he was usually somewhere with Sally. The two had become almost inseparable in the evenings. Charlie had a small flat above an insurance company office down the street from the hotel. He had been offered a room but decided he wanted some space between living and working. As far as Johnny and Brandy knew, Sally was in her room at night, but they couldn't be sure and didn't want to know if she wasn't. Johnny had to keep telling himself that his new son wasn't a kid and neither was Sally.

Sally broached the subject of the assets and payoff. Although Charlie had been vague about his plans, she decided that he needed her help if he was going to break away from the high desert town. He was bright, decent, and deserved better than spending a lot of additional years as a hotel clerk. They started meeting for dinner at the other cafe in town, sometimes driving to Alturas or other spots that were an hour or more distant. They split expenses for food and gas. They joked about where they might sleep, her place or his, but both knew it was not a serious inquiry. Tuesday evening, they were sitting in her car, parked two miles out of town.

"Charlie, in about a month, I am going to have a full share, my aunt's portion, of the trove. It will be a substantial amount, enough to get me to school, to travel, to start a life." She gave him time to mull it over. "How much will your part of Johnny's share come to?"

"We haven't talked about it. I didn't know how much Mr. Gonzales was going to give me."

"Do you think it will be half?"

He frowned and turned his head. "I don't know, Sally. I guess I could ask. I was surprised I would be getting anything. I mean, I haven't done anything to earn a share."

"Neither have I, at least not yet. You'll be helping get the gold to the buyers. That means traveling with Ray and Rod. Not something I'd look forward to."

"No, I guess not, but my dad and Brandy will be following close behind, so I'm not worried. For all of his sour looks, Rod isn't such a bad guy. He was a lot of fun at the bar Saturday night, remember?"

"Yeah. They are all nice people with the possible exception of Ray Gordon. I've met his brother and his wife several times, and they seem different from him."

"I think they are, but I have seen Jay working only a couple of times. He's big and strong and always friendly to everyone."

"Charlie, think about what you want to do with the money. Maybe we can do it together." He gave her the confused deer-in-the headlight look. "Just a thought, something to keep you awake on the road. We will still have a month to think about it and, if we want, to make some plans of our own."

"Okay. Yeah, I'll give it some thought. Speaking of which, tomorrow's the big day followed by a long night. I should get back to the hotel and get some rest."

She smiled a different kind of grin, semi-predatory, like a cat trying to seduce a songbird. "Sure that's what you need, Charlie?"

He looked at her, considering the possibilities. "I really like you Sally, a lot, but let's wait until I return. As you said, we'll have time. You might not want to be hooked up with someone like me, still not knowing what's what. You have some real ambitions and I'm not sure about anything."

"You will be, Charlie, wait and see." She drove him to his flat and returned to the hotel, satisfied that she had planted the right seeds. Now she had to tend to the garden and watch it grow.

Wednesday morning came dry and hot with a blustery wind that filled the streets with dust and tumbling brush. Brandy, Sally, and Johnny were having breakfast at eight o'clock. As he often did, Rod was sleeping in, having had his full share of liquid enjoyment the evening before.

Brandy was in a teasing mood, laughing and joking with her companions. She said to Sally, "Keeping some late hours are you?" She winked at Johnny, who listened and said as little as possible.

Sally was nonplused, scooping oatmeal as if nothing had been said. "I have the afternoon shift, so I am up earlier than necessary." She looked at Johnny. "Your son is responsible, you know, keeping me out on a working night."

Johnny smiled. "I believe it's your car and you are the driver, right? My son is being led astray by an older woman."

Brandy started to say something about "like father, like son" but caught herself, not knowing what Sally knew or where the sensibilities might lie. Instead, she said, "You two are probably planning something big for when the payoff arrives." She smiled at Sally, "Eloping, running away to Tahiti?"

Sally put her spoon down and reached for her coffee cup. She laughed. "Maybe Nepal, high in the mountains where nobody will find us."

Johnny looked from Sally to Brandy and back to Sally. *I've heard that type of banter before. Is Brandy already giving her lessons on how to handle men?*

Charlie came to work a few minutes before nine o'clock, and Brandy adjourned to her room. It seemed like another routine day in Sagebrush, but it was anything but.

———◆———

AT TEN O'CLOCK THAT MORNING, A MAN IN A DARK SHIRT VIS-ited Ray Gordon at his house. Ray opened the door and said, "Morning. Let's walk."

They took a trail behind the trailer and shop, leaving Barbara and Jay to their work for the day. The men sat down on a bench overlooking a pasture. Ray pulled out a cigar, offered another to Al, and they lit up.

"So what else do you know?" asked Ray, looking straight ahead.

"I know that things are getting busier and more complicated. A *lot* more complicated. It's going to cost you extra than what we agreed to."

"Oh? And how much more would that be and for what reason?"

"Your hotel owner called in the county sheriff. One of the cops, a young woman, went out to the Dodson place and spent over an hour there Sunday night looking around. Unfortunately, that happened before I could get there and finish cleaning up. I was going to do that on Monday. I wasn't counting on an investigation or the law."

"So what? Do you think they're gonna find anything? These are county cops we're talking about, not the FBI. Besides, why would they be snooping around? An autopsy is scheduled for this week, but you assured me there wouldn't be any evidence of anything unusual. We're clear."

"Think so? I don't know if they found anything, but I suspect they took some samples. That might have included her tea."

Ray looked at him for a long moment, his mind racing back to Thursday evening when he sent his associate to enter Emma Dodson's kitchen. The door lock was easy to pick. "Your roots were completely crushed, looking like the tea in her jar. I'd defy anyone to see anything different if you did what you were supposed to do." He puffed angrily on his cigar, daring Al to contradict him.

"I did the job, but the risks have multiplied, especially if you want me to follow through with the rest of your plan. Another two thousand should take care of it."

"Make sure you *do* take care of it. You're being paid from what I expect to be a bigger share of the deal, and that happens only if there are fewer participants. I didn't count on that wisp of a girl assuming her aunt's full share."

"We've got time. You told me the payouts won't happen right away. The old lady's will won't be read for a while, so the waitress has nothing yet. Things happen, don't you know."

"Yeah, I know. You going to follow the truck tonight in case there are unplanned distractions?"

"Yeah, I'll follow the two in the other car, staying out of sight. I'll be around somewhere until you make the delivery and drive out of the Bay Area. You'll see me again next weekend."

"Not during the day, not again. My wife and brother think you are one of my farm customers and no one else knows anything. I assume your stay at the hotel hasn't attracted attention?"

"We're good to go. I eat in the dining room and sometimes walk around town, but no one has any reason to think I have an interest in your little club. Just part of the background."

"Time to fade into it then. Wait on the highway going south. We should be showing up sometime between nine and nine-thirty. Wait until Brandy's car passes and pull out only after they're out of sight. There's not much on the highway between here and Susanville. From there, we'll cut over to I-5 and it's a straight shot down to I-80 and into San Francisco. By then, stay close, but you'll be hidden in the heavy traffic. Once we pull up to the agent's office in Chinatown, you can leave or do whatever you want."

"Okay. See you in a few days. I'll start keeping tabs on Mr. Gonzales and his waitress."

Still smoking their cigars, the men walked back to the shop by the road. Al drove away, satisfied that there was no resistance to his demand for additional payment.

⸻ ◆ ⸻

As usual, Ray ate at home on Wednesday evening, informing his family that he needed to be gone overnight, to transport some furniture for the hotel. Jay asked if he needed help, but Ray assured him he had plenty, including Justin's desk clerk.

It was an early, sober dinner at the hotel for the four travelers and for Justin and Sally. Sally kept looking at Charlie, giving him an occasional smile of reassurance. It wasn't so subtle that Brandy and Johnny didn't notice, but they said nothing. There would be time for speculation later that night.

One thing had been decided before dinner. Brandy and Johnny planned to share a room when they stopped for the night, somewhere on California Highway 36. That would leave Charlie with Rod and Ray, but Brandy suggested he join her and Johnny. The men could share a bed, and she would have her own—a provocative presence but only that.

Johnny was amused. "Couldn't we pretend like we were Mommy and Daddy, sharing a bed like always?"

"We ain't Mum and Daddy, are we? Besides, Charlie is already on a fast learning curve, if I know Sally, and he doesn't need any shortcuts to the Promised Land courtesy of you and me."

"Good, because that's one thing I'm not sure I could provide instructions on."

She didn't answer, but her eyes told him what he wanted to hear.

A few minutes before eight, Ray walked in the door. The group was gathering in the lobby and made their way to the back of the hotel. Justin descended the stairs with the master key to open the inner sanctuary. Ray had his truck along the back dock, and everyone stationed themselves as decided. Sally waited around the corner of the alley.

Loading the truck went smoothly, and they were ready to roll by quarter of nine. Justin handed out money for travel expenses. Charlie and Johnny conferred for a few minutes, and Charlie said goodbye to Sally.

Sally said, "Good luck, Charlie. I'll see you tomorrow. We can continue our discussion then."

"Your place or mine?" he said, with a conspiratorial grin.

"You're learning fast, aren't you? Take care of yourself." She hit him lightly on the upper arm, turned and walked into the hotel.

Ray slipped in behind the wheel, Charlie climbed in beside him, and Rod got in and closed the door. They waved to the others. As the van pulled out of the alley, Johnny and Brandy walked to the front of the hotel and got into her car. He took the first shift of driving and she lay back in the passenger seat with a satisfied smile.

"What are you so pleased about?" he asked, looking at her as he started the car and eased down the street, following the taillights on the dark road out of town.

"Life in general, Johnny-O. Finally something is happening and, guess what? We're going to be in the chips after all of these years. Hard to believe."

"It has been a while. A lot of water under the bridge." He looked over at her again. "For both of us. I assume you'll be leaving town again after the payoff."

Since he hadn't posed it as a question, she didn't answer right away. He knew she was looking at him but he kept his eyes on the road, keeping pace with the van and watching for coyotes, rabbits, and stray livestock. The road was paved but needed repairs, and the occasional large pothole was to be avoided. He heard Brandy take in a long slow breath.

"What is with us, Johnny? We've known each other for more than twenty years. We've been together, and we've gone our separate ways. We've had some great times and a few that weren't so great. Yet, here we are again. What now? What happens when we receive our money? Hit the road and say goodbye? What about your son? Does he change anything for you?"

A quick glance at the brunette before he answered. "Charlie does change some things. Of course, he is on his own or will be soon. If he wasn't in the picture, there wouldn't be any reason for me to stay in Sagebrush. I'd be heading out for somewhere again, but the last ten years *have been* different. I missed you, Brandy. Not just the wicked card games and the few nights we spent together. You intrigued me from the start. I don't know why I haven't pursued you. Shyness was never one of my attributes."

"There you go with the big words again. You been studying in your spare time?" She meant it as a joke and didn't expect his answer.

"I took some courses at a junior college in Mobile. I was there for almost three years, bumming along the Gulf between Florida and New Orleans. Had some odd jobs, building houses, industrial construction, even a turn or two for a gas drilling company onshore in Lafayette, but there was time to read and to attend classes. It seems I had a hankering for literature and even some writing. My instructors, a couple of them real sweet things, liked my creative efforts and told me I should pursue it."

Brandy sat up in her seat, put her knees up, and hugged them. "You? A writer? I can see the reading part, something to fill those long, lonely nights without me, but writing? Johnny, I would love to see what you've written. Do you have anything with you?"

"Nope. I travelled light, just a few clothes, I have a small storage shed in Austin where I spent part of the last year. My other belongings, including books and papers, are there."

The taillights lit up, and the van stopped, signaled, and turned right onto US 395, south toward Susanville. A minute later, Johnny did the same, and the road, with much better pavement, stretched out ahead. They would make good time, the weather was clear, and the traffic, except for the occasional semi, was light. The California Highway Patrol on this stretch rarely stopped anyone unless the driver was erratic or grossly exceeding the speed limit.

Johnny's revelation triggered something in Brandy. He could tell that her interest had taken a different tack as if he was a new man. Maybe he was. A father making first stabs at receiving a post-high school education. Something to think about during the long night ahead. While they were waiting for the money, what to do? Johnny's cash wouldn't last the month. Brandy had indicated she might pick up some bartending work around town, but she seemed to have adequate funds from her time in Vegas. She didn't want to resume her duties at the hotel.

She told Johnny she was paying for her room in Sagebrush. When he mentioned that he only had enough money for a few more days lodging and food, she offered to share her room with him.

"A kept man, huh? No one's kept me since my days with Sonya and I paid half of the expenses."

"You need someone to keep you, Johnny. You just won't admit it."

"And what about you? Have you reached for and gotten what you want?"

She looked at him as if intrigued by his question. "Maybe. Why are you asking?"

"Been thinking about what you were doing the past ten years, that's all. You never told me how it went. Obviously, you didn't do bad—your car and extra money tell me you did better than I did. What happened? Did you work in management or did you mostly just play big-time cards?"

"I had a job for about two years at one of the bigger clubs on the Strip, but I wasn't allowed to play anywhere in town. I was in the middle management set, some responsibilities, decent pay, but I wasn't going anywhere. You had to know the right people to climb higher. They call it being affiliated. I wasn't and wasn't willing to sleep with or marry the right people to achieve status."

He gave her a double take and a grin. "Married? You would have to marry some jerk in order to be promoted?"

"No. A ready, steady consort would be acceptable to some of them, but it was anything but a permanent position. Occupation by how the mood strikes them. I found it easier to hustle drinks now and then at the better nightclubs, nice tips for a smile and a wiggle. The best job was the familiar rituals and action at the table. Many of the old timers couldn't believe that a woman could outmaneuver them. Not always, of course. I lost my share of pots and there were occasional stretches when I didn't eat or sleep as grandly as I wanted to. You know how that goes."

"Yes, I do. Yes, I did." He stared straight ahead, following the distant taillight across the Madeline Plains desert. *She didn't mention any other men, guys who kept her company during those occasional stretches. I have no reason to think she was chaste or didn't have some companionship. I certainly had mine. Like she said, what are we doing? Where are we going? A lot to think about over the next few weeks.*

As she drifted off to sleep, he thought about trying to understand the new rules of engagement. *Maybe, just maybe, but I still need to earn my way. Is that what I want to do? Is she inviting me to be with her? What does that mean? Live together, travel together?*

Marriage, a family? It seemed ironic that things appeared to be headed toward a domestic relationship at the same time he was acquiring the funds to live as independently as he wished.

Brandy aroused as they passed through Susanville and then took over on their way to the Sacramento Valley. Johnny apologized for not keeping her company and awake and then crawled into the back seat and slept until they arrived in Chester at a lakeside motel off Highway 36. Rod was checking in at the office when Brandy pulled in alongside the van.

Johnny woke up, stretched and asked where they were. He went to the office, registered against his better judgment, and found Charlie waiting beside the room that Rod and Ray would share. They made arrangements to be up for breakfast at six o'clock. They were still several hours from their destination and wanted to arrive before noon. Brandy joined Johnny and his son. She had brought a modest nightshirt to sleep in. At first, Charlie was confused about which bed he was to sleep in, but Brandy smiled at him and said neither bed was big enough for the three of them. Charlie was mostly asleep by the time he and his dad hit the sack.

Johnny and Brandy had snoozed in the car. Both stayed awake for some time to mentally replay the past few hours and the conversational teases that had been offered.

⁃◆⁃

IT WAS OBVIOUS AT BREAKFAST THAT HARSH WORDS HAD PASSED between Rod and Ray. Neither looked at the other during the meal.

Outside, Johnny asked his friend what happened and Rod told him that Ray had spent the first half hour in the room grousing about the arrangements, Charlie's presence, Brandy and Johnny following in the car, and Sally's prominence in the group. Rod didn't say much, but he let Ray know he wasn't talking to sympathetic ears.

"Do you want me to ride with you instead of Charlie? He can go with Brandy, but I'm not sure about his driving skills, especially in Bay Area traffic," Johnny said.

"No, he'll be okay. Ray hasn't said anything to him or in front of him. I think even he knows better than to mess with your son, and Charlie might just keep him and me from tearing each other's throats out. Don't want to do that until we deliver the goods." Rod smiled. "We'll get by, until the job is done. Too much riding on it." He glanced at Brandy, who was coming out of the motel room with her small suitcase. "Comfy little family, huh?"

Johnny shrugged and they walked to their respective vehicles to hit the highway west.

The day was uneventful. Getting on I-5, the traffic increased steadily as they made their way to I-80. They arrived in San Francisco at eleven o'clock, hungry and tired. Neither Brandy nor Johnny liked big city driving and San Francisco could be one of the worst—crowded and chaotic.

They followed the van to the Chinatown address. With the help of several people from the warehouse, they had the gold unloaded at an inside dock within twenty minutes. Wei Li Chan was an older woman, sixty or more, but sharp as a whip. She had papers ready to sign and needed only the actual weight and bar count to be filled in. They delivered ninety-five bars, keeping one back at the hotel for possible interim expenses. The bars were weighed in the presence of Thomas Crenshaw, the Reno analyst Justin hired. He examined and tested the scales and watched as each bar was weighed. It only took a few minutes, and he provided a written marker to Wei Li, who included the numbers on their receipt. The five treasure trove transporters enjoyed a cool drink while they waited.

Handing the slip to Ray, Wei Li smiled and wished them good fortune. She had received the retainer fee from Justin by wire and indicated that smelting and purification would occur over the next few days, in Crenshaw's presence. In answer to Ray's inquiry, she confirmed that the final settlement, made out to the real estate investment company in Sagebrush, would be forthcoming within thirty days.

They left Charlie with Rod and Ray, if only to prevent bloodshed on the way back. The five departed the Bay Area and returned to

Sagebrush, arriving late that evening. Rod drove the van most of the way back and was beat, so he headed for his room as soon as they reached the hotel.

Brandy and Johnny had covered a variety of topics during their return, such as how exciting Frisco could be for a tourist, the scenery of northern California, especially in the Sierras, and the contrast with Sagebrush. They didn't discuss the previous night's conversation, leaving it for the days ahead. He talked about getting some work during the next month, possibly on one of the outlying farms. Brandy looked on with an amused smile, biding her time.

Charlie and Sally got together for dinner, and he told her about the trip, sleeping in the same room with his dad and Brandy, and the visit to San Francisco, his first to the City by the Bay. It was also the first time he had ever experienced bumper-to-bumper traffic and the throngs of people that seemed to come out of nowhere.

"I didn't realize you could pack that many people in such a small space," he said.

Sally nodded. She had been out in the world farther and more often than her innocent companion, but she appreciated the impact of discovering the urban landscape for the first time. She hoped to lead him to other amazing discoveries in time.

CHAPTER TWELVE

Accusations and Consequences

The autopsy report came to Dr. Willoughby on Friday morning, July 29. He called Justin and told him that Emma Dodson didn't die from a simple heart attack. Although there was evidence of ventricular defibrillation, something had affected her gastrointestinal tract in a severe way. Chemical blood analysis revealed large amounts of lactic acid and other signs pointed to severe convulsions or seizures along with neurological damage. The report couldn't be conclusive without further studies. Samples of her blood and tissues were being sent to Sacramento, but the initial summary mentioned food poisoning or ingestion of some toxic substance as a possible contributor to her death.

"You must have suspected something, Justin. What gives?"

"Don't know yet, Ben. It may be only coincidental, but we shouldn't take any chances." He told the physician about the county sheriff's visit and samples sent to Sacramento. "We'll see what the labs come up with."

"Do you think her niece had anything to do with this?"

"No, I think that's highly unlikely. Although she benefits from Emma's will, they seemed close and she has worked for me for almost a year. I have every reason to believe she is of good character and her distress over her aunt's death is genuine."

"Will you be getting a copy of the sheriff's lab reports?" asked Willoughby.

"Yes. Let me know when you get the autopsy blood reports. We'll exchange information."

"Take care, Justin. We don't need any more mysterious deaths in our little corner of the world."

"Amen to that. Thanks for your help."

Justin hung up, vindicated but more concerned than ever. Something unusual had happened at the Dodson house less than a week ago and it cast a deep shadow over everything else. If it was a poison, what type and how did it happen? No one was calling it homicide, not yet, but Justin was ninety percent certain it wasn't an accident.

It was eight-thirty in the morning. Justin had eaten and left, Sally was serving breakfast in the dining room, and Charlie sat at a table by himself. Although he had a small kitchenette in his flat and sometimes ate cereal or scrambled a couple eggs, he had started eating regularly at the hotel as he and Sally forged their friendship. A few other customers came and went, but Charlie lingered over his coffee until time to report at the front desk. She kept up a steady banter as she served him and others, making sure his cup was filled and that he had got all he wanted to eat. There was no meal charges for him, and the flirtatious smiles of an attractive waitress were provided as a bonus.

Justin walked out of the lobby and into the hallway to knock on Johnny's door. As he anticipated, Johnny was awake but not up. Justin was relieved to find him alone. He entered, grabbed a chair, and sat beside the bed to relate what the physician had reported. "We won't know anything more until the other lab reports come back."

"Then what? Suppose they do come up with something suspicious, something toxic?" Johnny sat on the edge of the bed, clad only in boxer briefs.

A short knock on the closed door, and it opened, revealing Rod, also wearing boxers and a ragged T-shirt. He walked in, closed the door, and sat on the edge of the bed. "What's up guys?"

As Justin repeated the information to Rod, there was another knock. Brandy walked in, barefooted but wearing a simple housecoat. She looked at Rod and Johnny, smiled and said to Justin, "Aren't you a bit overdressed for the occasion?" She noticed there was no place else to sit, and Rod started to get up, but she motioned him to stay and leaned against the door, her hands behind her back.

For the third time, Justin told what he knew.

Brandy was thinking hard, trying to recall what she had seen when she was with Sally on Saturday. All of them had been with Emma on Thursday evening at dinner and Emma entertained Sally and Charlie later that night when Rod, Johnny, and she partied at the bar. Whatever caused Emma's sudden demise must have occurred very recently, she stated. The others agreed.

"What about her niece? asked Rod in a quiet voice as if reluctant to raise the possibility. "She had the most to gain, being the old lady's only heir. Sally knew that a full share would be enough to get her out of Sagebrush and to anywhere she wanted. As far as we know, the girl was the last one to see Emma alive. If the autopsy report is correct, it seems she should have heard something Friday night or early on Saturday. Doesn't sound like the woman died peacefully in her sleep."

They sat and stood, considering Rod's words but not wanting to accuse or even suggest that Sally was responsible.

Brandy spoke up. "I agree it is a possibility, for both of the reasons you gave, but I have dealt with a lot of bluffers and downright liars in my life. If Sally was faking her distress that day, she is every bit a pro. If so, she had me fooled. We may know more if something shows up in the samples they took. Until then, we can't do much anyway." She looked at Johnny. "Do you think Charlie might know something and if he did, would he tell you?"

Johnny glanced at Rod and Justin and then back at Brandy. "He hasn't said anything. I don't know what he would tell me. I don't know how involved he and Sally have become. I feel good about him, but remember, we've known each other for a only a week. Not near long enough to be confidantes."

Justin stood up. "Jeff, the sheriff, will let me know when his office hears something. For now, we should relax. I should be getting a report back from Crenshaw on what the purity of our trove came to and the final value of the payoff to our investment company. Then we can decide when and how to disburse each share. I suggest that each of us decide how to claim the money. We will retain an informal holding company and the funds can be drawn as a lump sum or gradually over the years. It will be invested so that the amount should appreciate over time. However you want to receive it, I suggest you set up a bank account, here or somewhere else, for the money to be wired to."

"I suggest that some of us get dressed if our host and the lady will permit." Johnny stood and bowed politely to Justin and Brandy. She grinned, turned, and walked out the door, followed by Justin.

Rod looked at Johnny. "I mentioned Sally, I know, but I believe the same thing as our poker-playing gal. You know who I suspect. I just don't know what or how."

"Let's continue to be alert, buddy. Maybe we'll know more in a few days." Johnny frowned and rubbed his chin. "Speaking of being alert, there's a guy staying here in the hotel, almost always wearing a black or dark shirt. Seen him a few times in the dining room, several times around town. He drives a gray Oldsmobile. I happened to be at the other end of town yesterday, and he paid a visit to Ray. Do you know who he is?"

"I know the one you mean. I checked the register to scan names but couldn't match him up. I'll ask Charlie what room he's staying in and get a name. I'll nose around and see what I can find out."

They agreed to meet later for lunch, and Rod left to get dressed.

Although Brandy didn't know Barbara Gordon well, they had been cordial over the years. Barbara had her own circle of friends in town, one that had little to no overlap with Brandy or her hotel gang, but Brandy had an ace up her sleeve. Ken, the loquacious barber and frequent poker player, had a wife who was friends with Barbara.

Justin and the boys decided to have another game on Saturday night, and Brandy said she would drop by Ken's shop and give him a personal invitation. She would use the occasion to ask about Ken's wife, Rita, and see if she would like to have lunch, perhaps inviting Barbara to join them. Although Brandy was not Barbara's cup of tea, they had all aged and time had passed. Whatever reputation the brunette had with the more stalwart and upright women of the town ten and twenty years ago, it should have mellowed. It was worth a try.

Ken was delighted there would be another game. Not for the first time he asked how long the "out-of-towners," meaning Rod, Johnny, and her, would be around. She shrugged it off, had him shape her short cut, and casually asked if he thought his wife would be interested in lunch or tea. Ken looked at her, not expecting the question. He picked up the phone, dialed home, repeated the question to Rita, and gave Brandy the phone.

"How are you, Mrs. Williamson? Yes, I'll call you Rita. Ken is trimming my hair, and it occurred to me that in all of these years we've never had lunch or even tea together. Yes? Would today be okay? Great! Do you think Barbara Gordon would like to join us? Another person I don't know as well as I should. Oh will you? Your place? In about an hour? Perfect, I'll look forward to seeing both of you." She hung up and Ken, amazed at the conversation, put the telephone back on the counter. She teased him about the upcoming game, as she did all the men, and Ken felt that things had returned to normal. He couldn't wait to hear what Rita would say that evening.

Rod had a chat with Charlie before Johnny and he went to lunch. Charlie was never sure what to make of the gruff, balding man. He knew that he was an old friend of his dad's and had played poker at the hotel forever. He was confident that Rod was on their side, whatever that meant, and that from the comments and joking around, there was an undisclosed relationship between him, Brandy, and his dad.

Rod tried to be nonchalant, to the extent that it was possible for him to be casual about anything, when he approached the clerk in the lobby. Charlie was on his hands and knees cleaning an old-fashioned radiator that had been left in place as an antique display. Working or not, it gathered dust and benefited from some metal polish.

"How's it going, Charlie boy? Recovered from our trip to the big city?"

Charlie smiled and nodded. "I wish we could have spent more time there. There's a lot to see."

"Indeed there is. You'll get your chance soon, if I'm not completely off base. I have a question I hope you can help me with."

Charlie stood and dropped the cleaning rag on the radiator. "Sure, Rod. What do you need?"

"There is a man staying here at the hotel—has glasses and a thin mustache, usually wears a dark shirt. He came in the same day I did, and I see him around here and there. Can you tell me what room he's in and his name?"

Charlie laughed. "Another one who didn't sign the register. He pays cash every other day, and I don't know much about him, except he goes by Al. Didn't give me a last name and he's by himself as far as I know."

"Room?"

"Upstairs in 216, two doors down from where you guys play cards. Justin told me to never book anyone in the room next door on a Friday or Saturday night."

Rod smiled. Charlie the once-shy desk clerk, was now on a first-name basis with everyone. *Was it the drinking at dinner, the barroom ventures, or the trip to Frisco that sparked his sudden entry into collegial adulthood? No, probably the subtle swing of a certain waitress.* "Thanks, Charlie. Your dad and I were wondering about our fellow guest. I owe you a beer sometime."

Charlie gave a short laugh and bent down to finish his task.

Rod walked back to his room. A few minutes later, he and Johnny were walking down the street, trying to decide where and what to eat.

"Since we're having a game tomorrow night, it might be a nice idea for some of us to head off for a good meal and some carousing tonight, being Friday and all," Johnny said.

Rod accidentally dropped his cigarette. As he stooped to pick it up, he glanced back down the street and noticed the man in the dark shirt stepping out of the hotel. The man looked the other way and walked away from them. Rod straightened up, took a drag. "Yeah, that'd be nice. Um, Johnny, don't look back, but our mystery man just stepped into the street. Let's see if he follows us."

Rod told Johnny what Charlie had said as they continued walking. At the Pioneer Barroom, they turned and entered, taking a small table near a window where they could see the street. They ordered a beer and a couple burgers. A few minutes later, Al came strolling down the opposite side of the street, carefully examining a storefront across from them but avoiding a direct look at the bar. As he walked out of sight, Rod and Johnny studied his gait and his physical appearance.

"Might see Al again on a dark night or in a dark room some time," said Johnny.

"I might be doing some of the following myself," answered Rod as the beers arrived.

"If your observation is right, there seems to be a relationship between him and Ray. Do you think there's any connection to Emma?"

Johnny took a slow sip. "I can ask Sally if the man has ever been to their house. She will know who I'm talking about, because he often eats breakfast at the hotel. I mean, it's not like the place is overrun with tourists and he's easy to lose in the crowd. The black shirt alone provides a description."

"Yeah, Charlie came across with what he knew right away. I wonder if he'll say anything to Sally?"

"What do you think of those two, Rod? It's been way too long since I was that young, so I'm not sure how to gauge what's going on."

"You were never that young, Johnny boy. You went directly from your mama's arms to being a roustabout and no-good son of a bitch, if you don't mind me saying."

"Talk's cheap, buddy, but we better figure out what's going on with our mechanic friend, whether it involves this dark-shirt guy, and who might be in danger next. I see Sally as a prime target. Ray didn't do much to hide his disappointment that she will have Emma's share. By the way, Justin hopes to find out when Emma's will is officially validated and Sally can claim her portion."

"We might want to have a talk with her, depending on what the labs say, if anything. She might not realize what is going on. Does she or Charlie know about the Woodward accident?"

"Don't know. Brandy has been talking to her but probably has said nothing that would put her in a black mood. She seems to be recovering okay from her aunt's death and realizes that there are some complications with the so-called investment company, but I think Brandy is trying to shelter her from the storm until it's necessary."

"The storm's coming," Rod said, "sooner than we want. I hope we're ready."

Johnny left the table, stuck his head out the front door of the tavern, and returned to the table as Rod finished the last of his burger and most of Johnny's fries.

"See him?"

"Nope, street was mostly empty."

They finished another beer and left the bar about one o'clock after deciding they would venture to Alturas for dinner with Brandy and the kids. Johnny mentioned an Italian restaurant on the main street that had looked promising. They would invite Justin and his wife but doubted they would accept.

Back at the hotel, Johnny left a note for Brandy about dinner, and he invited Charlie and Sally. They knew that Saturday would be reserved for another card game, and they would have time alone then, so both eagerly accepted. As anticipated, Justin politely declined and wished them a good trip.

Brandy came back at four o'clock, read the note, and found Rod and Johnny in a small sitting room off of the lobby. It wasn't used often, but it had comfortable chairs and was more pleasant than their individual rooms. They were in a good mood, drinking root beer floats, like it was another day of vacation at a resort.

"Sally fixed us up," said Rod, sporting a white mustache of foam like those formed from beer on other occasions.

"I see that." She sat across the room from them. "Should I close the door?"

Johnny glanced at the opening into the hallway and lobby. "Nah, let it be. We'll talk later in the car. The kids will join us, but they're going to take Sally's car in case we decide to get reckless and carouse all night."

Brandy displayed her customary smile and eye flash. "With you two, anything's possible. Smart kids."

"That reminds me." Johnny leaned forward in his seat and kept his voice low. "Without saying anything specific," he glanced at the door, "have you talked to Sally about some of our previous concerns, you know, about Steve and Donna?"

"No, I haven't. She knows there is tension between us and Ray but not why, other than his general belligerence and demands for a bigger share of the proceedings. Why? Should I tell her?"

"Not for now. It may still turn out that her aunt died of natural causes. Rod and I agree that we need to keep a careful eye on her. She might be the most vulnerable of our group."

Brandy said, "Well boys, guess where I've been today."

Johnny replied. "I can see you've been to Ken and must have invited him to tomorrow night's game. What else?"

"Had lunch at his wife's house. In addition to Rita, we were joined by Barbara Gordon." She let the words hang, waiting for their collective curiosity. She told them it started out awkward, since she was the outsider, but she quickly warmed up to Rita with small talk and comments about her recent travels. Rita said Ken was always curious about their comings and goings and why they returned to Sagebrush, especially at designated times. "Like a class reunion," was the way Rita had phrased it.

"Barbara was reluctant at first to say much, but it must have been obvious to her that the reunions also involved Ray. Both Ken and Ray were regular members of the poker group, but Barbara knew Ray had a deeper involvement, one that she was not well informed about. It became a game of cautious deception between Barbara and me on what to say and how to say it." Brandy paused and smiled at her demonstrated resourcefulness. "Barbara knew her husband was a partner in a real estate investment that involved the hotel and a number of other people, including me. Rita also knew about the partnership but that Ken was not part of it. A casual remark by Rita about Jay Gordon must have caught Barbara off-guard because she indicated that Jay wasn't as mentally limited as most people thought he was. I was careful not to react, as if I had known it all along.

"After a second glass of wine around, I dropped a few hints about doings around town. By that time, Barbara had relaxed and was talking freely, as if she and I had been friends for some time. She confirmed what others had speculated about. Jay didn't have any disabilities, but his brother wanted to keep him close and it was Ray's idea to spread the word about Jay's supposed mental impairment. Publicly, Barbara went along with it because she didn't dare oppose her husband, and Jay didn't seem to know the extent of his brother's false claims. The ruse resulted in Barbara and Jay maintaining a close relationship. Some of the women in town knew this, but most of the men didn't."

"What else did you find out?" asked Johnny.

"Although Rita was generally well-informed on town gossip, she knew little about the school teacher's recent death. When I indicated that both the county and state were investigating, Barbara told us Ray was very upset about it. 'Her death?' I asked. 'No,' replied Barbara, 'the investigations. He believes it is all nonsense and an overreaction by Justin and some of the others.' Barbara didn't say who the others were, but I mentioned that Emma and Justin were close friends and that Emma was part of the real estate partnership. That was news to both Rita and Barbara. Barbara wouldn't talk any more about it and said she needed to get home and fix supper for "her boys." I stayed a while longer with Rita, chatting about nothing of consequence but cementing a relationship that might prove useful later."

Johnny and Rod would have questions and comments when the three were on the road, but it was not prudent to say more at the moment. The guys finished their floats and returned the glasses and spoons to the kitchen.

Sally was getting off her shift and was looking forward to the night ahead.

FRIDAY NIGHT IN ALTURAS WENT WELL. THE ITALIAN RESTAUrant filled all stomachs, the kids were able to enjoy some wine with the legal adults, and the two-car arrangement turned out to be unnecessary. After a nice dinner, the five returned to Sagebrush.

Neither Johnny nor Rod wanted a three-way party with Brandy, preferring to keep things as they were. They did bring Charlie and Sally in on what they knew and their suspicions. Johnny wasn't sure that it was time, but Brandy and Rod overruled him. Charlie, it turned out, knew about the Woodward deaths but not about Ray's possible involvement. The kids caught on quickly. They mentioned their impressions of Ray and his outbursts during dinner and at group meetings. Charlie confirmed that Rod and Ray were barely communicative during the gold transport.

"Now that the gold is out of the hotel and in someone else's hands, we can finally talk about it without having to worry that someone is going to steal it or cause a major uproar," Brandy said. She sat back in her chair, visibly relaxed. Rod had driven to Alturas, and Johnny volunteered to drive back, so she felt like the privileged princess, to be worshipped and served.

"Some caution is still in order," said Johnny. "We don't have the money yet and until each of us has put our share somewhere secure, we don't want to invite unwelcome questions."

Rod commented on the strange man at the hotel and told Charlie and Sally to watch out for him but to do so without raising any suspicions.

On the way back, Sally told Charlie that she needed to see her grandparents again. She had avoided contact with them since her aunt's death. Emma was the youngest sister of Sally's grandmother. Both of her grandparents were in their early eighties and doing okay physically, but the old man was slipping mentally. "I won't have them forever," Sally told Charlie.

"We don't have anything forever, do we?"

She nodded. "Let's go back tomorrow. I love them, but this…I need to get this over with. They need to know. It's going to hurt though."

Dinner had been joyful, and her gay mood of the past few days belied her darker thoughts. She realized that Charlie was the only one in her life she could turn to. Brandy was a comfort, but Sally didn't see her as a future confidante.

They returned to Sagebrush at ten o'clock and retired for the evening.

Saturday came and went. Sally and Charlie returned to Alturas and she told her grandparents about Emma. She didn't mention the circumstances surrounding her death, only that she died at home in her sleep. Charlie gave her emotional support before and after their meeting. She introduced him to the old folks and that helped ease the pain of their loss. He drove on the way back as she looked out the window. He told her he didn't have the words she needed, but she told him that they weren't necessary. Being there was enough for now.

The Saturday-night poker game hosted the usual participants, including Ray. Ken told Brandy that his wife was delighted to have her for lunch and hoped they would get together again soon. Ray made no comment about his wife being with Brandy, but Johnny and Brandy took note of his silence. As in days past, Brandy claimed more than her fair share of the pots—"Rethink fair share," was her parting message—and she spent the night in her room with Johnny. Charlie went somewhere with Sally that night, but no one asked where or what.

On Sunday afternoon, Johnny helped some farmers bale hay and fix fences, promising to help again during the week. It wasn't a lot of pay, but it helped replace some of his diminishing funds, which had been bolstered only partly by some luck at the table.

* * *

THE BIG NEWS ARRIVED MONDAY MORNING. JOHNNY WAS AT work, Sally was in the dining room, and Charlie at the desk.

Jeff Courtney called Justin with the forensic laboratory findings. He confirmed that the tea cannister didn't contain only tea. *Cicuta douglasii*, a Pacific Northwest species of water hemlock, was present in a concentration large enough to produce severe poisoning. The herb roots had been ground to mix in with the tea. It was no accidental poisoning as sometimes happened when a hiker mistook the toxic plant for wild carrot or parsnip. Cows were the most common victims, and farmers took special precautions to clear their pastures of anything that resembled hemlock. Most toxicologists considered any of the four water hemlock species to be among the most poisonous plants in North America.

Justin wanted to know if that meant further investigation and Jeff told him additional tissue samples had been requested to confirm that Emma had ingested the toxin. That report would be expedited, and he should have additional information by Friday. Justin thanked him, unaware that he wasn't the only one receiving the news at that moment.

Alfred Wallman stood at a telephone booth outside the Sagebrush drug store. On the other end of the line was a clerk at the Modoc County sheriff's office in Alturas. She had read the report from Sacramento and arranged to inform her cousin of the lab findings. She told Al that further autopsy material had been ordered and an official homicide investigation had been started. If the new findings confirmed hemlock ingestion, the State of California would be apprised and they would take over.

Al thanked her and made notes on a pad he kept in his shirt pocket. Despite the risks, he needed to communicate this to Ray immediately. He dialed Ray's number and told him he wanted to see him, and they agreed to meet at a small farm road out of town. By the mere coincidence, it was a road that served the farm where Johnny was repairing fences.

Justin gathered Brandy and Rod in his office and told them what he had learned. Neither was surprised, but Rod's anger was apparent. "I'll kill that bastard," he said louder than he intended.

Justin told him to leave it to the state authorities who would soon be on the job. He reminded them that they still didn't have evidence that Ray was the perpetrator.

"I'll beat it out of him, and when he confesses, I'll blow his worthless life off this planet."

Brandy turned on her sweetest pleading voice. "We'd miss you terribly, Rod, so don't do it. Justin's right. We'll know more later this week. In the meantime we can watch Ray closely and also this other guy, Al." She turned to the hotel owner. "Can you find out anything further on our man in black?"

"I don't even have his last name. Not sure I can do anything legal." He looked at Brandy. "Maybe he can be seduced to say something." When he saw the look on her face, he added, "That was a joke, only a joke."

Rod stood up. "Joking time is past, folks. Time to get serious while we still can."

Johnny had been working steadily since nine o'clock. It was almost noon, and he was ready to take a break. The sun was hot, and he was wearing a large straw cowboy hat and the jeans he bought at the local hardware store. He was on his hands and knees, attaching a bottom strand of wire to a post, when he heard two cars drive up and park fifty yards away.

Crouched in a small depression that bordered the field, he was out of their sight, but he took a quick look and recognized Ray's hardware van and the gray Oldsmobile. *Another meeting of Ray and Al, but why all of the way out here?* He wasn't going to be able to hear what they said as they stood by their vehicles, but he was certain that it was important and relevant to the week's events. He decided to forego a lunch break, finish another hour of work, and get back to town. He had borrowed Brandy's car for the day, promising to fill the tank when he returned it.

The afternoon meeting in Justin's office with Rod and Johnny was brief. The man in black loomed larger in the unfolding drama, but his role, if any, in Emma's demise was unknown. Rod didn't say much, other than voicing his determination to keep a close eye on Al from that time on.

Rod kept his word. Tuesday morning after breakfast, he followed Al to Emma's bungalow. Yellow crime caution tape was stretched across the driveway. The gray Oldsmobile was parked a block away, and Al was walking around the side of the house. Rod had a good vantage point from the same rise where Ray had spied on them earlier. Rod crept down the hill and followed Al's path to the back of the building. The rear door to the kitchen was slightly ajar and he was able to open it and enter without making a sound.

Al was in the kitchen, pouring the remainder of the tea leaves into a plastic bag. He turned as Rod's shadow fell across him. "What the fu…" was all the man in black had time to say before Rod grabbed him by the throat and slammed him against the kitchen counter.

"Talk to me," Rod shouted, one beefy hand clutched around the smaller man's neck and the other poised to smash his face. "What are you doing and what have you done?"

The man had lost his glasses and whimpered something about it wasn't his idea and not to hurt him. It was not a contest in size or temperament. Rod was ready to kill or at least do serious damage, and the man knew it.

Rod released his hold but stood over him as Al crouched on the floor looking up at him.

"What wasn't your idea, little man? What did you do and who did you do it for? Ray Gordon, is that who? You and he planned this together or are you just the stooge gopher?" Rod looked at the plastic bag and the tea leaves scattered on the floor. "Did you think you were getting rid of the evidence? Too late for that, ain't it? The cops will be crawling all over this place in the next few days, but they already have enough evidence to put you and your friend away for a long time or worse."

Al was looking up at him, but his glance was off to the side and Rod discovered why when another voice sounded.

"That's all we need to know, Rodney. Turn around, slow, hands on head."

Rod turned, doing as Ray Gordon said. Ray was holding a .45 at waist level.

Al stood, whimpering, trying to express his gratitude that Ray had intervened.

"Shut up. You would have told him and the cops everything. It wasn't your idea? You were the one who told me about the hemlock and brought me the roots, showed me how to grind them up. You put it in her tea jar. You're in this more than I am, you little bastard."

Rod looked at the door and the distance to Ray, trying to decide if he could gain any advantage. Ray was slightly smaller than Rod and about as tough, but with a gun, all he could do was wait.

Ray turned his attention back to Rod. "You carrying?"

"No, I'm unarmed. My gun's back in the car, in the glove compartment."

"Thank you." Ray fired point-blank at Rod's chest, killing him instantly.

"Oh shit, oh shit!" Al peed his pants.

"Go get Rod's gun from his car. It's on the hill above the house. Bring it here."

Al hurried out the door. He could either run for his own car or do what Ray said. He decided on the latter. Hurrying back to the house, holding the gun gingerly in front of him, he almost stumbled in the driveway. He entered the kitchen to see Ray sweeping the tea leaves from the floor into the plastic bag. He handed Rod's .38 to Ray.

"Well, that about cleans everything up. Almost." He smiled at Al. He looked at the pistol and confirmed that it was loaded.

"What are we going to do now? What about him?" Al indicated the bloody body of Rod staring lifelessly at the ceiling.

"We? We won't need to do anything." He gave Al the same smile and pulled the trigger of the thirty-eight, shooting Al three times in the stomach and lower chest. "Unfortunately, this won't be as instantly fatal as what Rod got, but then he was more of a man then you'll ever be. And I guess we can forget about that extra two thousand, if that's all right with you."

Al was barely conscious, hunched over and bleeding profusely on the floor a few feet from Rod.

Ray wiped the .45 with a handkerchief and placed it in Al's dying hands. He placed the wiped .38 in Rod's hand for a moment and then dropped it on the floor beside him. Placing the tea cannister on the shelf and taking the plastic bag with him, Ray left the kitchen and secured the back door. By the time anyone else entered the house, Al would be cold meat.

Ray was correct about cleaning up, but not completely. Al managed to reach the phone and summon an ambulance. Thirty minutes later, on the way to Alturas, he told the attendant what happened, identifying Ray as Rod's and Emma's killer. Al Wallman, the man in the dark, bloody shirt died before reaching the hospital.

After receiving the report from the ambulance team, Justin was shocked to hear that Rod was also believed to be dead. The crew that retrieved Al couldn't revive Rod, but because it was an obvious crime scene, no one could remove his body until investigators arrived. Jeff phoned Justin and told him what happened and to avoid contact with Ray. He was sending two armed deputies to Sagebrush.

Johnny was finishing the fence work at the nearby farm when Brandy brought him the news. She was in tears, the most distressed he had ever seen her. They hugged for several minutes, as if they were the last humans left on earth and were afraid to let each other go. "Do Charlie or Sally know?" asked Johnny.

"Justin said he would wait and let you tell him. I'm not sure about Sally, but maybe I will talk to her. The poor kid has been through hell in such a short time." She looked up at him with mascara-stained cheeks. "Oh, Johnny, I used to think I had it tough when I was young, but I never had to deal with anything like this. As much as I teased and sometimes resented Rod, he was a good friend. This should never have happened."

"What did happen? Apparently Rod and Al shot each other, but Ray was there?"

"From what little Justin told me, Ray was the one who shot both of them, leaving Al for dead. Rod is still lying there, until the police arrive. The CHP will probably show up first and they are going after Ray."

"They better before I do."

"No Johnny, no. I don't want to lose you too. Not now." More tears, shaking shoulders, tight hugs.

— ◆ —

Ray was at home, eating a late lunch with Jay and Barbara. It was another nice day and he was relaxed. He dropped the plastic bag off in a corner of the kitchen counter, intending to flush it down the toilet later. He and Jay were discussing the tractor repairs they were ready to submit a bid on with one of the larger farmers in the valley.

There was a knock on the door. Barbara answered, mystified that two CHP officers were standing on her porch, one with a hand resting on his sidearm. They asked for Ray and he came to the door, still relaxed as if they had come by to sell raffle tickets or inquire about a lost child in the neighborhood. They put him under arrest, handcuffed him, read him his rights, and put him in the back of the patrol car.

Jay and Barbara stood in silence, not believing what had happened—one minute a pleasant family lunch and the next an arrest for murder. Jay put his arms around his sobbing sister-in-law and they retreated into the house. He mentioned contacting a lawyer and she nodded, leaving him to go into the kitchen. She wasn't sure whether she needed a drink. She rarely consumed alcohol, but if ever there was a time, this was it. She spotted the bag of tea leaves on the counter. *Something Ray brought me.* She smiled, picked it up, and decided a good strong cup of tea would calm her nerves. She and Jay could then decide on their next course of action. *Thank goodness he isn't retarded*, she thought. *I will need him more than ever.*

That afternoon, Justin received good tidings for a change. Thomas Crenshaw phoned him from San Francisco with the results of the gold delivery. The 95 bars weighed 966.8 pounds. The average purity was 78.63 percent gold and a trace of silver. The total street value at the time of delivery was $183.40 per ounce, for a total of $2,836,978. Minus the handling fee of 15 percent, and metal processing charges, the net proceeds came to $2,311,400 and some change. The news was better yet: they could expect payment wired to the RBE account in Alturas within ten days.

Justin thanked Crenshaw for his no-questions-asked services, finished some notes on his account sheet, and hung up. Now he had an additional problem to solve. How many shares existed? If Ray was also out of the picture, it left himself, Sally, Brandy, and a share belonging to Johnny and Charlie—total of four. Should Charlie get his own share? What about Barbara and Jay? Should they receive Ray's portion regardless of what was in store for the mechanic? Another meeting to decide, another set of papers to formalize the partnership of the RBE holding company.

As he put the latest numbers in the safe, he gazed at the one remaining doré bar. It had been retained for emergency purposes, to hold them over while the proceeds were in process. That wasn't necessary now. The rock had become a precious souvenir, a memento of their hopes and dreams. Everybody would be relatively rich from the settlement—about a half a million per share, depending on the split. It would provide a fresh start for the kids and end the tragic partnership that had existed since 1957. Whether the secret would ever be told was not yet determined. It was possible that the feds or state could still lay claim to the original find, so the less they knew, the better. There was no physical evidence that linked the gold shipment, now on its way to Hong Kong, with Sagebrush or the poker-playing gang that had endured twenty years of turmoil and bad blood. However, questions could be asked about the sizeable amount of money wired to RBE.

Johnny returned to the hotel that evening and was greeted with the news of Ray's arrest, the transport of Rod's body to the county seat, and the forthcoming payment. Charlie, Sally, Brandy, and Johnny sat and faced Justin behind his desk.

"Sorry that we have to deal with this after all that has happened today, but I need you to think about how we dissolve the holding company and disburse the money." Justin explained his reasoning on division of the funds but left it to the group to reach a consensus on who had what shares. He still intended to use his for civic improvements including some for the school that Emma had wanted.

They thanked Justin for his work and said they would discuss the issues during the next few days and arrive at a decision. Outside his office, Brandy suggested the four of them eat at a quiet place in town. Charlie knew it better than any of the others because he sometimes ate there by himself. "Always quiet, usually only a couple of customers at any time," he told them.

They relaxed while Charlie finished his shift in the lobby. Justin had said he was free to go, but Charlie told him he needed the work, if not the money, to unwind. Justin put his hand on the lad's shoulder and told him to unwind all he needed. Sally went to her room.

Brandy went with Johnny to his room. She sat on his bed while he changed from his work clothes and took a shower. He left the bathroom door open and she watched him. He stepped out of the bathroom wrapped in a towel, and she looked at him but remained silent.

"Deep thinking, are you?" He snapped off the towel, threw it on the bed beside her and pulled a pair of shorts out of a drawer. "Let me hide my distractions and maybe you'll share some of your deep, dark thoughts."

She had her left hand over her mouth and a furrowed brow, as if she was burning up gray matter at a furious pace. "My share and Justin's share haven't changed, just the number of players. I assume we are in agreement that Sally gets Emma's, right?"

"Umm, sounds right so far. That leaves Charlie and me."

"Yes it does. We don't know what he is going to do or wants to do, right?"

"Uh-huh, spot on."

"What if we cut him in as a full partner, giving him what would have gone to Ray? That would allow him to make his own decisions, whatever."

"Instead of him and me splitting a share?"

"That would give us each four hundred and sixty two thousand, plus a few loose dollars."

As he dressed, he said, "Well, that does allow us a lot of freedom of movement. I assume that Justin is the only one committed to stay in Sagebrush."

"There is the issue of Jay and Barbara. Although it was a late discovery, I found her more interesting, substantial if you will, than I had thought. If Ray is charged and found guilty of murder, Jay and his sister-in-law will suffer the penalty."

"I know from some other sources that Ray had a decent bank account, much of it left over from the sale of his business. If what you say about Jay is correct, he is still a viable breadwinner and will have the family business. Were you thinking about cutting them in on Ray's share?"

"No, just to be mindful that they are most likely innocent of whatever evil Ray has brought down on everyone. Suppose we have Justin give them the remaining doré bar. It won't be a full share, but it is some compensation."

"Point taken. You about ready to go out and deal with the kids?"

"Almost. There is one other thing I'd like you to think about. Almost a million dollars, two shares, would go a lot farther than one. Do you think we should form a holding company of our own?"

Johnny stopped in the middle of the room, gazing down at the serious brunette on his bed. "Darlin', I've faced off with you when you *were* a holding company, holding some mighty powerful hands. A holding company? Hmm, can I trust you?" He reached for her hand.

She got off the bed and tumbled into his arms. "Earlier today, I got your dirty shirt all wet. I can do better."

"Yeah, but can I trust you?"

"Poker players' honor, you can trust me."

"Guess that'll have to do." He kissed her and they walked down the hall to the lobby.

The four of them were at dinner and discussing their respective futures when Jay called an ambulance to come for Barbara. She was having severe seizures and vomiting, unable to catch a breath. He rode with her as the ambulance sped past the hotel.

Now what? thought Johnny. *This town has seen more police and ambulances in the last two weeks than during its entire existence.* He later learned that Barbara Gordon didn't make it to the hospital. The symptoms of her poisoning led to the discovery of the discarded plastic bag. Jay identified it as one his brother left there earlier that day.

The next day, Wednesday July 3, Ray was formally indicted on a charge of first-degree homicide. Facing the overwhelming evidence against him, including ownership of the .45 and the accidental loss of his wife, he pled guilty and was later convicted of second-degree murder. Jay attended his hearings and later his trial. He said little of comfort to his brother, and all pretense of his mental infirmary was abandoned. Ray told Jay about the gold and that he might try to bargain for a lesser sentence by revealing the twenty-year-old scheme. Jay informed him that if he ever said anything to that effect, he would never see his brother again. He took over the family business and, after Barbara's funeral, rebuilt it into a better hardware establishment, eventually hiring two employees.

July 4 was celebrated in Sagebrush, like in many small communities around America, with fireworks, kids running around front yards and playgrounds with sparklers, a country and western fiddle group playing at the school auditorium, and lots of shared picnics, barbeques, and family get-togethers. Jay was in Alturas, Justin was with his family, and the Trove Treasure Four, as they now designated themselves, spent it together at a quiet creek near Fandango Pass.

"This is where it all started," Johnny told Sally and Charlie. "We still have some big decisions to make, all of us. Better be thinking."

On Saturday afternoon, July 5, Emma Dodson and Rod Haas were laid to rest in the Sagebrush Methodist Church Cemetery. Emma's funeral was attended by a large crowd of community people including former students who gathered from around the area. Rod's burial was witnessed by a significantly smaller group. Both had plots near those of the Woodward family. Brandy had her arms around Sally at both ceremonies. As the final words were spoken over Rod's casket, Brandy said, "Here rests half of the tontine group." She looked at the remaining five. Sally's eyes were a mess. Johnny was watching Charlie, trying to interpret his mood. Big decisions for all of them would be coming soon.

On Monday, July 8, they met again with Justin. Brandy spoke for the four. She told Justin that Charlie and Sally should receive a full share, making five shares for the company. He agreed and had another set of papers prepared. He would retain the holding company centered on the hotel for tax purposes and as an investment platform for the community. They would receive their payouts in the next few days. She recommended that Justin give the remaining gold bar to Jay Gordon and he agreed.

Justin was notified on Friday, July 12, about the arrival of the funds at his bank in Alturas. He transferred four-fifths of the money to the Sagebrush Bank and informed the group that they could obtain the money in whatever form suited them. The moment of truth had arrived!

During the next two weeks, Brandy and Johnny spent most of their nights together—sometimes in his room, sometimes in hers, occasionally in other towns. Between passion and serious discussion they mutually arrived at a truth that some people bravely face but many others ignore. They were proud of their independence, cherished it and had few regrets about times past or opportunities missed. They were of similar philosophy, natural-born gamblers, willing to take the risks and face the uncertainties. The crucial question was, whether they wanted to continue doing it alone?

They examined it from every angle they could conceive. What would they gain, what would they lose? Like all of life and like the game they loved so well, they knew no ultimate answer provided only benefits. It would be a compromise and they each had to decide what price they were willing to pay.

Similar to a union–management negotiating session, they discussed the issues that were of primary importance. If they stayed together, was it a travelling companionship, a common-law residency somewhere, or were they considering the big banana: marriage and all of the legal obligations it entailed? They decided against making an immediate choice. They would leave Sagebrush with their individual shares, travel together, and possibly find a place where Johnny could continue school and Brandy could be gainfully employed, or not, occupation to be determined at a later date. Johnny wondered why he was bothering with college at his age, but Brandy convinced him he might live another decade or two, especially if he stayed out of bar fights and avoided loose women. They were resourceful. They were survivors. If it didn't work, it wouldn't be a tragedy, would it?

The discussion between Sally and Charlie was parallel but separate. Sally was more focused, wanting to pursue college and prepare for the career she felt was her calling. Charlie was the unsure cog in the wheel, but he was a malleable cog, subject to her influence and willing to consider any reasonable outcome. They agreed that marriage or any semipermanent arrangement was not what they wanted or needed at the moment, but living together was not out of the question. In addition to their windfall, sharing expenses would allow them to be interdependent and pursue separate objectives. Sally was aware of Charlie's growing confidence and maturity, even if he had not decided on where he wanted to land. She would help him start the flight.

Brandy had money left over from her previous employment in Vegas. She gave Justin a check for $50,000 for his community improvement projects. "For Emma and Steve," she said, remembering that they were the real sources of the trove. As she presented him with the money, a thought occurred to her. *Who were the real sources of the gold? Who were the miners and why had they buried their cache at Willow Creek? What happened to them?*

Justin hosted a farewell dinner for Sally and Charlie on a Sunday night, and he presented plaques to his clerk and waitress for their years of service. Each was signed by the rest of the hotel staff and by Brandy and Johnny.

The next morning, a bright Monday, July 22, they piled their few belongings into Sally's car and headed to Eugene. She had been accepted at the University of Oregon as a freshman in English. They would share a nice apartment, and he would take a few courses, starting at Lane Community College.

Johnny wished his son the best of luck and promised he would stay in touch. "Expect a lot of post cards," he said, as they parted.

Brandy and Sally hugged and the girl thanked the brunette for her help and support. Brandy told her she regretted not being able to give her poker lessons before they parted. "Can be a useful tool if you play it right."

"It isn't San Francisco, but it's pretty exciting," Charlie told his dad before they drove off.

As Brandy and Johnny watched the taillights disappear, he turned to her. "He has no idea, but he will."

Friday night, July 26, marked the last card game at the Sagebrush Hotel. Justin, Brandy, Johnny, and Ken were the only players. The excitement and frivolity were subdued. Each of them knew that an event of more than twenty years was fading into history. There would be no more games, no further legends of the brunette queen who ruled the table and made grown men weep. They drank, bluffed, and did their best to take each other's money, but a four-handed game was a much different dynamic than one with six or seven players.

They knew Brandy and Johnny would soon be leaving. Ken had decided it was time to retire and move south to be near his grandkids. Justin said he would continue to operate the hotel for the foreseeable future. He made no mention of his once ambitious desire to be the mayor of Sagebrush.

Ken looked at the others after the last hand was played. He won the pot, one of the biggest of the night. "I guess this is the last reunion, huh?" He was still unaware of the nature of their enterprise, the secret they had shared and what brought them back over the years.

Brandy pushed her chair back and quietly said, "You never know." She looked at each of them for a moment and finally at Justin. "Anything is possible." She stood and gave Ken and Justin a prolonged hug.

On Monday, she and Johnny finished loading her car. Johnny shook hands with Justin in front of the hotel. "Good luck with everything in Sagebrush. Hope the hotel prospers and that you are able to accomplish what you, Steve, Donna, and Emma wanted for so long. Too bad they're not here to share in it."

Justin said, "It'll live on in Charlie, Sally, and in a lot of other young kids who will grow up here. It isn't paradise, I know, but it's home. We'll do just fine. I hope you'll have a chance to visit some time and check up on us. Good luck, you two, in poker and in all things."

Brandy gave him a kiss on both cheeks. "The kids are not so far away, so we may well be in the neighborhood sometime. Again,

Justin, thanks for everything." The tears had started. She brushed them away, turned and got behind the wheel.

Johnny smiled at Justin, gave him a small wave, and got in beside her. With the roar of the engine, they were off.

Justin stood on the wooden porch for a few minutes. He would be training a new waitress and new desk clerk that day. It would be another hot one according to the sleepy dog on the wooden bench.

Epilogue

1985

A WIND BLOWS CLUMPS OF SAGEBRUSH DOWN THE MAIN STREET. It competes with little traffic, although there is some. A nearby highway connects other towns, destinations with more purpose, more reason to attract visitors.

The hotel remains as it has for almost one hundred years, but more weathered, more beaten down by the elements than ever. Shingles are loose at the corners and some of the windows appear crooked, as if hanging in desperation, trying to retain respectability. The building is obviously vacant. A board and a lock bar the entrance and if you go to the rear by the loading dock, you would see the same. A large sign proclaims that the building is for sale and a realtor contact number is listed at the bottom.

The owner? He was still around a few years ago but hasn't been involved with the hotel since 1981. He moved out of town a year ago, says an elderly woman at the tavern down the street. Pulled out early one morning without saying nothing to no one, as if they had been strangers for the several decades. The business? There hadn't been much. The hotel served some food and had some occasional guests, but like the rest of the town, its better days were far behind. The owner had wanted to spend money on the school and add some enhancements that would bring new business to the town, but a declining population said otherwise. The school closed and with it, the town slumbered into slow oblivion.

A few people remember the nights of the hotel poker games that the town barber, now retired and gone, had glorified as the "last of the best in the West." What had happened to the others, the players and drinkers who had brought a touch of notoriety to the high desert community? Especially the pretty brunette, the one they called the queen of the table. Didn't she run off with Johnny, the carpenter and traveler? What about the Charles boy? A nice kid, an orphan and clerk at the hotel. Some say he ended up with a waitress from the hotel. Kids, they leave town and never come back. The bar owner doesn't know.

There are rumors though—there is always speculation in a small town. The brunette and her man-friend are in Baja California, some say. They're down in Mexico, hiding out, but from what or why, no one knows. Jay, the auto mechanic, knows some of the more sordid details, but he says little. His business is also failing and he talks of moving to a larger town. His brother Ray is still serving time for murder. That they remember, because he had killed a retired school teacher and another man, right there in Sagebrush.

Other rumors circulate from time to time, about Emma and others who had found a horde of stolen gold. It is usually dismissed as wishful thinking and as "just one of many Western myths" to excite the occasional tourist or reporter. Some talk about a secret club, a group of people at the hotel who knew about the gold and helped Justin Gonzales purchase the building that still bears the faded letters of The Sagebrush Hotel. Whatever the group was or why it held reunions over a twenty-year period, no one is sure, but they agree that the members were strange, together or apart, bound by some secret from the past.

———————◆———◆———————

A NEW JEEP CHEROKEE XJ SITS UNDER A LARGE WILLOW TREE by a small creek. A trim brunette with short hair, youngish looking in her mid-forties, sits with a man on a blanket, sharing a basket of food and a bottle of Chardonnay. He is a few years older but also neat in appearance. They laugh, occasionally hold hands. It is a bright spring day and the water flows freely from the nearby mountains to the east.

They have already forgotten their recent visit to a small, dusty town in the middle of nowhere, a community clearly in steep decline with closed stores and offices, buildings that badly needed paint, and a two-story hotel that will never reopen. A few people could be seen here and there, mostly older folks with nowhere to go. They drove by a closed school, a closed bank, and one open bar. They stopped and asked a few questions, but the barmaid had few answers. The ones she had were mostly wrong. They each had a beer, thanked her, and left. There would be no need to return.

The two talk about a former desk clerk and waitress and the two children they are raising. They look at each other and inch closer. He puts his arms around her. A gold ring on her hand sparkles in the sun. The stream also sparkles, like it did 121 years earlier.

THE END

Author's Notes

1. Tontine. A tontine, named after Lorenzo Tonti, a French financier who established an insurance plan in the 1600s, is a written agreement for a group of investors or participants to share in a common asset, usually over a specified period of time or until one or more surviving participants remain. The tontine agreement in Sagebrush includes different people from 1957 to 1977 as the story progresses and people either die or are added.

2. Geography. Fandango Pass, the Lassen Trail, and many of the other names mentioned in the prologue are real. The small army garrison in Surprise Valley was known as Camp Bidwell in 1863–64 but designated later as Fort Bidwell. It was primarily established at the request of area settlers to help quell uprisings by bands of Paiutes. The fictitious gold heist from the Hatcher brothers at Willow Creek would be a few miles east of where County Road 4 joins US Highway 395. This is near the eastern shore of Goose Lake, several miles north of Alturas.

Sagebrush is a fictional community about thirty miles south and west of Alturas, in an agricultural valley near the South Fork of the Pit River in Modoc County, California. Water hemlock, a species of *Cicuta*, can be found in marsh areas and wetlands where it has not been eradicated by ranchers.

3. Gold bullion. It was illegal to possess large amounts of gold between 1933 and 1974. This included bullion, gold coins, and gold certificates. President Franklin D. Roosevelt signed into law an executive order on 5 April 5, 1933, and became official on 1 May 1, 1933. Congress enacted a law, proscribing criminal penalties for withholding gold, the following year. Repeal of the measure, permitting the legal ownership of gold, was enacted by President Gerald Ford and became official on December 31, 1974. The price of gold had been relatively constant at $35 per ounce during the years it was forbidden, but it rose in response to market demand after it became legal. Silver bullion was also included in the ban, but exemptions for both metals were made for antique collectibles, existing jewelry, small amounts for jewelers to make into jewelry, and industrial use. Foreigners also had their gold confiscated if they attempted to buy, sell or trade it within the United States. Foreign gold coins were included in the ban.

Doré bars were used during the gold rush years to concentrate gold flakes and nuggets for transport to smelters and buyers. Purity and weight varied, as did shape, but a ground mold could produce the shape of the bars described in this story and illustrated on the back cover. The gold bar Justin retained at the hotel and given to Jay would have been worth about $95,000 dollars in 1980.

4. The great game of poker. The origins of modern poker are lost to antiquity. Forms of it arose at various places during the eighteenth century. The rules of card play are similar to many other games, but betting and bluffing give the game its unique and characteristic flavor. Modern forms, involving more than two players, use a fifty-two-card deck, with or without wild cards. Jokers are extra cards, but certain cards (deuces, one-eyed jacks, etc.) can be designated to add variety to the games. The standard games are five-card draw, five-card stud, and seven-card stud. Many authorities believe that Mississippi River boats and the gambling casinos they featured helped spread the game across the developing United States. By 1950, most of the conventions and variations that are now common had been introduced. Family and community games, as opposed to those at casino tables, often have more variety and additional rules. After 1970, large tournaments and professional events became prominent, especially at casinos on the Atlantic and Gulf Coasts and in Nevada. Texas hold'em, a seven card community flop game, became the leading variant for large poker tournaments during this time, but the Sagebrush Hotel group usually played draw, the two stud games, and variants such as high–low pot splits and no see 'em, where the gamblers bet on blind hands, similar to showdown. For these nonprofessional games, drinking, trash talk, and bluffing are the main elements of the social setting. The amount won or lost over the long run, provided none of the players are terrible, is usually not as significant as the social benefits of sharing in an evening of craziness.

5. Small towns and legalities. I took some liberties with the law and their investigations. Charlie's adoption by the Charles family was never officially registered, and they had someone local draw up papers for his later use. His birth certificate would be real, however. Jurisdiction between the Modoc County sheriff and the California Highway Patrol during both homicide investigations was not as formal in the story as it might be in reality, nor was submission of the autopsy and household samples to a forensic lab in Sacramento. Sometimes you can get bogged down in detail. This was before computers tracked everything distinctly and instantly.

Acknowledgments

THIS IS ALWAYS ONE OF THE MOST ENJOYABLE SECTIONS OF A manuscript for me. Despite all of the commentary about writing being a lonely art or living on a literary island, I have never found that to be true. Relatives and friends have provided support, as one might expect. Their critical appraisal and objective scrutiny become the invaluable assistance to edit, rewrite, and shape a story into something that will fly free from the confines of the author's imagination. Beyond the close family and friends, there is a community of writers, colleagues in suffering and triumph, who share in the creativity and fully understand the challenges and obstacles to producing the published work. They give a collective voice to who we are and what we are about. I especially thank the individuals of the Northwest Independent Writers Association (NIWA) for their unselfish time, enthusiasm, and inspiration.

Norm King Brady Jr. and William J. Cook again provided much-needed feedback and helped immensely with revisions of earlier drafts. Alla Vichurina Powers, my gracious and ever-helpful spouse, an English major and librarian, read multiple drafts, helped clarify points of view, and corrected numerous grammatical issues. Cover designs are the creation of Roslyn McFarland. This is the third cover she has rendered for my books.

As always, the publisher and staff of Luminare Press in Eugene, Oregon, have proven to be the very best: Patricia Marshall, Kim Harper-Kennedy, Claire Flint Last, Nina Leis, and Lori Stephens.

About the Author

L. WADE POWERS, UNDER THE NAME LAWRENCE W. POWERS, PhD, has published books and articles in the fields of medical technology, ecology, marine biology, and animal behavior. He authored a critique of *The Winter of Our Discontent* for *Steinbeck Review* and several articles for *Oregon Encyclopedia Online*. He was a contributing editor for the *Journal of the Shaw Historical Library* for several years and served as creative nonfiction editor for *Timberline Review* for two years.

As L. Wade Powers, he has published three previous novels—*The Home* (2017), *The Party House* (2019), and *New Albion Sunset* (2020)—and two collections of short stories, *Falling in Love and Other Misadventures* (2019) and *Confronting the Boundaries* (2020).

A revised edition of *The Home* was published in November 2019. Like the characters in this novel, Powers enjoys low-stakes poker and occasionally makes the drive down US 395 to Reno, passing through the Alturas-Likely high desert area to indulge his passion. He is currently at work on a fifth novel set in a dystopic future.

A retired professor of natural sciences, Larry lives in Eastern Oregon with his wife, Alla, with the gracious permission of their cat, Mollie. He is a member of the Northwest Independent Writers Association (NIWA) and Willamette Writers. For further information about the author and his works, please visit his website at lwadepowers.com.